Stories

- of the -

NIGHT

Stories
- of the -
NIGHT

LAUREN SMYTH

AMBASSADOR INTERNATIONAL
GREENVILLE, SOUTH CAROLINA & BELFAST, NORTHERN IRELAND
www.ambassador-international.com

Stories of the Night

ISBN: 978-1-62020-821-2
eISBN: 978-1-62020-827-4
Library of Congress Control Number: 2019939887

Cover Design and Page Layout by Hannah Nichols
eBook Conversion by Anna Riebe Raats

This is a work of fiction. Names, characters, and incidents are all products of the author's imagination or are used for fictional purposes. Any resemblance to actual events or persons, living or dead, is entirely coincidental. Any mentioned brand names, places, and trademarks remain the property of their respective owners, bear no association with the author or the publisher, and are used for fictional purposes only.

AMBASSADOR INTERNATIONAL
Emerald House
411 University Ridge, Suite B14
Greenville, SC 29601, USA
www.ambassador-international.com

AMBASSADOR BOOKS
The Mount
2 Woodstock Link
Belfast, BT6 8DD, Northern Ireland, UK
www.ambassadormedia.co.uk

The colophon is a trademark of Ambassador, a Christian publishing company.

Dedication

To Grace, my wonderful fellow-writer and alter ego who inspired and encouraged me all the way.

I'll trade you some edamame for a chocolate stir!

ACKNOWLEDGMENTS

With special thanks to my mom, Kelli, without whom this book would not exist. She helped me edit, made me great writing snacks, and taught me everything I know about writing. Her love and support convinced me to create this book, and I could never have done it without her.

Thanks also to my dad, Ryan, who made time in a busy week to help me fine-tune this book. Without him, I wouldn't have made it this far.

CHAPTER I

ALISEN FINISHED BRAIDING HER HAIR and wound it into a bun. She admired herself in the mirror for a moment before giving a last twitch to her bun and starting down the stairs.

She was dressed in a spotless blue uniform, her silver rank insignia sparkling on her shoulder, her black shoes shining as brightly. She looked much like a young Army lieutenant, but she was only fifteen. She was a cadet member of the Civil Air Patrol, which met on the local Air Force base, to which she went mainly to be admired for her beauty and remarkable strength. She paid little attention to the careful lectures in leadership, aviation, or other activities; she did not attend the meetings for friendship; she merely went to see and be seen, and because her parents had long ago decided that she should go.

A car pulled up in front of her house. Alisen saw it from the window, and with a brief farewell to her mother she was out the door and knocking on the car's window.

Someone inside the car, laughing, unlocked it. Alisen clambered inside, taking care not to wrinkle a fold in her uniform. Her best friend smiled at her and said, "You'll get a good rating on the inspection today. You always do. I wish I had half as much care as you."

"Right," said Alisen. "You're a neat freak, McKenzie, and you know it."

McKenzie poked her slyly. "I'm neat, but not so careful. You wait and see. Before inspection, I'll have fallen on the stairs, fought with one of the boys, or rolled in a mud puddle. It always happens."

McKenzie's mother looked back at them from the front seat. "It's true," she said. "Last time it was the mud puddle. That was the end of her starched uniform, and I had spent an hour on it the night before!"

McKenzie and her mother laughed. Alisen crossed her arms and rolled her eyes, half wishing she could join in their laughter.

"Tired today?" asked McKenzie, observing her silence.

"No," snapped Alisen. "Just . . . well . . . what can I blame it on? Everything went wrong today. Before school, I tried to curl my hair, and ended up with a big frizzy mess. At lunch, I tried to put it up so no one would tease me, and it fell out in PE class. While we were waiting for the bus, some stupid kid was chasing me, grabbed my sweater, and tore it from top to bottom. And—yeah, the whole day was like that."

"At least nothing happened to your precious cell phone," teased McKenzie. "Then what would you do?"

"Probably pulverize whoever did it," Alisen smiled ruefully. "I still don't know how you manage to exist with that flip phone of yours."

"Better than the colonists did," said McKenzie. "They didn't even have GPS. Now you have to wonder how they got here at all."

"They were smarter. Who cares anyway?" said Alisen. "I bet it was dirty on board the ship."

"Probably true," agreed McKenzie.

By this time, they had arrived, and McKenzie's mother was pulling up to the guard shack. The tired-looking Air Force guard looked at their IDs, then saluted wearily. Probably he had done a great deal of that today, since all the local Civil Air Patrol members came onto the Air Force base to meet. Alisen felt that she had found a kindred spirit in those lackluster eyes, and immediately felt better about herself.

McKenzie's mother let her daughter and Alisen off in front of a hangar. "I'll meet you out here as soon as you're done. Have fun!"

Alisen and McKenzie waved and started toward the hangar.

McKenzie paused in front of the door to stare up at the sky. "That's where I want to be," she said wistfully. "You know, I'm going to get my pilot's license soon. Two years . . . "

"Flying is so . . . unnecessary," said Alisen, searching for a word that would convey her feelings and not offend her friend. "Why would you want to?"

McKenzie stared at her. "Have you ever even been flying?"

Alisen shrugged. "No," she admitted. "Didn't see a need for it."

McKenzie laughed cheerfully and opened the door. "Some time, when I get my license, I'll take you," she said. "My family owns the best little plane— a Stearman. Dad is so proud of it."

Alisen attempted a smile and followed McKenzie inside the hangar.

Jay, the Patrol secretary, was standing at check-in holding out a clipboard and pen. Alisen disliked her extremely, though McKenzie had always admired her. What had Jay done to earn her high rank?

"Good evening," said Jay quietly. "Write your names here."

McKenzie lifted the pen and smiled up at her. "Thanks, Jay. You're wonderful, as usual. Do you ever get tired of doing this?"

"No. Why should I?" she said, returning McKenzie's smile.

McKenzie shook her head and gave the pen to Alisen. "I'll see you later."

Jay nodded quietly.

Alisen followed McKenzie into the middle of the hangar, where chairs and desks had been set up in front of a large oblong whiteboard. "I don't see how you can be so nice to Jay," she whispered, as soon as she caught up. "She's so—well, she's higher ranking than us, but she's no kind of a leader!"

McKenzie looked at her in surprise. "Really? Nearly everyone I know has expressed the opposite opinion. She's considered the best role model in the squadron—except, maybe, for how quiet she always is. Sometimes I wish I was more like her, but I could never stop talking for more than a few minutes at a time."

"That's just it," complained Alisen. "She won't talk to me."

"That doesn't mean she doesn't like you," said McKenzie. "That's just the way she is."

Someone behind McKenzie tapped her on the shoulder and started talking to her. It was an airman—someone Alisen was not interested in—so she turned away and focused her attention on the rest of the group.

Across from her, a group of boys were talking about computer science in terms which Alisen did not comprehend. In the first row, two girls were whispering secrets to each other, and a solitary sergeant named Kale was sitting by himself. Alisen should have known everyone there, but making friends was not something she always excelled at.

A cheerful voice behind her made her turn. "Where'd you go, Alisen?" It was McKenzie, resurrected from her conversation.

"ATT'N HUT!!" came from the back of the room; at least, that was what it always sounded like to Alisen. She never bothered to know what the slurred words meant. All she knew was that she had to stand up suddenly, a process which might wrinkle her uniform. Reluctantly she bounced up with the rest of the class and remained standing until a friendly but unusually quiet voice bid everyone recover.

Flight sergeant Jay stood in front of the class and said briefly, "As you all should know, we will be having inspections today. Everybody needs to go out to the parking lot."

"And woe to him who shall have spilled coffee on his uniform!" came a misplaced cry from the back of the room.

Everybody, including Jay, laughed, and those closest to the commentator wrestled him playfully to the floor.

All the cadets stood, teasing each other, talking, and enjoying themselves, making their leisurely way out to the parking lot. Jay walked toward the back of the group, clipboard pressed to her chest and apparently looking for someone. She looked slightly annoyed, if it was possible for someone as taciturn as Jay to show any emotion. Alisen sidled up to her and asked who she was looking for.

"I'm not usually in charge of inspections," Jay replied. "I am looking for Ethan. He should have been here by now."

"Who cares about him anyway," muttered Alisen, and left Jay without another word.

When everyone had left the hangar and the cadets were milling around in the parking lot, Jay shut the door with a loud slam that made everyone jump. "Fall in!" she ordered, and the cadets scrambled to their positions.

Inspections gave Alisen a chance to show off her invariably immaculate uniform. She had never bothered to notice who was in charge of them nor did she care enough to understand the purpose or the commands. She merely copied McKenzie, who always knew what was happening.

Jay and Kale, acting as her secretary, inspected each cadet carefully and wrote the result on Jay's clipboard. When the inspection was finished, Jay allowed the cadets to recover and return inside to their desks. It was leadership night, her least favorite night. Jay was to make the first appearance.

"Why did it have to be Jay?" asked Alisen under her breath.

"I told you," whispered McKenzie in reply, "she's the best leader. Why do you think she takes care of all the paper and drills and PT?"

"I don't know," said Alisen. "I'd much rather it was somebody else. Lisel, for example."

"Lisel!" scoffed McKenzie, after looking around to ensure that the girl in question could not hear them. "She's so stuck up, all she thinks about is making friends with the airmen! Surely you wouldn't want to follow her lead?"

"If she was really the leader, we wouldn't have to," said Alisen. "She would lose her marbles." Both girls laughed quietly.

"ATT'N HUT!" The familiar cry brought them to their feet until the cheerful voice bid them recover. It was a senior lieutenant colonel, who usually had good things to say that were well masked under a veil of silliness. It was impossible not to like him, and Alisen was relieved that Jay was not speaking after all.

"I'm here to replace Jay tonight," he began, turning to face his audience. "She's on the phone with someone in the office, and she's a much better secretary than I am. It's always best to talk to me in person, by the way, and not on the phone. Keep that in mind when you're asking for favors. So, let us begin with—"

"Sir," Jay interrupted, standing at the back with a strange expression on her face. "I think you'd better listen to this."

"Can it wait? I'm rather busy at the moment. The cadets are absorbing many life lessons." There were a few stifled giggles from the back.

"No sir, I'm afraid not," said Jay. "I think you need to hear this."

The hangar door opened, and a young man walked inside.

The lieutenant colonel glanced hastily up at him. "Ah, there you are, Ethan," he said. "You are late, but I will excuse it if you will say something about leadership. I was supposed to give the seminar tonight, but Jay is calling me away on urgent business." And with that, he followed Jay into the rear office.

Ethan looked puzzled for a moment, then he walked up to the front and stood in front of the whiteboard.

"Leadership," he began slowly, "is being able to step up and accomplish a task even when you think you're not prepared . . . "

*****   *****   *****

Alisen was tired of Ethan's lecture. McKenzie thought it was interesting, and she listened carefully, but to Alisen it was a mere waste of time. She scrunched back in her seat and absently counted the rings on the desk in front of her.

A loud slam from the back interrupted Ethan's lecture.

"Everybody out!" cried the lieutenant colonel frantically. "Out! Quickly!"

"Sir," protested Jay, "what are we going to do with them? Where are they going to go?"

The lieutenant colonel turned to Jay and said something in a low voice. Then to the cadets he added, "You heard me! Move out of this hangar and look for somewhere to hide!"

"Find shelter outside," said Jay coolly. "It doesn't matter where you go, just go somewhere! Hurry! And when this is over, meet back here. Go, now!"

The cadets had looked confused at the lieutenant colonel's words; when Jay spoke, they moved. Everyone got up and ran for the door, though none of them had any idea what was happening.

Alisen suspected this was a drill of some sort and was reluctant to get up.

McKenzie pulled her to her feet, her eyes wide with fear. "Hurry up, Alisen!" she cried.

Alisen shrugged. "You know the C.A.P. does drills. This is probably just another one. No need to hurry."

McKenzie turned to face Alisen. She placed her hands on Alisen's shoulders and stared straight into her eyes. "I'd believe you if it wasn't for Jay," she said. "She's serious if ever anyone was."

Alisen darted a glance at Jay, ushering the cadets out the door.

"Right," she said wearily. "Come on then."

Jay stood watching them as they ran outside. Alisen stopped. "Where do we go? Why are we doing this?"

"You're going to find out soon if this is real," Jay replied. "Make sure you cannot be seen either from the sky or from the ground. And hurry."

"Where could we—"

"If you can't find anywhere else, get in the basement levels of one of the office buildings," interrupted Jay. "They'll let you in this time."

Suddenly a loud siren shattered the still air and made her ears ring. Jay motioned them to hurry on, and then returned inside the hangar.

Something must really be happening. Alisen clung to McKenzie, who dragged her away from the hangar.

"Hurry! Hurry!" she kept repeating, and Alisen had to follow her.

Jay, Ethan, and the lieutenant colonel were the last to leave the hangar. Alisen looked back at them. A few yards from the door Jay paused and looked up at the sky. Over the siren Alisen could not hear what she said, but she distinctly saw her lips form the word: "Planes."

Alisen stared upwards. "McKenzie! Wait!" she screamed.

McKenzie paused.

Louder and louder, a slight vibration of the atmosphere grew and increased until the ground seemed to shiver, and the noise was overpowering. Both girls turned their eyes upwards and saw military jets speeding towards them.

"Whose?" shouted McKenzie over the noise.

"I don't know, but they're not ours," said Jay, appearing suddenly behind them. "You two are the slowest evacuees I've ever seen. Get moving."

She ran behind them, spurring them onward to a low building up ahead. The door was opened by a dusty Air Force airman, and then shut behind them with a click.

Alisen and McKenzie stopped short. The hall was guarded by several rows of men with machine guns, who did not seem to notice them. They all stared at Jay.

"Jaylis!" said one of them. "What did you find out? What's going on?"

"Hard to say," she said, looking at Alisen and McKenzie.

"Sergeant Jay, what's going on?" she whispered.

Jay looked down at her. "The Civil Air Patrol received a phone call," she said. "The man on the phone said only four words, 'An attack is coming.' Then he added the name of the organization."

"Which was?" interrupted the airman.

"The I.P."

The name sent a shiver of dread down Alisen's spine. She had heard the horror stories of what the I.P. did in the Middle East, where they killed, maimed, and destroyed countless thousands of people. Everyone feared that name, no matter who they were or where they were. Daily the news was spattered with incoherent reports on the violence they caused, which was all done in the name of . . . of what?

Alisen could not take the time to think about it. Everything around her became indistinct somehow—Jay's set face, McKenzie's frightened squeak—and there was no longer a connection between her and them. All she heard was the planes overhead and—

Jay's hand on her shoulder snapped her back to reality. "Alisen? Wake up!"

Tears rolled down Alisen's face. "What is happening?" she whispered, looking up at Jay.

"God is on our side," said Jay, without answering her question. "Our God . . . He will surely save us."

McKenzie took her friend's arm. "Come on," she said. "The airmen want us to stay in the basement, where we'll be out of the way."

The last thing Alisen saw before beginning the descent of the stairs was Jaylis taking a heavy black machine gun from the airman nearest her.

CHAPTER II

THEY HAD DESCENDED SIX FLIGHTS of stairs before the airman had left them and returned to the main floor. Alisen and McKenzie huddled together in the corner, both in tears, listening to the strange noises upstairs. They thought they had heard some explosions, but they were so far underground they could not tell for sure.

There was nothing either of them could do but wait and try to understand what was happening above them.

Suddenly McKenzie stood up and stamped her foot on the dirt floor. "I can't stand this!" she cried. "Jaylis, those airmen—they're all up there doing something, and we're in this dirty basement sitting and hoping they succeed in keeping the I.P. out! This is stupidity."

"What are you thinking?" Alisen looked up at her. "You can't shoot a gun!"

"Whoever said I couldn't?" demanded McKenzie. "I spent hours at the shooting range with my father. My—oh!"

There was a moment of silence as they wondered what had happened to their parents.

"Where could they have gone?" asked Alisen at last. "Do they know about . . . this?"

"My mother had a gun," whispered McKenzie. "She could defend herself."

Alisen didn't say what she was thinking. What good was one small gun in the hands of a woman going to do against the entire army of the I.P.?

"My mom and dad stayed at home today," she said aloud. "We live pretty close to the base. I'm sure they know at least a little of what's going on."

McKenzie's eyes widened. "Got your cell phone?"

"Of course!" cried Alisen. "Why didn't I think of that sooner!"

She pulled it out of her pocket and turned it on. "Should I call my parents first, or yours?"

"Call yours," said McKenzie. "Hurry, please!"

Alisen tapped in the numbers. Both girls waited anxiously while it rang and eventually went to voicemail.

"No!" Alisen was about to hang up, but McKenzie stopped her. "Wait! Listen to the message!"

They listened closely.

"If it's Alisen, stay somewhere safe!" said the voice of Alisen's mother. "If it's anyone else . . . I'm sorry, I can't help."

"Try my mother!" cried McKenzie. "It's—"

Suddenly the ceiling above them shook and plaster fell on their heads. A moment later a deafening explosion rent the air above them.

"Bombs!" shrieked McKenzie. "Jay, the airmen!"

"The ceiling!" Alisen grabbed McKenzie and pulled her violently under a nearby desk. It was just in time. The ceiling shook, cracked, and began to fall.

"This is the end!" shouted Alisen, beginning to believe her own words. "Hold on, McKenzie!"

The ceiling cracked audibly. The side opposite them fell inward with a loud crash.

"Look!" screamed McKenzie, pointing.

Alisen tried to see over the wall of fallen plaster and concrete. She twisted and turned until she was able to see the still body of an airman lying atop the rubble.

McKenzie tried to climb out from under the desk to reach him, but Alisen restrained her. "Back, you idiot!" she shouted above the noise. "You can't help him now!"

With one final, terrifying split, the entire ceiling gave way and fell on top of them, burying them and the desk beneath the rubble.

There was a long moment of silence, during which Alisen was convinced that, if they had not died already, they would do so in a matter of seconds. She held her breath and wondered where she would be in the next five minutes.

Suddenly she felt something soft slipped over her mouth.

McKenzie had torn a piece of dark blue cloth from her long military pants and covered both their faces. "Breathe through it," she said, her voice strangely muffled.

Alisen's mind returned to earth with a thump. "How are we going to get out of here?"

"We can't get out of here," said McKenzie. "Either we suffocate, or the I.P. finds us, or . . . "

"Or?" Alisen prodded.

"Or, somebody digs us out, I suppose . . . "

"How long must we wait? Can't we make a noise?"

"I guess," said McKenzie reluctantly.

They were about to raise their voices and call for help when a sound from above froze them mid-shout.

At first, she could not tell what it was, but after a moment she recognized a voice speaking an odd and very guttural language. Then, very suddenly, it switched to English.

"That was a good job they did with the bombs," it said. "Cleared nearly everything out for us."

Someone else said something that Alisen did not catch.

"It must be some sort of acoustic effect," whispered McKenzie. "Otherwise we would be too far down to hear them."

"Right," said the first voice. "Say, there's somebody over there. Let's see if they're still alive."

"If they are?" said another.

"Then we have one more prisoner. The more the better, you know. It will save us trouble later."

There was the sound of feet crunching on rubble.

Alisen slipped her hand over McKenzie's mouth.

"They must be I.P.," whispered Alisen. "Keep still, or we're finished!"

McKenzie nodded, her eyes wide with fear.

"Looks like a girl," said the first voice. "Living?"

"Yes," said a third voice, female this time. Alisen recognized it as Jay's. "What was the plan, anyway? Concerted attack across the country? Or was it here that you were primarily targeting?"

The first voice laughed. "Acquainted with the ways of the I.P., are you?"

"To my infinite regret," said Jay. She added something else, in the same language the first voice had been speaking earlier.

The conversation continued incomprehensible to McKenzie and Alisen for a few moments. Then they heard Jay's voice raised. "That cannot be true! It is well known that the I.S., which sponsors your army, has not the resources for such an expedition!"

The first voice coldly cut her off. "The I.S. sponsors our army," it said. "True. But we have another, much greater assistant than them. They are, well, you might call them our aide-de-camp. It was not the I.S. who supported this attack. They refused to have anything to do with it, for they said it was sure to fail." He laughed bitterly.

"Who was it?" demanded Jay.

"See if you can guess. You seem to know the policies well."

There was a moment of silence.

"We should have seen this coming," said Jay at last. "You have only confirmed what I knew in my heart already."

"Which is?" The voice was insolent and sneering.

"Your support comes from the country you have attacked, the United States itself." Jay became louder. "Traitors! All along you planned this so—"

"You do know!" cried the voice. "No one was supposed to know—not yet!"

"What do you hide?" Jay's voice was sharp and bitter. "Who could look, and not see what you intended? You wanted only one thing, to annihilate the people who believe what I do."

"You," said the voice, slowly, "you are an ex-agent. You could not have known what you do—unless you were once I.P."

"What I have done does not enter into this discussion. Only what you are doing now matters."

"I don't think so," said the voice. Then, after a moment's pause: "I begin to recall to my mind the story of an ex-agent, who was nearly executed for abandoning the I.P."

"Abandoning? Strange choice of words."

"Perhaps it is time for justice to be served."

"God forbid your kind of justice is the right one," said Jay. "But so be it. Death has no terrors for me, any more than it did then."

"You would have made a brave agent," said the voice, accompanied by a thin rustling of metal against cloth. "There is still that choice."

"I have seen who you are. I know you, and I will never go back."

"That choice will cost you your life."

"So be it!" cried Jay.

There was a loud, sharp explosion, and then a forbidding silence.

"The rest of you, take heed!" cried the voice. "This is what becomes of the I.P.'s enemies! They shall all die! On everything we believe in as men, I swear it!"

There were more footsteps, and then silence again.

McKenzie and Alisen looked at each other in horror. "Jay!" they both whispered.

"How did this happen?" Tears ran down Alisen's face unheeded. "We left our house for a meeting of cadets and friends, and now . . . "

"Now," finished McKenzie drily, "now they're all dead. And we're about to suffer the same fate."

"Poor Jay!" cried Alisen. "I was wrong to hate her so . . ."

"What happened to this world?" whispered McKenzie. "And what did Jay mean when she said that our own country was supporting the I.P.?"

"I don't know," said Alisen. "One thing I do know. We found the safest place on the entire base, and we'd better stay here."

"Except that we're going to suffocate if we don't get out," said McKenzie. "One way or the other, we're going to end up where Jay is."

Alisen squinted at her. "What?"

McKenzie shrugged.

"That doesn't sound like you."

Finally, McKenzie burst out, "Where's God now? Why are we here? Why did Jay have to die?"

"McKenzie . . . "

"What?" The word came out as a strangled shriek.

"I don't know . . . "

"Isn't He supposed to help us when we're in trouble?" said McKenzie. "We're under a building, Jay is dead, and the I.P. is taking over our country! What is happening? Where is He?"

"God?"

McKenzie stared at her silently.

"Maybe this is supposed to happen," Alisen offered weakly. "Maybe there's some purpose in this."

"What could it be?" McKenzie had lowered her voice as if it was an effort to speak. "Why?"

"I'm not God!" exclaimed Alisen angrily. "I don't have any answers! Stop asking me!"

"What's the point?" asked McKenzie.

"I swear, I don't know!"

"And how are we going to get out of here?"

Undoubtedly McKenzie had raised an important point. Already the scarcity of air was starting to affect them. It was necessary that they should escape as soon as possible before their coughing became audible to the I.P.

McKenzie, holding her cloth over her mouth, started scratching at the back of the desk. Alisen watched her for a moment, then started on the other side.

After a few moments they gave up in exhaustion. It was like trying to dig out of a rock. The weight of the entire building held them trapped and pinned beneath it. They made no headway at all except to disturb the delicate balance of the plaster and send it crashing on their heads.

"At this point I don't care if it's the I.P. that finds us," said McKenzie. "Better them than nobody. I say we yell."

"Agreed," said Alisen, her dread of the building beginning to outweigh her dread of the I.P. attackers.

They pressed their cloths over their faces and started to call for help again.

"I'm coming," said a muffled voice above them. "Stay where you are. Don't move."

Alisen and McKenzie looked at each other with hope. "Doesn't sound like the I.P.," said McKenzie.

"I'm not I.P.," said the voice. "Stay where you are." There was a strange cough and then the sound of rubble being moved.

Alisen grabbed McKenzie's arm and said, "What about the airman? Maybe whoever this is can help him, too."

McKenzie nodded. "Say," she called up, "there's another man trapped about ten feet away from us on the other side. Can you help him, too?"

There was a moment of silence above. "Wait," said the voice, tramped away over the rubble.

The sounds of digging resumed on the other side of the basement. Then it stopped, and the footsteps came back to them. "He's dead."

Alisen lowered her head.

The digging continued above them, occasionally interspersed with a loud, hacking cough. At last, not directly above them, but a little to the side, Alisen could see a speck of light. She and McKenzie cheered and started climbing up to meet it.

"Stay where you are," cautioned the voice again, more hoarse now than muffled. "You move, and the entire pile comes back down on you."

Alisen and McKenzie immediately subsided.

The coughing and the digging recommenced. Still neither of the girls had seen their rescuer's face through the hole, but, as McKenzie pointed out, they would owe whoever it was an enormous debt of gratitude when they got out.

"We could take them somewhere for lunch sometime," suggested Alisen.

McKenzie scoffed at the idea. "During a war?"

"Well, perhaps we should just ask them what they want. I'm sure our parents would help us get it."

"Probably," said McKenzie. "I can't wait to know who it is!"

"Likely it's one of the airmen," said Alisen. "Somebody from another building who happened to make it out."

"But the cough?"

"Could be a patient from the hospital. It's not far from here."

Alisen's cell phone rang loudly, interrupting their conversation.

"You have a cell phone?" said their rescuer's voice from far above them. "Answer the call and then get rid of it. That's how they can track you."

Alisen put the phone to her ear and answered. "Mom?"

"Alisen!" said a male voice on the other end. "It's me, Lieutenant Colonel Krakoff. I'm calling all the C.A.P. members to meet at the wreckage of the hangar . . . as soon as you can get here without being spotted. I.P. patrols are all around."

"I'm trapped under a building, sir," said Alisen. "Only McKenzie is with me. Where is everyone else? What's happening outside?"

Krakoff paused. "I don't know where everyone else is," he said. "You're the only one who's answered my phone call."

Alisen shivered. "I'll be there as soon as I can. Thank you."

"Right," said Krakoff. "And let me say it again—don't let yourself get caught by a patrol. Better to stay under that building for all eternity than to be caught. You hear me?"

Alisen and McKenzie looked at each other. "Yes, sir. We'll be very careful."

"Right," he repeated. "Hurry, then."

Alisen hung up the phone and stared at it. "What could he have meant about the patrols being so dangerous?" she said. "Surely . . ."

"I don't know," said McKenzie. "But I do know that if the I.P. hacks or bribes or induces the cell providers, then they'll be able to track you by your phone. Let's see. We want the phone to work without the tracking systems, so . . . let me see it."

Alisen gave her the phone.

McKenzie took off the back cover and removed the battery. She pulled out another grey chip and waved it in front of Alisen's eyes. "See this?" she said. "That is your GPS receiver. Now your phone will still do everything but receive GPS. And we will go into the phone and turn off mobile data and cellular, and then you'll be invisible."

Alisen blinked. "How did you know all that?"

"Just because I don't have a big, fancy phone doesn't mean I don't know how they work," said McKenzie. "There. The ideal phone for wartime."

"Is this really a war?" asked Alisen. "After all, if they only attacked this state, then surely the army will come, and we'll be saved? Somehow?"

"The I.P. won't have made that mistake," said their rescuer's voice breathlessly. "I can't say what they've done, but they're out for blood this time."

"Do you know very much about the I.P.?" questioned McKenzie.

There was a brief pause. "Yes," said the voice above. "Yes, I do."

"Then can you tell us what the lieutenant colonel meant when he said it's better to stay under this building for eternity than to fall into the hands of one of their patrols?"

Again silence. "No," said the voice. "I know the answer, but I will not tell you. Knowing would do you no good under the present circumstances."

There was another round of coughing from above, then the voice said faintly, "All right. You can try climbing out now. Be careful."

"Go ahead," said McKenzie, pushing Alisen forward.

Alisen got a grip on a pile of bricks and pulled herself up. She froze for a moment.

"What are you doing?" complained McKenzie. "Let me out!"

Alisen moved out of the way. "You'd better come see this," she said.

McKenzie climbed out and stared. "Jay!"

CHAPTER III

FROM HER SITTING POSITION ON the ground, Jay smiled up at her. "Yes, of course."

"How'd you dig us out?" said McKenzie. "We thought you were killed!"

Jay coughed and put a hand to her side. "The building was built on a hill," she explained, her voice faint and distant. "I was able to get to you from the back side." She put her hands on the ground beside her and seemed to be trying to hold herself up.

"Are you okay?" asked McKenzie worriedly, sitting down beside her. "Jay?"

Alisen pointed suddenly to Jay's side. "Look!"

It was covered in blood, which poured out from the deep wound and stained the white plaster beneath them.

Jay lay back, her head on McKenzie's lap. Her eyes were closed and marked with dark rings that had not been present a few hours earlier. Her face was pale, and her hands twitched convulsively by her side, as if she was trying to fight her weakness for a few minutes longer.

McKenzie supported Jay against her chest, tears pooling in her eyes, and then dropping down her nose. "Why did you do it for us?" she whispered. "You could have gone to the hospital."

Jay shivered and coughed again. "No," she said. "I had to save you."

Alisen was scared, more frightened than she could ever remember being. She had watched horror movies, where there was blood everywhere and people died violent deaths, but it was nothing like the reality. And this was her friend, the one person they knew who could protect them.

"I'm sorry for being such a prig," Alisen said, kneeling beside Jay and crying bitterly into McKenzie's shoulder. "I was so hateful to you!"

Jay smiled. "You weren't," she said. "I didn't give you a chance."

She tried to sit up, but fell back, coughing. A thin stream of blood trickled from her lips. "Go meet Krakoff," she said. "Leave me behind."

"We won't leave you," said McKenzie. "Come with us. We'll help you get there."

Jay's eyes closed for a moment, then fluttered open again. "No," she whispered. "I would never make it all the way."

"We have to try!" McKenzie struggled to stand and help Jay to her feet.

"Stop!" Jay gasped and tried to stifle a cry of pain. "You have to go without me. You cannot move me."

"You're going to be fine," Alisen tried to believe it was true. "We'll get you to the hospital or something."

"I'm sorry, Alisen." She grimaced against her spasmodic shivers. "You have to let me go."

McKenzie abandoned all efforts at keeping back her tears and turned away.

"You dug us out," said Alisen through her strangled sobs, "with that wound in your side. You gave your life for ours. Why? You should have been saved, not us!"

Jay's breathing had become hoarse. With a great effort she said, "It was only justice."

After a moment's intense inward struggle for breath, her head fell back and rested against McKenzie's shoulder. Her dark eyes became wide and sightless, staring up at the clouded sky where jets crossed back and forth.

McKenzie looked up at Alisen, her face fearful. "I think she's dead, Alisen."

Alisen reached for Jay's wrist, soaked in blood from her wound, but drew her hand back before she touched it. "Why did it have to be her," she whispered. "Why Jay?"

McKenzie gently stood up and let Jay's body slide to the ground. "I don't know. Her courage, her knowledge. It would have helped us so much. She deserved life!"

"What did she mean," said Alisen, rising to her feet, "when she said that it was only justice for her to help us?"

"I don't know," said McKenzie again. Then she wildly shouted, "The I.P. will pay for this!"

"Shut up!" hissed Alisen, terrified. "You're going to get us killed!"

"What price?" She savagely pointed to Jay's still form. "Look at what they left behind!"

"The I.P. did this," said Alisen, desperately trying to stay calm. "But you can't stop them all by yourself. Jay would never have wanted you to do something stupid like this. She said to go meet Krakoff. And if we have to defy the entire I.P., then we'll honor her last request."

McKenzie stared at her coldly. "You try to sound all courageous. We'll honor her last request, all right. We'll avenge her death."

"McKenzie! What's got into you?"

For a moment McKenzie was silent. Then she fell to her knees and wept without restraint. "I've never seen anybody die before," she said. "Not even in movies. We never watched anything. And it had to be Jay, the one person I looked up to more than anyone else in the Patrol."

"I'm so sorry," said Alisen. There was nothing else she could have said. Nothing and nobody could bring Jay back.

She stood on top of a pile of rubble and looked around. She was on the highest visible point on the horizon. The bomb had made an immense hole in the ground, hardly two hundred yards away. Anyone who had been there was beyond their help. Nowhere could she see an entire building still standing; all were like the hangar, or the barracks they had taken shelter in.

A bright speck caught her eye. It was the red stripes of the American flag, fluttering nearby on top of a loudspeaker system. The flag was being hauled down, replaced by a green and white canvas—the I.P.'s signature.

McKenzie, still kneeling, looked past Alisen at the flagpole. "At least Jay didn't live to see the American flag replaced by the I.P. flag."

Alisen wanted to tell her to stop talking about Jay, to stop reminding her of the pitiful sight behind her. But she couldn't bring herself to do it. Fear had nearly mastered them; now was the time for action.

"Hurry," Alisen stumbled across the wreckage, "before we sight another patrol. We've got to get to the hangar."

"Right," said McKenzie. "Alright. Let's go."

They grabbed hold of each other's hands, took a mutual deep breath, and began to run across the road.

Every moment Alisen expected to hear shouts behind them. She thought she heard gunfire, and nearly overturned McKenzie trying to look back.

"Come on!" cried McKenzie breathlessly. "We have to make it there!"

Alisen turned back around and tried to keep up with McKenzie. She pulled too hard, and their hands separated.

An I.P. patrol rounded the ruins of the barracks and came into the road, not thirty feet from where McKenzie and Alisen were.

McKenzie saw them first. "Look out!" she screamed, pausing and turning back to look for Alisen. "Run!"

The patrol seemed so surprised to see anyone living that they did not immediately react. It gave Alisen and McKenzie time to scatter and make it off the road.

Cold sweat dripped down Alisen's face. Never had she run for her life before, and she was surprised at how slowly she seemed to move. The trees flitted by, what few of them there were, and Alisen thought she heard pursuit. A moment later she was sure of it. She looked around in desperation, until she spotted a ruined building she thought she could crawl under. She darted towards it and slid underneath.

A hand slipped over her mouth.

She tried to scream, but no sound came out.

A voice arrested her frantic struggle. "Quiet, it's me, Kale." He removed his hand from her mouth. "Are they following you?"

"I don't know," said Alisen, sniffling miserably. "I think so."

"Did they see you come under here?"

"I hope not," said Alisen. She squinted and tried to see him in the darkness. "Kale? Kale, from Civil Air Patrol? I can't see you."

"Yes," he whispered back. "Are you okay? Hurt or anything?"

"I'm fine," said Alisen. "But I lost McKenzie, and Jay—"

"Jay?" repeated Kale. "Where's Jay?"

"Dead." She shuddered. "I saw it."

Kale took a deep breath. "I'm guessing this is the first death you've ever seen?"

Alisen nodded and ducked her head.

"I'm so sorry," he said gently. "I know how you feel because . . . because I've seen it, too."

She looked up at him, surprised.

"Do you want to talk about it?" she added, after a brief awkward pause.

"Not now," he said. "I hear people coming."

They held their breaths as the sound of rapid pursuit came closer and closer.

A voice began to speak in the mysterious language that Alisen did not recognize.

"That's Arabic," whispered Kale.

"You speak Arabic?"

"No, I just know. It's the language of the I.P."

"But what's he saying?"

Kale raised a finger.

"Quit talking like that," said another voice in accented but precise English. "You know the orders—assimilate. It's why you were chosen. You all speak English, so do it."

"I'm saying, where could this girl have gone? You know the patrol leader is going to be angry if we don't find her."

"He won't," said the other voice. "He knows as well as I do that one small girl or another isn't going to make much of a difference. After all, when one takes over a country, there still should be people to rule over and to work the land, wouldn't you say? She'll learn to her cost what it's like to meddle with the I.P." There were a few sardonic laughs.

"But what about Jay?"

"Jay? Who's that?"

"You know," said the first voice, "the ex-agent who escaped us a few years ago. This girl was coming from where Jay was killed."

"Perhaps they were friends," said the second voice. "We can easily find out."

The footsteps grew fainter, and at last passed out of hearing.

Alisen turned to look at Kale. "Why me?" she whispered nervously. "Where am I going to go?"

"You're going to get rid of your cell phone if you've got it," he replied. "There's a GPS chip in the back."

"Was," corrected Alisen. "McKenzie took it out."

"Good," said Kale. "So, they can't track you. Anything else electronic? Fitbit, watch—anything?"

Alisen felt in her pockets to be sure. "Nothing," she said. "Why?"

"Well, for example, if you're wearing a Fitbit, they can track the Bluetooth signal," said Kale.

"Why are you so calm?"

Kale smiled bitterly. "I'm not," he said. "Inside, I'm cursing this day and wondering about my family and my school and my house. But that's not going to help me, so I try not to focus on it."

"You have such strength," sighed Alisen wearily. "I wish I was like you."

Kale did not reply.

"Must I leave?" asked Alisen. "Where will I go?"

"We can't very well stay under this building," said Kale. He paused to think. "I know my way around this base. If the bombs haven't levelled it, we might be able to get to the commissary for supplies. Then . . . "

"Supplies?" The familiar word made Alisen feel the tiniest bit better.

"How long do you think it'll be before we make it to a grocery store again?"

"I haven't thought that far ahead," said Alisen, hiding her face in her hands so that Kale would not see her cry. "The commander told me to try to get back to the hangar. I was on the way there with McKenzie when the patrol found us. I really just want to go home. Can't we at least try to get back? There's plenty of food there, and my house is only a few miles away."

"But what about the patrols?" asked Kale. "Almost everything got flattened by the bombs, and they can see for miles. They'll find us if we try to travel too far."

"I just want to go home," repeated Alisen. "I really, really want to go home."

"We can always look for temporary shelter," said Kale, "and make our way back to your house after dark, or in a few days when the patrols relax a little. For now, I think we need to hide as much as possible and not travel if we can help it."

"We were supposed to go back to the hangar as soon as we got free," said Alisen. "Maybe someone has supplies there or can help us get back home. I need to make sure my family is okay."

"Then we'll go to the hangar first," said Kale. "Follow me."

He darted out from under the building and into the shelter of some trees. He turned back to look for her, and she had no choice but to follow.

"Keep your head down," cautioned Kale in a whisper. "I'm going ahead to see if the road is clear. We can't afford to mess this up. When you see me wave, you follow."

Alisen was shivering too hard to reply, but she nodded her head vigorously and Kale started off.

He was halfway down the slope before he waved to Alisen. She came down with a tumble and nearly fell into the road.

"Careful!" said Kale, steadying her. "I think we are safe to cross. There are no patrols in sight either direction."

Alisen followed him as they cautiously descended the rest of the slope. They were nearly to the road when Kale said suddenly, "Somebody's coming!"

"McKenzie!" shrieked Alisen, louder than she had intended. The forlorn figure limping toward them sped up at her cry and embraced Alisen vigorously.

Alisen held her friend at arm's length and scanned her curiously. "What happened to you?"

Kale broke in, "This isn't the time for reunions. Someone could come along any minute. Hadn't we better save this for the hangar?"

"Kale's right," said McKenzie. "I'll tell you when we get there. You owe me a good story, too, seeing that you found one of the missing C.A.P. airmen."

"Hurry!" hissed Kale.

They crossed the road at a trot and observed the state of the hangar. The rear part had collapsed, burying the planes, but the front part was intact and looked safe to enter.

Kale held the door open, and they rushed inside.

It was eerily empty. None of them had ever seen it without the cheerful voices of the cadets inside. The whiteboard had been overturned as if by an earthquake; various items belonging to the members were scattered around the floor where they had been suddenly abandoned. There was no sign of the lieutenant colonel.

Kale called out in a fierce whisper: "Lieutenant Colonel Krakoff?" There was no reply.

Then, raising his voice, he tried again. "Lieutenant Colonel Krakoff?"

One of the closet doors opened, and an unfamiliar man stepped out, dressed in an unfamiliar light brown uniform. He smiled in a friendly manner, then picked up a machine gun that had been lying unobserved at his feet and slung it over his shoulder.

"You did not really think that your commander would tell you to come back here?" he asked. "Apparently you have never heard his voice over the phone. I did rather a good job counterfeiting it, I think. How lovely it is to see you all, though I rather hoped more would show up."

"Who are you?" McKenzie's voice shook.

"Good question. My name is Dalek, and I am a commander in the I.P. army. I have come here to see how many of you I could round up."

"Us?"

"You, precisely, my lady," said Dalek, "along with the other Civil Air Patrol members. There is one specifically that we are looking for. Well, as you can see that it would be useless to resist, perhaps you had better come single-file into this closet, so I can contain you. Hurry up now."

"Wait!" said Alisen, with a sudden premonition. "Who are you looking for?"

Dalek crossed his arms and looked at her in mock surprise. "What, a possible informant? Would you tell me where she is hiding?"

"I don't know where anyone is hiding," insisted Alisen. "Who are you looking for?"

"We are looking for a girl named Jaylis," replied Dalek. "Her last name, in your peculiar English language, would be something like Jennison. Have you perhaps seen her?"

Alisen and McKenzie exchanged glances.

"She's dead," said McKenzie softly.

"Really?" said Dalek, with diabolical cheerfulness. "Well, then, my task is already half-way accomplished! That would also mean that you, as informants, are no longer of any use. Into the closet, all of you!"

There really was nothing they could do. Dalek was armed and very determined, and they could not hope to gain anything by storming him. One by one they entered the closet.

Dalek waved to them before he closed the door. "Goodbye," he said. "I hope we shan't meet again."

The door slammed shut and darkness enveloped them.

"Now what?" asked Alisen, trying to sound calm and failing utterly.

"Now," said Kale, "we wait and hope the lieutenant colonel is around here somewhere."

"Can we depend on him? For all we know, they may have caught him!"

"Well, Jay did say to return to the hangar after . . . oh." Kale paused awkwardly. "I'm sorry."

"We have to wait for the commander," he added, after an uncomfortable pause. "We can't get out of here by ourselves."

McKenzie, who had been scratching in the corner, spoke up suddenly "We can't wait for the commander."

"What do you propose we do?" Alisen asked sharply.

"Smell," said McKenzie, turning and glancing back at the corner.

They sniffed, and suddenly fear took hold.

Kale was the first to say aloud what they all knew. "Fire."

"Then we have to get out of here," said McKenzie. "There has to be a way out!"

Kale put his hand to the metal door and drew it back quickly. "The fire's inside the hangar," he said. "If we're going to get out, it won't be through that door."

Alisen ran into McKenzie as she was crossing the room to feel at the door. She stumbled back, fell against the wall, and crashed through.

McKenzie and Kale rushed to look at her, eyes wide. "That's what we need! A battering ram!" said Kale. "Is there a door in there?"

Alisen turned to look and saw that she had gone completely through the weakened drywall and into the next room. There was a door on the back wall.

McKenzie helped Alisen to her feet. "Come on!"

Kale pulled Alisen through the opening and ran toward the door. It opened, and they hurried outside, then froze suddenly while still standing on the doorstep.

Dalek was standing there, a machine gun pointed at them.

CHAPTER IV

ALISEN WOKE WITH A SCREAM. She sat up in her bed, tears of fear running down her face from what she had seen and the pain and horror of it all.

And yet, everything had been only a dream. Alisen was not a member of the Civil Air Patrol, she knew no one named Jay, and her friend McKenzie had long since moved away.

Her door opened and her mother, her eyes wide and anxious, looked inside. "Are you okay, sweetie?" she asked.

Alisen lay back down. "Yes, I'm fine. Just a bad dream."

Her mother came in and sat on the bed beside her. "Tell me about it."

"I'd rather not."

"Alisen, we're going to have to do something about these dreams. You have one almost every night, and you've never yet said what they're about."

"Really, I don't want to talk about it," Alisen sighed. "It's just a scary dream. Maybe I ate too much pizza last night."

"We had salads for dinner."

"Salads. Whatever." She paused, feeling uncomfortable. "Fine. I'll tell you about it." Alisen took a deep breath. "I was at this thing called Civil Air Patrol—I don't even know what that is—and McKenzie was with me. There was also this girl named Jay. We were having a course on leadership, when suddenly Jay came running in telling us all to get out. She said this organization called the I.P. was coming after us, and they'd kill us if they found us. Funny thing is, I've never heard of the I.P., yet in the dream I knew all about them—they were a sort of terrorist organization from the Middle East. We all ran. They tried to catch us. They found Jay, and—and killed her. McKenzie and I were there when she died. At the end of the dream, we were in a hangar with this boy named Kale, trying to get out before the fire got to us. It was all so . . . so real. No empty places, no skips—everything seemed real." Alisen dropped her head and tried to hide her tears.

"That's strange." Her mother wrapped a protective arm around her. "Your father was a member of the Civil Air Patrol when he was little. Perhaps he's told you about it."

"But that doesn't explain the rest of it."

"That's true," said her mother. "Let's pray about it."

Alisen shrugged.

Her mother put a hand on her shoulder and began speaking softly. "God, we pray for Alisen right now and these dreams she's been having. If they're from You, then please help us to know what they mean. If they're not, then please take them away and keep all evil from her. In Jesus's name, amen."

Alisen looked up at her, realizing that her mother was not simply curious; she truly cared. "I'm okay," she said, her voice softening. "I'll go back to sleep."

Her mother kissed her and left the room.

For hours she lay awake and stared at the ceiling, remembering and yet trying to forget the dream she had. Maybe it had some meaning. It was always the same, every night—except that details were added, and the dream always became longer and more complex than the night before.

Alisen was terrified of it, but she never could prevent it from coming. She had tried everything she knew, down to counting imaginary sheep, but the result was always the same; the dream would come, and she would suffer through it, feeling real physical and mental pain, until at last she woke up in terror.

Her alarm clock went off. It startled her, and she got up to turn it off. As she looked at her phone, she noticed a text from her friend McKenzie.

This seemed to her eerily prophetic and she clicked the icon to read it.

Alisen! Good news! the text ran. *We're moving back there this summer. Dad finally got a job, and I can't WAIT to see you!!*

Alisen's eyes opened wide. She collapsed on the side of the bed and stared at the phone.

This was one of the things that had to happen for her dream to come true.

She shook her head. It wasn't possible. Nobody had dreams that came true, so there was no reason for her to either. Anyhow, the only thing she would get by worrying was a reprimand from her teacher for being late to school. So, she got up and began to dress.

Her friend Sadie met her at the bus stop. "How are you this morning?" she asked. "You look tired."

"Yeah. I didn't sleep much last night."

"Having those dreams again?"

Alisen glanced around. "Worse than usual," she whispered. "Do you know anyone named Jay, or Kale?"

"You've asked me that before," said Sadie. "I can't think of anyone."

"Who knows," said Alisen. "It's probably just something I ate before I went to bed. Or a book, maybe. It's just so frightening."

"I bet," said Sadie. "You been reading Sherlock Holmes lately?"

Alisen stifled a smile. "Why?"

"Well, it's a good book, but sometimes it can be creepy—and I've been nagging at you to read it for months now. I'd think you'd take my advice eventually." Sadie laughed. "I was hoping that maybe you were finally reading it, which might cause your dreams, you know?"

"I will, I promise," Alisen silently shook her head at Sadie's preferred list of literature. "I don't have much time to read right now. Besides, I don't think it would help with the dreams." She opened her backpack and rummaged for her phone.

"Oh, well," said Sadie. "Look, the bus is coming."

Alisen looked up from her backpack and saw the yellow bus approaching them.

"Come on," said Sadie, and they ascended the steps together.

They went all the way to the back to the last three seats. It was an uncomfortable ride. The back seats vibrated badly, but at least she and Sadie could sit together without being sandwiched by fellow students.

Alisen moved through all her classes that day mechanically, feeling both sleepy and still frightened. She got half her math questions wrong, and, though she studiously pretended not to care, she was feeling irritable by lunch.

As she was standing in line, she heard loud voices behind her, and turned to see what was going on. Two boys had surrounded a third, and it appeared that they were about to fight him. Alisen watched without much interest while they circled, and finally pounced at the same moment. The third boy fought hard and threw them off again and again.

Things might still have ended badly for him had not one of the teachers, prowling around for signs of dissention in his domain, observed the struggle and arrived in time to intervene. The wrath of the two assailants turned suddenly on him until they realized who he was. Then, with startling suddenness, their facades crumbled into ingratiating obedience, and they made a few vain attempts to deny their participation. The teacher was unsympathetic and rumbled off in disgust to convey the offenders to the principal's office.

The remaining boy got up and dusted himself. He saw Alisen staring at him, smiled at her, then winced painfully. He stood up straight, looked around, and stood uncomfortably on one leg. It was obvious that he was feeling unsure of himself, and that he was probably new to the school.

Someone poked Alisen. It was Sadie.

"You're ahead of schedule," she said. "Go and see if you can help him. He's new here, I can tell."

Alisen started to reply, but Sadie had already gotten a tray and joined the line. She glanced back at the boy, who still stood looking forlornly around, rather like a lost puppy. Alisen smiled and went over to talk to him.

"Hello," she said. "Are you new to this school?"

He turned to look at her, smiled immediately, and replied, "Yes, I'm new to this whole state. My family just moved here last week."

"Oh . . . well, glad you're here," said Alisen, not knowing exactly what to say. "So, um . . . do you know how this works?"

"No." The boy shrugged slightly. "I've always been homeschooled until recently."

"Okay," said Alisen. "Follow me. I know every twist and turn of this school. What grade are you in?"

"Ninth," said the boy. "I've been in class with you all day so far."

"Cool! I guess I didn't even see you," Alisen laughed at her own shortcoming. "I'm not always the most observant. Well, lunch is waiting for us. This way."

By the time she had instructed the boy on the various rules and unwritten customs of the cafeteria, she found herself cheering up more than she had thought possible. Her fears from the night before were beginning to disappear, and she was singularly amused by her new friend. He had a way of saying serious things in a sarcastic way that could not help being both silly and hilarious, and she was attracted by his cheerful demeanor. Alisen was glad that Sadie had convinced her to talk to him.

They met again after school while waiting for the bus. "Have fun?" Alisen asked him.

He shrugged, seeming singularly quiet as a contrast to his earlier cheerfulness. "Yeah," he said. "I liked it okay."

"Is something the matter?" asked Alisen.

He smiled again, but Alisen thought she detected a hint of insincerity in it. "No," he said. "Just thinking. I do a lot of that some days."

"I see," said Alisen, puzzled by his apparent personality change; but she was prevented from saying anything else by the arrival of the bus.

"By the way," said the boy, as they boarded the bus side-by-side, "we've been together all day and haven't asked each other's names. What's yours?"

"I'm Alisen," she said, taking hold of the bar to pull herself up and earning a disapproving glance from the bus driver. "How about you?"

"Kale," he said. "Yeah, yeah, like the vegetable." He rolled his eyes.

"Kale," Alisen repeated mechanically. "Right. Actually, it doesn't remind me of a vegetable."

"Really?" he said. "What does it remind you of?"

"My dream," she said. "My—oh, you don't even know about that. Never mind, I'll explain some other time."

"Oh," he said. "Interesting. What do you dream about?"

"Lots of things," said Alisen evasively. "Tomorrow. Meet me at lunch."

"Okay," said Kale obligingly. Then his face clouded. "On second thought . . . I'll be absent tomorrow."

"Absent?" said Alisen, interested in any break of the monotony of school. "What for?"

Kale looked her directly in the eyes and smiled bitterly. "A funeral," he said. "And a couple of other things."

"Oh . . . " Alisen's voice trailed off. "I'm sorry. I suppose I should learn to keep my mouth shut sometimes."

Kale nodded. "Thanks. And it's no problem. It was a fair question."

"Well, whenever we see each other again, I'll explain about the dream. Funny that your name should be connected with it."

"Yeah," said Kale. "Oh, look. I get off here—I think." He smiled, sincerely this time, and picked up his backpack. "See you soon."

Alisen waved goodbye, and Kale stepped down outside the bus. Alisen watched him walk until the bus came to life again and sped away in the opposite direction.

CHAPTER V

ALONE IN HER BEDROOM, ALISEN was determined not to have this dream again. She couldn't imagine what to do to prevent it, but she knew she couldn't keep existing like this, awakening in terror every night and being utterly unable to control the cause of her fears.

She stood in front of her bookshelf, trying to resign herself to reading only 'bonnet books', as she called them, books with no action or violence whatsoever. She didn't have very many, but if she tried to read them for a few days, maybe the dream would disappear.

She seized one from the shelf and returned with it to her bed. She turned her light on, opened it, and started to read, but found she couldn't concentrate on it. She hated bonnet books anyway, so why bother? She put the book on her nightstand and lay back on the pillows.

Her phone, sitting next to her, blinked on. She picked it up and saw that another message had come from her friend McKenzie. It read: *We're coming sooner than I thought . . . the company really wants Dad and they're rather impatient. The sooner the better! I can't wait to see you again!!*

Alisen smiled at the phone, remembering how naively cheerful and happy McKenzie had always been. This reminded her a little of Kale, and she felt sure they would get along well together. She clapped her hands together silently. Even if her dream did have a meaning, she was glad McKenzie was coming back. It would be like old times again.

She typed: *I'm excited too! I'm going to take you to that old ice-cream shop the very day you get here. Remember what you used to order?*

The reply came in a moment: *Banana split, of course. With extra straw-berry sauce.*

Alisen smiled again. *You're up late tonight*, she texted. *I have to go to bed, otherwise I won't be able to get up tomorrow.*

Alright. See you soon!! came the message back, with a little wide-eyed smi-ley at the end.

Alisen put the phone on top of the book and lay back in her bed, glad that McKenzie was coming back. Her thoughts were cheerful and happy, and before she knew it she was sound asleep.

*****   *****   *****

The scene was suddenly different. Alisen found herself standing in front of a tall brick building, looking in through dusty glass windows, and hear-ing everything that was said inside. It was like she was really inside with the people, though she could put her hands to the glass and tell that she was not.

Immediately she noticed that the room was set up like a court trial. On one end was an elevated box with one empty chair and one large seat, upon which sat the judge. Along the right side was the jury box, populated with people Alisen didn't recognize. The back of the room was all seating for on-lookers, and there was a wide empty space between them and the judge's seat. She could hear the people whispering, but nobody was talking loudly—and nobody was speaking English.

Alisen stepped back from the window and looked around, wondering if she could go inside. She saw a group of people dressed entirely in black walk up toward the building and enter by a door on the front. Alisen followed and slipped in behind them before the door closed.

She walked in between the two doors and froze. Two guards were stand-ing there, armed with machine guns slung across their chests. Alisen did not know how she could get past them. They were sure to notice her as soon as she approached. She crept timidly towards them, but they did not move a muscle. Did they even notice her?

She passed them carefully, but they did not turn. Looking back, she saw that they still did not move. It was like they were rooted to the ground.

In front of her was a pair of great wooden doors, standing open and leading into the room she had seen from outside. She inched toward them, glancing back every once in a while, to the still motionless guards. Then she darted inside.

She slid into one of the long rows of benches and sat down on the end. The room was filled with a confused murmuring of voices, slightly louder now that she was actually inside, and they were speaking in some Eastern language—possibly Arabic. It sounded like what the I.P. had been speaking in her previous dream.

Dream! Was this a dream? Alisen wondered.

She looked around; the people looked real, and she could easily see their faces. Could they see her? She walked toward one of them and gingerly touched their arm. They neither turned toward her nor seemed to notice the intrusion.

Alisen sat back down, relieved. That must have been why the guards at the front had not challenged her. Nobody could see or sense her. A strange thought flitted through her mind. Would it be possible for one of them to walk right through her, since she could evidently neither be seen nor felt?

Whether this was a dream or not, this strange sort of protection might be useful—indeed, it already had been. She would have a chance to see what was happening in this room, unhindered by the doubtful clarity of the glass windows.

In a moment everything became suddenly quiet. The judge, who had erstwhile been reclining in his chair, rose and raised a hand. The people took their seats, and the big wooden doors behind them closed.

He turned his head toward the front left of the room. A pair of guards approached, holding two ends of a chain that connected a prisoner's handcuffs.

The prisoner walked between them, head held proudly high, long dark hair streaming loosely behind.

The prisoner was Jay.

The guards bowed to the judge, and it was obvious that Jaylis was expected to do likewise. But she made no move, and the guards had to force her to her knees.

The judge spoke to her once she was in this position. "You are Jaylis Jennison?" he said, in accented but clear English.

"I am," she said. She made an effort to rise, but the guards held her down.

"Do you know what are the charges against you?"

"I do."

"I will then inform the court." He turned gravely to the jury and the onlookers. "This Jaylis Jennison is accused of treachery and refusal to obey direct orders from a superior. She is also accused of accepting the religion of our enemy."

Alisen wondered who the enemy was.

Jay's voice sounded rather shrill after his. "Who brought the accusation, Your Honor?" Alisen fancied that she put a rather sarcastic emphasis on her last words.

The judge nodded. "Bring forth the prosecutor."

A tall and beautiful woman was brought in from the same direction as Jaylis had been, almost as if from the wings of a stage. But she was not dragged along by a chain; instead, it was almost as if the guards who accompanied her were escorting a dignitary. She stopped in front of Jay, looked down at her, and said icily, "I'm sorry." Then she paused. "It didn't have to be this way. We might have been friends."

"You aren't really sorry," said Jaylis drily. "If you were, you would have done things differently."

The girl shrugged and sat down in the front row.

"The prosecutor's name is Ave Genine," said the judge. "She has taken her place. Jaylis, you may rise and be seated on the opposite side."

Before Jay could move, the guards pulled her chains and dragged her to the bench.

The scene was filled with mystery for Alisen. Why was Jaylis in custody? Who was this Ave person, and what did she have to do with anything? And what on earth was this strange court? Who had Jaylis betrayed?

She couldn't help feeling that whatever Jay had done, no matter how terrible, she was being treated cruelly. She was very thin, as if she had not eaten in a long time, her beautiful hair was tangled, and her clothes—which looked as if they had once been a uniform of some sort—were ragged and worn. In addition, the guards pulled her mercilessly by the chains around her wrists, and even from her seat in the back Alisen could see where they were bleeding.

Once Jaylis was seated, the ever-present guards behind her, the judge asked her whether she had anything to say.

"I do," she said. The guards led her to the platform, and she stood up in front of the entire room. Alisen saw dark rings around her eyes.

"Why are you putting me on trial?" she cried passionately. "Is it just a show? Everyone in this room knows what I did, and everyone knows what the punishment is going to be. When Nathan first brought the Bible to this place, you gave him no chance, you immediately told me to go and kill him. Did you think I had so far forgotten myself that I would? And you took me prisoner and had him killed by someone else's hand. What is the point? I know what you want!"

The guards interrupted her by pushing her down to the ground and kicking her hard on both sides. She remained for a moment on her hands and knees, panting, before looking up and saying softly, "I am ready!"

The guards augmented their cruelty, and nobody in the room interfered. Alisen hid her head in her hands, unable to bear the sight before her. If this was a dream, it was worse than all the other ones before. If it was reality . . .

At last the judge stopped them. "Leave her alone," he said. They stepped back and left the still form of Jaylis lying across the platform. The judge bent over her, and said, "Somebody go get water to revive her. There is still more to be done. This trial is not yet finished."

Some water was brought and poured over Jaylis's face. She blinked sleepily, then tried to sit up.

Someone else Alisen didn't recognize was brought in from the side. Jay's eyes fell on him, and she cried, "Nathan!"

Alisen craned her neck to see and froze in horror.

If it was possible for anyone to appear more miserable than Jay herself, it was this man. He had obviously suffered excruciating treatment for a very long time and was the worse for it. His eyes were surrounded by dark rings, his skin was rough and red in patches, and the blood from his torment had not been washed from him. His face was covered in a horrible mask of it.

Alisen averted her eyes but drew them back again at Jay's cry.

Jay struggled, broke loose from her guards and embraced him, throwing her arms around his neck and burying her head in his shoulder. He smiled immediately and squeezed her tightly. But before they could say anything, they were torn apart and pushed back to their places—Jay to one side of the platform, Nathan to the other.

Nathan's guards situated themselves in front of him, unslung their guns from their backs, and held them across their chests in a threatening manner.

The judge turned to Jay. "You can save him," he said. "We'll let him go free if you tell us who else is involved in this."

Jay looked across at Nathan. He smiled at her and shook his head.

She bit her lip and looked up at the judge. "I can't tell you."

"What if we throw your life in the pile?" he said, with a cruel smile. "Would that raise the value of the deal?"

With a last agonized glance at Nathan, Jay wordlessly shook her head.

Alisen knew what was going to happen, and she knew that if it did, she could never stay to watch. She was just getting up to run from the room when she saw the judge signal to Nathan's guards, and her ears exploded in a simultaneous explosion of the two guns.

Her scream echoed through the building, but nobody heard it except her.

CHAPTER VI

IT WAS THE SAME AGAIN. Alisen woke with her own scream ringing in her ears and her body covered in sweat. But at least it had been a different dream. A very different dream, with a very different meaning.

As Alisen grew calmer, she realized that she ought to write down the details of her dream, so she could remember them later.

She seized a sketchbook from her desk and started writing.

DREAM #1

> McKenzie and I are members of the Civil Air Patrol.
>
> There are also people named Kale, Jay (who also seems to go by Jaylis), and a lieutenant colonel.
>
> A mysterious organization called the I.P. (who I thought was a terrorist group from the M.E.) attacks the base.
>
> McKenzie and I are trapped under a building and rescued by Jay, who gives her last strength to dig us out and dies of her wounds soon after.
>
> We meet Kale again.
>
> We are caught by Dalek who traps us in the hangar and sets fire to it.

DREAM #2

> A court is in session; a person named Ave is the prosecutor and Jay is the defendant.
>
> Jay is accused of treason.
>
> Jay refers to Nathan having a Bible.
>
> Guards bring Nathan in.

The judge offers to save Jay's life and Nathan's if they betray their friends.

They refuse, and Nathan is killed.

She paused and thought for a moment, then added another column:

QUESTIONS

Who were the people in the court case?

Why was it wrong for Nathan to have a Bible?

How could they get away with shooting someone in a public court?

What did Jay mean when, before she died, she said she was 'very familiar with the I.P.?'

She stared at the paper, wondering if she had really seen all those things, or if they had simply been part of her overactive imagination. Anyway, she would have a long story for Kale next time she saw him.

*****   *****   *****

"And it was like I was standing right there." Alisen sat across from Kale at the lunch table, her sketchbook in front of them, finally feeling safe to tell someone what she had seen. "Why am I having these crazy dreams? Do you think they mean something?"

Kale hesitated. "Well . . . " he began. "You said your friend McKenzie is moving back here?"

Alisen nodded.

"And you know . . . I am a member of the Civil Air Patrol."

"Really?" Alisen sat up straighter. "Around here?"

"Not yet," said Kale. "But my mom wants me to start soon. And my squadron would be on the Air Force Base, like the one in your dream."

"So maybe things are beginning to come true!" Alisen tried her best not to look scared, but she knew that her face must be unusually pale.

"Maybe," said Kale cautiously. He hesitated. "I've been having strange dreams, too," he said finally.

"Really?" Alisen became suddenly dizzy but she leaned forward with intense interest. "What about?"

"They're mostly the same—like yours—about this woman who comes and takes over the government."

"Then what happens?"

"Then she helps this organization called the I.P. get into the United States, they take over and get rid of her, and the national government passes into the hands of a single man. I know they say his name in the dreams, but I always forget it when I wake up."

"Like Jay said!" Alisen cried. The whole room quieted suddenly, and the nearby students turned to look at her; she lowered her voice. "She said that our own government—America's government—had helped the I.P. get here."

"Right," Kale said. "It sounds like our dreams match up perfectly."

"So, what's the common thread?"

"You mean, why are we having these dreams?" asked Kale gloomily. "I wish I knew. Something must be going to happen."

Alisen had remembered something. "You know," she said slowly, "in my dream, you said that you were familiar with tragedy or something, after I saw Jay die. Are you?"

Kale's head dropped, and his fingers began playing nervously with his zipper. At last he said, "Maybe. But I'd rather not talk about it yet. It's a little too close."

Alisen nodded. "Sorry," she said. "I should learn to keep my mouth shut. Seriously, that's the second time I've had to say that. I really am sorry."

He looked up with a quick smile. "Don't worry about it."

"But what should we do?" continued Alisen. "Our dreams are so similar. There has to be something going on here."

"Maybe," said Kale. "Or, maybe we read the same books, think about the same things, and so influence our dreams the same way. We can't just jump to conclusions. After all, miracles don't really happen anymore."

Alisen was inclined to challenge his view, considering the evidence, but he seemed suddenly reluctant to talk. She did not want to press him.

The bell rang, and lunch was over. They got up and took their trays to the station before heading back to class, sliding into their seats and exchanging a few last words.

"Talk about it again tomorrow," said Kale, just before the teacher arrived. "Let's see if we have any more dreams between now and then."

Alisen nodded.

Classes seemed to pass slowly that day. For the first time since these nightmares had begun, Alisen found herself curious to see what would happen next. She actually wanted to know what would happen to Jay, to the mysterious I.P., and to all the Civil Air Patrol members. And more than anything she wanted to know what it all meant. Her fear was half dominated by intense curiosity.

When she got home, she flung herself onto the bed, finished her homework as quickly as possible, and then pulled out her sketchbook again to look over her columns.

There were some details about her dream that she could easily verify or check in some way to see if they were real. The I.P., for example. Organizations like that did not spring into existence without anyone knowing about it. She pulled her computer toward her by its charging cable and quickly typed in the acronym.

The first page that appeared was mostly irrelevant, but on the second page she found an article titled "What you need to know about joining the I.P." Alisen clicked on it and read the introductory article.

According to the web page, the initials I.P. stood for International Policy, and the organization was not at all a terrorist organization. Rather it said that it was a group of young people who stood up for what they believed in—a perfect world and a perfect life.

Alisen made a mental note of the fact that it elaborated by saying, " . . . and those who are not perfect will be weeded out." That seemed to be a bit ominous, and in accordance with the fear everyone exhibited in her dream.

The next thing she researched was the Civil Air Patrol. What exactly was that? She imagined it as something only adults with driver's licenses could participate in, but in her dream, she had certainly not been sixteen.

It turned out to be a national organization that trained young people in leadership skills, aviation, and military introduction. It looked like good community, and quality training. Alisen found herself wishing she could go and at least see what it was like, for it looked like a close-knit and friendly community. But that could not be. Her dream must never come true, and to even visit the Civil Air Patrol seemed to be tempting fate.

Alisen's phone rang, and she glanced over at it. It was Sadie.

"Hello?" she said, quickly picking up the phone.

"Been getting along with that kid, have you?" asked Sadie, without a preface. "I have literally been invisible to you for days."

"Not days," corrected Alisen, hoping her smile was not betrayed in her voice. "One day and a half. What's bothering you?"

"Things have to bother me for me to call you?"

"I know you way too well for this. What is it?"

"I have spent about three hours on this stupid math problem and it won't work out. Not only that, but I've spent an equal amount of time trying to balance a chemical equation and it won't work out either. Can I come over and get help?"

"I guess that depends on how hard the equation is," said Alisen. "Just kidding. Come on over!"

"Thanks." Sadie hung up with a final annoyed sigh.

She arrived on her bicycle a few minutes later, with a bag of heavy textbooks on her back. Alisen momentarily felt a pang of regret. She would have preferred to spend her evening alone, but she felt she ought to help Sadie with her homework. She had no excuse to avoid it.

Sadie left her bike in the traditional bush by the front porch, which grew sideways and offered excellent support. "Hey, Alisen," she said. "I brought all my books."

"I can see that," said Alisen, eyeing the backpack warily. "Want to sit outside?"

"Sure!" said Sadie. "It's awfully pretty. I love your maple trees."

"Thanks," said Alisen, looking toward the front yard where the flaming trees stood in autumnal red glory. "This is the best time of year for them."

They sat down on the porch swing, and Alisen listened while Sadie explained her woes. Alisen happened to be rather good at chemistry and math, so she was able to explain what was wrong and finish the problem easily. Sadie, who had yet to touch the pencil, sighed with relief.

"I wish I could get you to do my homework for me," she said. Then she slyly added, "What's for dinner?"

"Meatballs," said Alisen. "Meatballs with cheddar cheese. And you're invited."

Sadie laughed. "Thanks," she said. "Not that I was hinting or anything . . . let me call Mom and tell her where I'll be."

While she was waiting, Alisen went around to the backyard and climbed up into the crook of a drooping oak tree. She found a book she had accidentally left behind a while ago. It was damp, and the ink was badly smeared. The only words she could still read were 'Christian' and 'difficulty', which conveyed no meaning to her mind. She sighed and wondered gloomily how much the book had cost before it became soaked through.

Sadie appeared suddenly around the corner. "Mom said it's okay for me to stay," she said. "She's got some work going on tonight."

Alisen slipped down from the tree and stood beside her. "Ever get tired of her being gone all the time?" she asked.

"Always," said Sadie, shrugging her shoulders. "Since Dad died two years ago, everything's been different. We used to have friends at the church, but when we stopped going they all seemed to disappear. Now it's just you." She smiled and poked Alisen's shoulder. "Not that I'm complaining."

"Well, you're always welcome to stay as long as you want," Alisen said. "How about we go upstairs and find something fun to do?"

"Sounds good," said Sadie. "Maybe you can tell me about your time at school when I haven't seen you. Guess you and What's-His-Name get along quite well, right?"

They both laughed and headed for the back door.

CHAPTER VII

IT WAS LATE WHEN SADIE left, pedaling her lonely way down the dark street. Alisen should have been in bed earlier, and she wished they could have made it a sleepover, but that was impossible with her recent nightmares. Nobody would have slept.

She actually had to compel Sadie to leave, because that incorrigible friend had preconceived notions about how the night would continue into the early hours of the morning. But at last she took the hint and left.

As curious as she was to know what her dream would be about tonight, so she could share it with Kale the next day, her fear of what would happen returned. She hoped that tonight would be less violent than the courtroom scene she had witnessed . . .

Soon she drifted off to sleep.

*****   *****   *****

Alisen was in her familiar seat at the Civil Air Patrol. Things were different. Everyone looked pale and disheveled, and some were missing altogether. Alisen sensed the fear that pervaded the room, yet she did not know why it was there or what they were afraid of.

The lieutenant colonel walked between the desks to the whiteboard. "As you all know," he began, his voice oddly shaky, "these last few days have been a horror none of us could have predicted or imagined. The I.P. has taken over our country. However, they are trying to revert from their sudden attack to facilitate the return of law and order as quickly as possible. That is why we were allowed to meet here tonight."

He paused and looked anxiously around the room. "Some of the members of this squadron are never coming back . . . "

Alisen remembered Jay's tragic death and shivered suddenly. What could it mean?

" . . . and we will never forget them."

The entire room became deathly silent.

"There is a young member who wishes to address you tonight. I'm going to let him come up to the stage here and tell us what he thinks of this devastation. Anyone who can make sense out of this is welcome."

A young cadet came through the aisle and stood before the whiteboard. He made a contrast to everyone else in the room, including the lieutenant colonel. He stood up straight and seemed to look everyone in the eye at once. He, too, seemed overshadowed by that ghastly paleness, but at least he did not look afraid.

"I'm sure you're wondering what I could possibly have to say," he said. "Did I know this was coming? Could I have warned you? No, but I should have been able to."

He paused. Nobody moved.

"All these events are predicted in the Bible."

Somebody in the back stood up. "You're going to preach now?" screamed a wild voice. "When the I.P. is out there killing people?"

"'You will hear of wars and rumors of wars, but see to it that you are not alarmed. Such things must happen, but the end is still to come.' Quoted from Matthew 24:6," said the cadet quietly.

"What has that got to do with anything?" said another voice from the back.

"This verse from the Bible seems to summarize what's happening, doesn't it?" he said. "Wars and rumors of wars. And if we ever needed God, it's now."

"Get promoted to chaplain, did you?" sneered the first. "Preaching to us about the end times? Is that what you think this is? The end of the world?"

Alisen realized with horror that was exactly what he had meant. Timidly she raised her hand.

The cadet in front called on her. "Yes?"

"I was wondering," said Alisen, "what did you mean about that rumors of wars thing? I mean, I've heard that before somewhere, but . . . "

"Well," said the cadet, "it's considered to be a sign of the end times. Another thing that many people believe will foretell the end is the disappearance of all people who believe in the one true God. This could happen any time."

"So, you're saying—" Alisen stopped in astonishment.

The cadet had suddenly been enveloped in a white light, painful to look at. Alisen felt heat on her right shoulder; McKenzie, who she had not noticed until now, was shining brilliantly next to her. Alisen screamed and fell back out of her seat into the aisle, covering her eyes with her hands and desperately trying to shut out the painful light. It seemed to slip through her fingers, enveloping and warming and hurting her, too.

Just as suddenly as the glow had begun, it vanished.

With it vanished the people who had shone so brightly.

The cadets around the room cried out with terror. There began a mass scramble for the door; everyone ran over top of each other, heedless of protocol, rules, or regulations. It was a horrible moment. Alisen was run down in the middle of the aisle and trampled on; she could not rise, much less make for the hangar door. Nobody cared about her. Nobody cared about anybody but themselves.

She put her hands back over her eyes and screamed in pain and terror.

*****   *****   *****

Kale sat across from her at the lunch table. Neither spoke; both were subdued and quiet.

"It was the dream, wasn't it?" asked Alisen suddenly.

"Yes, unfortunately," said Kale. "It was the most terrifying thing I have ever seen. I'm only glad it wasn't real."

"Tell me what you dreamed."

Kale poked his fork listlessly into his rice. "Everybody vanished," he said. "Well, not everybody. Some were left. But most people got this glow around them, and then they were gone."

"Why?" Alisen asked, her voice sinking to a whisper. "Why do you think it happened?"

Kale shrugged. "I don't know. Even in the dream I didn't know."

"I was at a Civil Air Patrol meeting," said Alisen. "Obviously it was after the invasion of the I.P. This kid came up and started talking about the end times, how they're predicted in the Bible and how one of the signs is 'wars and rumors of wars'. And he also said that another sign many people believed was that everybody would disappear. I was asking him a question, when suddenly there was that glow, and he vanished." Alisen paused. "So did McKenzie, and a bunch of other people."

"You said that he thought it was predicted in the Bible?" asked Kale. "I never knew much about the Bible. Always seemed like a book of legends. There were some good stories, though. Maybe he was referencing one of those."

"Maybe we should see what we can find out about it," said Alisen. "I never thought much about it either, but if people who believe in God are going to disappear, then we ought to be the first to know."

"Nobody ever said these dreams were prophetic," said Kale quickly.

"You think it's a coincidence that we're both dreaming the same thing?" asked Alisen irritably. She put her elbow on the table and leaned on her hands. "Really?"

"No, I guess not," admitted Kale. "It can't be, can it? They fit together so well."

"Assuming that these dreams are really prophetic," said Alisen, "what has to happen before they can come true?"

"Well, there has to be a presidential election," said Kale. "Everybody knows they've started campaigning already. And for the scenario to fit my dream, a woman has to be elected."

"Is there a woman running?" asked Alisen.

"I don't know," said Kale. "Look it up on that fancy phone of yours."

Alisen took her phone from her pocket and pulled up the news. "Sure enough, there is," she said. "Diane Schultz."

"Another thing that has to happen," continued Kale, "is that we both have to join the Civil Air Patrol squadron on the Air Force base."

"Which I'll never do," shuddered Alisen, "if it pertains to the dream."

"Right," said Kale. "Thirdly, your friend McKenzie has to move back here."

"And she is," said Alisen, "very soon."

"And there has to be an organization called the I.P. I've never heard of anything like it."

"There is," said Alisen. "I looked it up on the computer. 'I.P.' stands for International Policy. Best I could tell, they're some kind of organization for world peace."

"But why would a peaceful organization show up in our dreams as a bunch of crazy murderers?" Kale asked. "If what they really want is peace . . . "

"It said on their webpage that they would accomplish world peace by . . . what was the word . . . something like 'survival of the fittest'. You could read that phrase in many ways, but if that's really what they mean, it would go right along with our dreams."

"Another thing," said Kale, putting his fork on his plate and staring thoughtfully past Alisen's head. "What could be prophetic about people disappearing? I mean, people don't disappear. It's not logical. It defies all those laws of nature that Mr. Miller is always going on about."

"The kid at Civil Air Patrol said it had to do with the Bible, remember?" said Alisen. She leaned forward and tried to draw Kale's gaze back to her. "I've never read it, but isn't it supposed to be about God? God is all-powerful, so maybe He could make people disappear—if He exists."

"I have read some of the stories," said Kale. "At least a little. But I didn't see anything about people disappearing."

Alisen looked at her phone. "Tomorrow's Saturday, right?"

"Yes," said Kale.

"You're free?"

"I guess, if you want me to be."

"So then, why don't we go somewhere where they know about these things? Let's see if we can't find a pastor, a politician who knows about the I.P., and somebody from the Civil Air Patrol."

"Let's divide the projects," said Kale. "You won't be allowed on the Air Force Base without an ID, so I'll take the Civil Air Patrol and find out if there's anyone there named Jaylis. The politician is also going to be harder to find, so we'll both look for him. You find the pastor who can explain the Bible mystery."

"And then you come over and hang out for the evening. I'll make popcorn, and we can talk about what we find." Alisen was excited. "We might find the key to these mysteries!"

"We might," said Kale cautiously. "It's just possible. You sure your parents won't mind if I just show up at your house?"

"Dad won't be home, but I guess Mom might," said Alisen. "She works from home, and sometimes she gets busy and needs the house to be quiet. Why don't we meet down the street at the basketball courts? I'll give you the address right now if you want."

She fished a paper out of her pocket, scribbled a few words, and handed it to him. "Do you know where that is?"

Kale studied it. "Yes," he said. "It's not too far from my house. How about five o'clock? That gives us both time to snoop around town."

"Lucky it's a small town," said Alisen, "and we're allowed to walk around. Imagine what we could do if we could drive!"

"I hope it has everything we need," said Kale. For the first time during their conversation, he smiled. "This is getting interesting."

"Right," said Alisen. The bell rang, and other kids started putting their trays away. "Until tomorrow then."

"See ya." Kale waved as they separated into lines.

CHAPTER VIII

ALISEN WOKE UP EARLY IN the morning. Her parents were already awake, and they had no objection to her leaving as long as she took her pink pepper spray and phone with her.

She put a lunchbox in her backpack and got on her bicycle. The evening before she had found directions to the town's local church, and that was the first place she was planning to go. She hoped that the pastor there would have something to say about this mysterious biblical prophecy, and she hoped that the church was of the right religion. Theology was a bit out of her depth.

She slowed to a stop right in front of the door. It was a beautiful building, towering tall above her with big, colorful windows that sparkled in the sunlight. The rounded wooden doors were open, and she walked straight in, looking all around and up and down at the pretty architecture.

There seemed to be nobody inside. It was deathly silent. Alisen walked all the way to the front and stood before the pulpit, gazing at the splendid decorations and beautiful gilded arabesques. Then she peered into all the side doors, but still she found nobody.

She heard footsteps behind her. She turned quickly in surprise and found herself face-to-face with a nice looking young man, carrying what appeared to be a Bible.

"Hello," he said with a smile. "Do you need anything?"

"Well, yes," stammered Alisen. "I mean, I was looking for the pastor. I had a question for him."

The man sat down in the pew next to her. "I'm not the pastor, but I might be able to answer your question," he said. "Unless of course you'd rather speak directly to him."

"No. That's okay," said Alisen. She sat down beside him on the pew. "So . . . I was wondering, is there anything in the Bible about . . . about people disappearing at the end of the world?"

The man looked surprised, then laughed cheerfully. "That's an unusual question," he said. "Well, there's a big debate about that. There is a verse in the Bible—in Corinthians, actually—that says, 'In the blink of an eye, we shall be changed.' 'We' refers to people who believe that Jesus Christ is the Son of God. This verse is talking about what will happen when Jesus returns to take His followers up to heaven to live with Him forever, which of course indicates that this will happen at the end of the world. To 'be changed' means that these people will have their bodies changed from mortal to immortal. So, from this verse you get: in an instant, anyone who believes in God will be taken to heaven. Does that make sense so far?"

Alisen nodded.

"This event—the changing and the taking to heaven part—is usually called the rapture. Many people believe that all believers will be taken up to heaven, and after that there will be a time of hardship for seven years for everyone left on earth. After that, Jesus will return to the earth and set up a thousand-year kingdom.

"Some people, however, do not think this is clearly indicated in the Bible. They say that Christians may not be taken, but instead will remain on the earth to live through the seven years of hardship. Some say they will be taken in the middle of the seven years. The truth is, the Bible says that no one will know when this event will occur. It's a mystery."

"So . . . " Alisen paused and thought hard. "The good people get taken to heaven? But what happens to everyone else?"

"Not the good people," he corrected. "It's the people who believe that Jesus Christ is the Son of God and that He can save them from their sins. Everyone who is left must endure the seven years of tribulation. Many will not survive. During this time, God will judge the earth, and there will be many unexplainable occurrences that are predicted in the Bible, such as an earthquake that will be felt around the entire world. Many people will come to believe, but many will not. They will follow the leader who will arise to rule the entire world. Then—"

"Wait," said Alisen suddenly. "A world leader? What will his name be?"

"The Bible doesn't say," said the man. "In fact, it is difficult to understand this part. But most people believe that he will be a leader who will end by dividing the entire world into ten kingdoms, each with its own ruler. Then he will rule over all of them, being the one power in control of the entire planet."

"What else will he do?"

"He will require that every man, woman, and child receive a mark on their forehead or their right hand. You will have to take it to buy or sell anything. But the Bible says that if you take this mark, you will have chosen sides with the devil and will not be able to receive eternal life with God in heaven. We don't know what kind of mark this is, but since the creation of biotechnology, people usually think of it as a sort of computer chip."

Alisen shivered. "That's scary," she said. Then she stood up. "Thank you for your answer," she said. "It was exactly what I needed."

"May I ask why you are curious about this?"

Alisen stared at him. He looked back at her, candid, full of confidence, and not too annoyingly outgoing. She felt that she could trust him, and she sat back down.

"I've been having these dreams," she said. "They're terrifying, and they frighten me so much every night. I dreamed that an organization came from the Middle East and took over our country. They killed my best friend. Then I dreamed that I managed to meet with some people, one of whom said that this kind of thing was predicted in the Bible. He said something about 'wars and rumors of wars'. Then he said it was also predicted that people would disappear. And right after he finished saying it, he vanished. It was like nothing I've ever seen before."

"Wow," said the man. "What else? Do you have any idea where they're coming from?"

"I thought they were just nightmares, like I had been reading something too scary before I went to bed. But then I met a friend at school, whose name was actually in my dream. In real life, he looked just like he did in the dream. And he said he's been dreaming the same sorts of things. Where there were gaps in my dreams, his could fill them in. We started looking into things, seeing if the things we dreamed about were real. So far, they all have been. What you just said verified another piece of the puzzle."

"Maybe it's a warning," said the man. "A prediction of things to come. You could be having these dreams to prepare you for the end times."

"But you're saying I don't have to be here at the end of the world," said Alisen, "as long as I believe in Jesus."

"Right," said the man. "Here, take this Bible with you. You can use it to do some more research."

"Thanks," Alisen took the book and flipped thoughtfully through the thin pages. "You really helped."

"Call me if you have any more questions," he said, smiling. "My name is Peter Giller. Here's my number." He gave Alisen a card, and she tucked it into the book.

"Thanks," she repeated. "I probably will talk to you soon." She waved and headed for the doors.

Once outside she paused to reflect. She scribbled down everything Peter had told her in her sketchbook and put it in her backpack. There would be a lot to tell Kale in the evening, and she did not want to forget a single word.

The next challenge was to find a politician of some kind, somebody who could tell her the truth about the mysterious I.P. Alisen didn't know where to go, but she did know that she wanted to get the better of Kale by finding the politician first. So, she decided to ride her bicycle around town and see if anything presented itself.

As she biked down Main Street, she noticed two new buildings that had previously been empty. They were right across the street from each other, and when Alisen read their signs she couldn't help but laugh. The one on her left was the 'Democratic Party' and the one on her right was the 'Republican Party'. This seemed so ironic, despite her lack of knowledge concerning politics that she stopped, left her bicycle on the sidewalk, and went to look in the windows of each one.

They were both decorated inside, but the Democratic Party's design was much less formal than the Republican Party. In addition, Alisen noticed a Christmas tree in the corner of the Democratic Party's main room. She wondered why anyone would have a Christmas tree up in the middle of September. Maybe the Democrats liked to give things away, and that seemed like a promising sign.

She might be able to find the desired explanation in one of these two buildings. Alisen stood in the middle of the road and looked uncertainly back and forth. Which ought she visit first? She knew her parents were Republicans, but she knew little about politics and didn't know the difference between the parties. Finally, she ran to the left toward the Democratic Party.

The door was open, and she went inside. A very jovial man who seemed to be the secretary greeted her loudly. She was rather taken aback by his friendliness, but she asked, "Is there anyone here who can answer a few questions? I'll be quick."

"Well," he said, "that depends on what you want to know. I'm probably exactly who you're looking for."

She paused. "Well, I'd like to learn a little bit about International Policy. Who they are, what they do. That kind of thing."

"I see," he said. "International Policy. This is a peaceful organization who wants to reform the world government. They haven't been very active yet, as they are in the process of—well, of reforming their own government."

"What country are they headquartered in?" asked Alisen.

"Syria, I believe" replied the secretary. "A wonderful group of people. In fact, the money they donated to Diane Schultz's campaign helped buy the signs for this building. Don't they look wonderful?"

"Diane Schultz?" Alisen was interested. "The Presidential candidate? What can you tell me about her?"

"She's a wonderful woman," gushed the secretary, waving his hands. "She is all for limiting violence, giving a woman the right to choose, and allowing unfortunate refugees to enter the country."

Alisen shook her head in confusion. She had no idea what the secretary was talking about. "What are all those things?"

"Goodness, child, where have you been these past few years? These are the latest developments."

"I need more specifics." Alisen was frustrated. "What are you talking about?"

Instead of answering her directly, he swiveled his chair around and rummaged under his desk. Alisen stared at his back for a few moments before he swung back around, his arms full of pamphlets.

"This one is about abortion," he said, planting a poster-sized image of a sad-looking young woman under her nose. "This one is about refugees, and this one is about gun control." He looked up at her in satisfaction, as if he had answered all her questions.

Alisen picked them up and leafed through them. "I'd really rather hear your opinion," she sighed, putting the pamphlets in her backpack. "That's alright. These are helpful. Thank you for your time."

"Certainly," he said, standing up and coming around the desk. "It was nice talking to you. Come see us again."

"Or not," muttered Alisen to herself.

Once outside, she found herself rather discouraged. She hadn't uncovered anything of real value, except that the I.P. was busily 'reforming their own government'—the government, presumably, of Syria. What did that mean? What did the verb 'reforming' indicate, and was it a sort of revolution? Maybe the Republicans could tell her, though, after her uncomfortable experience with the Democrats, she was feeling much less sure of herself.

She entered the building, and at once felt the difference in atmosphere between the two. And she felt rather more comfortable here, especially after a very nice secretary asked her what she needed.

"I need to talk to someone who can tell me about the I.P., International Policy."

His brows lowered at once. "The I.P.," he began. "I'm sure I can tell you everything you could possibly want to know about them. They are an organization of infidels, a group of wild revolutionaries who wish to take over the world's government. They are headquartered in Syria, where they are showing who they really are by taking over the government and killing its leaders. In fact—"

"I was just at the Democratic Party across the street," interrupted Alisen. "That's not what they said."

"That is because the favorite Democratic candidate, Diane Schultz, is supported by the I.P.," he said. "Of course, they don't want to lose their support."

"How much power does the I.P. have?" asked Alisen.

"Not much right now," he said. "That could change, however, especially if they get control of the oil."

"What oil?" Alisen asked curiously.

"Crude oil deposits in the deserts of the Middle East. You know how expensive gasoline has been lately. It's worth a lot of money."

"But what exactly does the oil have to do with the I.P.?" Alisen pressed.

"The United States produces most of its own crude oil," he explained. "But we also depend on other countries, such as Canada and Mexico. Syria and the countries around Syria have large supplies of this oil, and revenue—that's incoming money—from the sale of this oil makes them incredibly wealthy. Right now, the oil is partly in our control and partly in the control of the governments of those countries, but if the revolutionaries get hold of it, the money will be diverted to them. And we will have lost a percentage of our supply of crude oil."

"Crude oil?" Alisen paused. "And by that you mean gasoline?"

"The oil that is refined to make gasoline, yes," he said.

"And we depend on gasoline every day," said Alisen. "It would be a major problem if our gasoline supply were cut off or even reduced."

"Exactly."

"And it would weaken our country because we'd have to spend more time and money getting the oil from somewhere else."

"Correct," he said. Then he added, with a smile, "You're good at this logic thing."

"But what makes you think the I.P. is trying to get hold of the oil?" said Alisen, trying to pretend she did not notice the compliment. "And what makes you think they could even have a chance?"

"I know they're trying because it's the only way they can grow their power, which is what they're after," he said. "I know they have a chance because of a deal that was made recently between the United States government and the I.P. By this deal, our country has sold airplanes and military-grade explosives to them. We know they are building their army with these things. And we know that we have sold them nearly enough to make good the attack on the Syrian government."

"That's completely different from what the Democratic secretary said."

"What did he say?"

"He said the I.P. was a peaceful organization who was reforming their own government. He also said something about Diane Schultz. Something about her support of a woman's right to choose, ending violence, and allowing refugees to enter the country. Then he wouldn't explain what those things were." Alisen paused and thought. "It's almost like he didn't want me to know."

"I guess not," said the secretary. "In fact, I highly doubt he wanted you to know. And I can tell you why, phrase by phrase. 'A woman's right to choose' refers to abortion. Do you know what that is?"

Alisen nodded. "And?"

"Perhaps I'd better define it anyway," said the secretary. "It is the killing of unborn children by their mothers who for some reason or another do not wish them to be born," he said. "Right now, abortion is protected by law. In other words, it's lawful to kill your baby if you don't want it, as long as it has never seen the daylight."

Alisen's eyes widened. "I've never thought about it that way before. That sounds an awful lot like murder, not just another random choice."

"I know." There was a moment's pause before he continued.

"'Ending violence' probably refers to the outbreak of gun violence in big cities. In order to end the violence, Diane wants to take everyone's guns away. If by law you aren't allowed to own a gun, who do you think will end up owning guns?"

"The government and the criminals," said Alisen. "I get it. If she takes the people's weapons away, they can't defend themselves."

"Exactly," he said. "Finally, 'allowing refugees to enter the country' means that refugees from countries like Syria would be allowed to come into the United States without vetting—that's like checking to make sure they aren't dangerous—and become citizens."

"What would that mean?"

"It would mean that terrorists from the Middle East, and organizations such as the I.P., could enter, assimilate, and possibly attack without warning," he said. "The reason Diane wants to allow this is because most of the immigrants, grateful to her for the favor, would vote for her and other Democrats who approve of the immigration law. But everybody knows it will be dangerous. The thing is, this influx of refugees won't be fast enough to cause problems in Diane's lifetime. It's the next generation who will have to repair the mistake, and by then it will be impossible."

"That's crazy," said Alisen. "I can hardly believe I listened to that Democratic Party secretary. You've told me far more than he did."

"The difference between Republicans and Democrats is that, while they want to hide things from you, so you can't always see where they're corrupt, we try to show you what it's supposed to look like so you can choose for yourself," he said. "At least, that is how it is supposed to be. Often the Republicans get carried away by greed and selfishness, but we're still more transparent than the Democrats." He shrugged and smiled.

"I see," said Alisen. "You've given me a lot to think about. Thank you so much."

"It is my pleasure," he replied.

Alisen ran outside, then paused in thought before she reached her bike. Suddenly, obeying an inexplicable impulse she ran straight across the road, and into the Democratic Party building.

The secretary was still inside. "Why, hello," he said. "You're back with another question?"

"In a way," said Alisen. "I want to know why you support abortion."

"Why, because . . . because . . . a woman should be able to choose whether she wants to have children or not." The secretary looked flustered and confused, almost as if he hadn't had time to prepare his answer.

"If she doesn't want to have children, she shouldn't get pregnant in the first place," said Alisen. "Nobody has the right to kill babies because they aren't wanted. That's stupid. Anyone can see through your lies if they look hard enough. You might as well hang a sign in the window saying, 'We support child homicide'."

"Look, kid—"

"If my parents bought into your lies," said Alisen, "I wouldn't be here. I'd be in a box where the rest of those aborted children are."

"You don't know what you're—"

"You know why?" continued Alisen, her face hot. "Because I was born into a poor family. They barely had the money to keep me alive, until my dad got the job he needed. That was years after I was born. If they had believed in abortion, they could've just gotten rid of me, or thrown me in the river, or dropped me into the well. It's the same thing. And I think you're villains for supporting it."

And then Alisen left the secretary and slammed the door behind her, feeling better inside.

After these two interviews all she could think of was getting to the park to meet Kale. She had learned much that day, probably more than she had intended. At least she had the information she wanted. She wondered how Kale had done with his own research and pedaled a little faster.

When she arrived at the park, though it was a little before the specified time, Kale was already there, sitting on top of a basketball goal.

"What are you doing?" asked Alisen, squinting up at him against the fading light. "You're early."

Kale slid nimbly down the pole. "Well, so are you," he said. "I didn't have anywhere else to be today."

"Right." Alisen pulled her sketchbook out of her backpack and sat down on the curb. "You first. What did you find out about the Civil Air Patrol?"

"Just like in our dreams, there is a squadron on base," said Kale. "It's headed by a senior lieutenant colonel named Krakoff, also just like the dreams. And get this." Kale's voice lowered to a near whisper. "The secretary's name is Jay."

Alisen's eyes opened wide.

"I pretended that I was interested in joining the squadron," continued Kale, "and arranged a meeting with her tomorrow afternoon. I'll get a picture somehow, and you can tell me if she's the one you know from your dreams."

"Strange how this is all coming together," whispered Alisen, after looking around as though she was afraid someone would hear her. "What is going to happen if our dreams come true? The whole world is going to fall apart!"

Kale hesitated. "Have you ever heard of dreaming something because you've seen it before?"

Alisen rolled her eyes. "I've never been in a war zone before, you freak."

"I know, but I mean, what if we've seen all these people and places before? They say that everything you see in your dreams you've seen before in real life. So maybe we're just adding in the details of the battle from our imagination and the rest is reality."

"One thing I know for sure," said Alisen. "I've never met anyone named Jay, and I've never heard of the I.P. organization."

"But maybe your parents were talking about it one day, and you forgot you heard it," argued Kale. "Maybe you saw Jay in a grocery store."

"That doesn't explain why we're dreaming the same dreams."

Kale took a deep breath. "No. It doesn't."

"Why do you so desperately want this to be chance? What's wrong with this being a message?"

He turned to look at her. "Because if these dreams are real, the world is going to be changed, Alisen. Our entire lives are going to be altered, and we may not even survive what's coming."

"How do you know?"

"Jay didn't last even one day, and she was stronger than us."

There was a long moment of silence, as much of fear as it was of deep thought.

"Why don't I tell you what I found," said Alisen slowly. "This is a subject that is morbid and deserves to be changed."

Kale nodded.

"First I went to the church. I met this guy who said that the idea of people disappearing is really in the Bible, but not everybody agrees about it. Some people say that everybody who believes in Jesus will disappear before a seven-year period of hardship, some say they will disappear in the middle, and some say they will not disappear at all. He said—"

"When is this supposed to happen?" interrupted Kale.

Alisen paused. "At the end of the world, I think." She continued, "He said that in order to be one of the people who disappears—one of the people who gets taken to heaven—you have to believe in Jesus. I don't really know what he meant by that. He explained, but I've forgotten now."

"Interesting," said Kale. "Our dreams definitely looked like the end of the world. But the Bible? Really? It's just a book of myths and legends, isn't it?"

"This man talked about it as if it were real."

Kale nodded. "I guess he would. Anything else?"

"I found someone to tell me about the I.P." She smirked, glad to have gotten ahead of Kale. "He said they are an organization of terrorists who support that woman running for president—Diane Schultz. He said they're currently trying to overthrow the government of Syria, and that the United States sold them the weapons to do it. And he said that when they finish, they're going to take over the supplies of crude oil, because—"

"Because it would affect the entire world," finished Kale. "Not just the United States. Cut the crude oil, that's little short of a global economic disaster."

"That's exactly what he said," said Alisen. "They're trying to get the power."

"But why?" Kale wondered aloud. "Why would they go to the trouble?"

"Why did Hitler try to take over Europe?" retorted Alisen.

Kale shrugged. "I guess you're right. Where did you meet this person?"

"At the Republican Party building downtown."

Kale smiled. "Republican Party, yes. Did you consider the Democratic Party?"

"Indeed." Alisen shrugged. "They wouldn't tell me anything."

"Alright then." Kale got up and stretched. "What else?"

"What's going to happen if our dreams start coming true?" asked Alisen, looking up at him.

Kale's mouth drooped. "Lots of terrible things, obviously," he said. "Let's look at our dreams so far."

Alisen pulled out her sketchbook. "I dreamed about the bombing and the I.P. Then I dreamed about some sort of a trial with Jay and a man named Nathan. Finally, I dreamed about the mysterious disappearance of half the Civil Air Patrol, which according to what they said must have happened sometime after the first dream."

"And I," said Kale, "dreamed about a presidential election in which the winning candidate was a female. I dreamed about reading a newspaper that said she supported the I.P., and I dreamed that the writer of the article was executed for the statement. Finally, my dream skipped ahead to a time when she was no longer the ruler, and someone far more terrifying had taken her place."

They both sat silently, thinking deeply.

"There's something wrong with the sequence of your dreams," said Kale. "The second dream you had tells more of Jay's story, but in the other two dreams she had been killed. So that second dream must have taken place before either of the others."

"But what could Jay have been on trial for?" wondered Alisen aloud. "They said she had committed treason, that she had refused a direct order from a superior, and that she had accepted some sort of religion. She herself said that she had refused to kill the man, Nathan, who had brought her a Bible for the first time so the order she disobeyed must have been the order to kill him, and the religion she accepted must have been Christianity. Isn't that right?"

"Probably," said Kale. "But that still doesn't explain why they wanted her dead, nor does it explain why she was supposed to kill Nathan in the first place."

"Maybe they wanted to kill her because of her religion," suggested Alisen. "They said one of her crimes was accepting the enemy's religion."

"And refusal to obey an order," said Kale. "But that would mean a court martial, not execution."

"In a lawful government," said Alisen gravely. "But what if this government was illegal? What if they had taken over the country?"

"That would make sense," Kale nodded. "They would obviously never be allowed to execute capital punishment for no good reason, certainly not on the basis of religion, if they were an ordinary government."

"And who were 'they'?" asked Alisen. "Do you suppose, since the rest of the dreams have been centered around the I.P., that it was them?"

"Possibly," Kale glanced at her. "Or it could even have been the United States' government, under that female president from my dream."

"I guess the only way we could get evidence is by figuring out if the I.P. tolerates Christianity or not." She paused. "It's kind of strange how everything keeps tying back to that, isn't it? I mean, if it's not even real?"

"Which? The I.P or Christianity?" asked Kale absently.

"Christianity, of course. We know the I.P is real." Alisen started typing a search on her phone. "If Christianity is just a myth, then why does everything seem to circle back to it?"

 Kale shrugged. "I guess there were a lot of people who believed in it and who were willing to die for it." He smiled lopsidedly. "Not something I'd do."

"It doesn't matter about what you'd do," said Alisen. "We're only talking about Jay and Nathan here."

"And all those people who disappeared, if they were 'believers' like you said."

 Alisen looked up briefly. "I can't think about all this at once."

 Kale kept silent.

"Alright, here's their webpage," said Alisen. "Now—"

"They're not going to have records of executions on their webpage. Let me see it."

"They won't have a record of this execution anyway, since it probably hasn't happened yet," said Alisen, handing him the phone. "What are you looking for?"

"Anything about the imprisonment of someone named Nathan," he said, taking the phone and bending over it. "I think he's the key to this puzzle. He was the one who brought Jay the forbidden Bible, he was the one she was ordered to kill. You've got the idea."

After a few minutes he dropped the phone in the grass. "Nothing," he said. "I guess that's to be expected. Well, now what?"

"We've got to find Jay," said Alisen. "You're going to meet with her tomorrow?"

"Right," said Kale. "I'll pretend I'm interested in joining the squadron. I'll also get a picture of her for you to take a look at."

"Perfect," smiled Alisen. "Then all we have to do is wait."

Kale stood up. "This meeting could prove or disprove the dreams."

"Disprove?" Alisen was incredulous. "Really? After all the evidence?" "Okay," Kale paused. "You're right. Obviously something is going on here."

"Something," said Alisen. "Kale, you're way too literal with your words."

"Maybe." He looked down the street. "I'd better be getting home soon. You want me to walk with you to your house?"

"No, I'm fine," said Alisen. "It's only right up the road."

"Okay then. I'll see you tomorrow, same place, probably around one-thirty?"

"Perfect," Alisen smiled up at him. "I'll be here."

Kale waved and started walking along the sidewalk, back toward the entrance to the neighborhood.

She watched him round the corner and descend the hill before she mounted her bicycle and rode back to her house.

CHAPTER IX

A FAMILIAR PURPLE BICYCLE LEANED against the hedge, and Alisen smiled when she saw it. It meant that Sadie had come to study, or really to watch a movie.

Alisen went around to the back yard and found Sadie in the hammock, reading a chemistry book and eating an apple.

"Hey, Alisen." Sadie looked up. "I've been waiting for you."

"I was at the park." Alisen, sat on a stump beside her. "Didn't you see me when you were coming in?"

"Nope. Not too observant, I guess. You didn't see me either."

"Well, I'm here now. What chemistry equation has you stumped today?"

Sadie shut the book. "Luckily, none." She grinned. "I'm here to hang out for a while, if you don't mind. My mom had to run to town for a meeting."

"Sure," said Alisen. "I'm glad you came. There's a new movie out I've been meaning to watch. Unless, of course, you'd rather do your homework."

Sadie laughed. "What's it called?"

"*The Invaders*, I believe. It has something to do with the dollar crashing and rioting and the end of the world and airplanes and—"

"Slow down," interrupted Sadie, a puzzled look on her face. "How's all that going to fit in two hours?"

"We're going to find out," said Alisen. "But we've got plenty of time before it gets dark. How long are you staying?"

"Your mom invited me to stay until tomorrow morning," said Sadie. "Unless you've got a different opinion."

"Good! Then we definitely have plenty of time," said Alisen, though she still worried about her nightmares. "What shall we do first?"

Sadie got off the hammock. "I've got a script to practice for the school play," she said. "Want to read the other dialogue part?"

"Sure," said Alisen. "What's this one about again? I'm terrible at remembering."

Sadie pulled the script from the pages of the chemistry book and spread it out on the grass. "It's just Romeo and Juliet. You remember? We studied that in literature class."

"Got it." Alisen picked up the script. "What part are you?"

"Juliet." Sadie smiled modestly.

"That means I have to be Romeo?"

Sadie nodded.

Alisen looked at it with a resigned air. "Can I be as dramatic as I want to?"

"I guess," said Sadie dubiously.

They read the script through, with Alisen playing Romeo and finding her role tremendously funny. She had never been a great actress, which was why she did not participate in the school plays, and she was highly amused to find herself in the spotlight at last. The rehearsal ended inevitably in giggles and hilarity.

***** ***** *****

Alisen couldn't sleep. Afraid that her dreams would wake her up and that she would have to explain her terror to Sadie, she waited until Sadie's even breathing told her that she, at least, had no trouble sleeping, then crept out of the room.

She spread her blankets on the sofa downstairs and set her alarm for early in the morning, before she knew Sadie would wake up. Then she curled up, pulled the blanket over her ears, and fell sound asleep.

***** ***** *****

When she woke up in the morning, something was different, and she couldn't tell what it was. She looked around, wondering if maybe the sounds of Sadie's early morning shower had woken her.

Then she realized that the mixed fear and curiosity she had felt every morning after she had her dream was gone. She had slept the whole night through without a single dream of any kind.

She waved her arms in silent excitement and danced up and down the room. She felt rested as never before. It was a relief not to have to puzzle out the meaning of her nighttime visions, not to have to wonder what terrible thing was going to happen. She felt freer than ever before.

She tiptoed to the kitchen, trying not to awaken anyone by her excitement. Sadie was already at the counter, hair wet and dripping on the floor, pouring milk into a cereal bowl. She looked up when Alisen entered.

"Where were you?" she whispered.

"Downstairs," said Alisen vaguely. "Came down in the middle of the night. You look sleepy."

"I am," said Sadie, ignoring the change of subject. "You, on the other hand, look like you slept ten hours instead of six."

"Yeah. I feel like it." Alisen poured some cereal into a bowl. "Going to church this morning?"

"We never go to church, Alisen, and you know it," said Sadie, with a wide yawn. "Don't see much point. It's going to be a lovely day outside."

"Maybe we can take a hike down to the creek before lunch," said Alisen.

"Or we could take lunch with us."

Alisen shook her head. "Got somewhere to be around one-thirty," she said. "I can meet you again after that though."

Sadie yawned again. "Okay," she said. "Here, why don't you turn on the TV and let's see what happened while we were asleep last night."

Alisen didn't care in the least about the news, except as it pertained to her dreams, but she turned it on anyway.

For a few moments Sadie watched in silence, while Alisen fried sausages. But suddenly she said, "Alisen, come look at this."

Alisen propped the spatula up on the side of the pan and came to look.

" . . . by order of the president," the news anchor was saying. "Some say the U.S. is not taking care of its own citizens by leaving the borders open, but others say they are performing a charitable act by allowing refugees to enter the country. The country they left behind, meanwhile, is being slowly destroyed by International Policy. They say they are working to rebuild it again, but . . . "

"What was that?" asked Alisen, staring at the screen which showed pictures of beautifully colored buildings, burning relentlessly.

Sadie turned the volume down. All the sleepiness had gone out of her voice. "The International Policy organization has been trying to take over the Syrian government for about a year now," she explained, a bit proud of her knowledge. "They just did."

"But what was that about the refugees?"

Sadie looked at her, surprise written across her face. "The refugees are people fleeing from Syria to escape the I.P. What he just said," she motioned to the TV, "is that the United States opened its borders, temporarily of course, to allow these refugees to enter without papers of any kind. Only problem is, we won't know if the people coming in are really refugees or if they are International Policy spies." Sadie shrugged. "Who knows who might take advantage of it."

Alisen did not say anything. She merely walked back to her pan with a deep terrifying feeling. The sausages were nearly overcooked. Mechanically she slid them off the pan onto a white paper plate.

"Is something wrong?" asked Sadie curiously, waking Alisen from her daze.

"No, nothing," she said hastily. "I'm just thinking about the news."

"Since when have you been so worried about the news?" laughed Sadie. "Who cares anyway?"

Alisen smiled ruefully and shrugged.

They spent the morning at a creek near Alisen's house, playing in the water and eating the lunch Sadie had finally convinced Alisen to pack. It was so fun that Alisen had nearly forgotten her appointment with Kale; but now she remembered, and it was nearly time.

Sadie's mother came to the house to pick her up, and Alisen set out immediately for the park.

Kale was leaning against a basketball goal, playing idly with the strings of his jacket. Alisen noticed that something was strange about him. When he turned toward her she saw what it was. He was wearing glasses.

Kale smiled at her surprised face. "Like the look?"

"I didn't know you wore glasses."

"I don't." He took them off and put them in his pocket. "But I had to get a picture of Jay somehow."

"What?" asked Alisen. "Do you mean that there's a camera in those glasses?"

Kale shrugged. "I used to be interested in spying when I was younger," he said, with a half-smile. "These came in handy today."

"Can I see the picture?" Alisen stared at his glasses and sat down against the goal.

"Not yet. First thing's first. Tell me what you dreamed last night."

"Nothing!" Alisen shrugged. "Nothing at all. It's the first night I have slept well for two months."

Kale looked at her strangely. "I dreamed your dream," he said at last. "The one where we're all at Civil Air Patrol and the people disappear."

"You heard everything the cadet talking said?"

"Everything, just like you described." He rubbed at his head. "This is getting weird."

"And you just now noticed that?"

"C'mon, I'm trying to think it through," he said. Then he pulled the glasses out of his pocket. "Want to see the pictures?"

Alisen hopped over a line and stood beside him. "Yes!"

He sat down on the ground and carefully took a small SD card out of the glasses. Taking his phone from his pocket, he gently pried the back off, inserted the card in a slot, and replaced the cover.

"There you go," he said, holding the phone up to Alisen.

The photo was grainy, but she could easily make out the girl's features. They were strong and dark, without a hint of a smile but not unfriendly either. She had long black hair, deep eyes, and suntanned skin. Alisen recognized her immediately.

"That's her," she said. "She looks exactly like she did in my dream."

Kale looked at the picture. "Obviously I didn't tell her about any of this," he said. "Really, I didn't learn much from her. I already know plenty about C.A.P."

"C.A.P.?"

"I mean Civil Air Patrol," said Kale. "Anyway, if that's the girl you saw in your dream, then we know we're onto something." He paused. "I think," he said at last, very slowly, "I think it might be worth going to this place—at least for a couple of meetings. Maybe we can recognize some of the cadets, maybe we can figure out where all this is going to take place and warn the people."

"Ah," said Alisen snidely, "so you're finally starting to believe in this?"

Kale turned to face her. "I have to."

"But your idea is crazy," protested Alisen. "You know what's going to happen if I join."

"Maybe," said Kale. "But how are we going to prepare for it if we don't at least see what's going on? Besides, don't you think we should maybe tell them in advance?"

"Like they're going to believe us?" Alisen shook her head. "Would you believe somebody who came up to you and told you the world was about to end?"

Kale frowned. "What about Jay?"

"What has she got to do with this?"

"If your dreams about her were true, then she must have a key to this mystery because she could tell you who the people were that she was on trial before, unless that hasn't happened yet. Maybe we should talk to her together."

"You really think she'd just tell you? For no reason other than you think you might know something about them?" Alisen was more amused than annoyed. "Seriously, you're living in your own world. If Jay is anything like she was in the dream, she won't be very talkative, and that definitely won't be her favorite subject."

Kale sat down. "You're probably right."

"Probably? I *am* right." She stood up a bit straighter and nodded. "Besides, how can we warn the people at this Civil Air Patrol place unless we understand a bit more? I mean, we still don't have a handle on those people who disappeared. We can predict that there's going to be an attack, but we don't know when it will be."

"Is there anything in the dream that could tell us?"

Alisen thought for a moment. "My friend McKenzie will have moved back here," she said at last. "I got a text from her last night. She'll be here in a month."

"Well, there's a start," said Kale. "And in order to be a junior cadet in Civil Air Patrol, you have to be less than twenty-one years old. So, it will definitely happen in less than six years, because in the dream I was a junior member."

"That's quite the timetable," said Alisen. "Plus, everything we've found so far depends on the result of this presidential election, right?"

"Right," Kale agreed, "because I saw a female president—"

"—and the only female running is Diane Schultz." Alisen paused. "What's so bad about her, I wonder?"

"Everything," said Kale. "I found out a lot about her from my mother. She's been in politics for many years. Her husband was once a senator, and while he was served as senator there was this huge law scandal involving Diane. All the evidence—and there was plenty of it—pointed to her as the criminal, but she was never convicted. Do you know why?"

Alisen did not, but she felt no need to answer.

"Because nearly everyone else who had been involved wound up dead." Kale's voice had lowered to a whisper. "For all kinds of reasons. One got killed in an armed gas station robbery. Some had heart attacks. Others died for 'no known cause'. And yet Diane is still here. No criminal charges against her, nothing. And since her husband has been out of the Senate, things have continued like that. If you become too friendly with her, you're likely to wind up dead one day."

"How can such a person become the president?" murmured Alisen. "How can we let this happen?"

"The answer's very simple," said Kale. "We can't let it happen. If it does, the I.P. wins. Jay's going to die, and you and I—"

"—are going to have a terrible time keeping out of their hands." Alisen's eyes widened. "How can we stop her?"

"I don't think we can," said Kale. "Contrary to popular belief, it's not the people that elect the president, it's electors they choose to vote the way they tell them. And besides, fifteen-year-olds aren't allowed to vote in any state. I guess the only thing we can do is run ads at the school. Maybe the kids will convince their parents one way or another." He shrugged and smiled.

"Like I could convince my parents to vote Democrat," sighed Alisen.

"You don't want to," said Kale. "That's how Diane is running."

"Right." Alisen paused. "What do we do now? Now, as in the present moment in time?"

He thought for a moment. "I wish we could get some more information out of this Jaylis person." He looked Alisen up and down. "You know the only way we could do that, right?"

"No." Alisen scowled. "Stop being so secretive."

"You'd have to join the Civil Air Patrol and make friends with her. Get her to where she's comfortable with you. And then maybe you could get her to tell you a little about her life."

Alisen nearly rolled her eyes. "We've been over this! If we join the Civil Air Patrol, we put another puzzle piece in place for the prophecy to come true!"

"Just until your friend McKenzie gets to town," begged Kale. "After that, we can leave. Hopefully she gives us enough time to accomplish our mission."

Alisen crossed her arms and looked away. "Fine," she said, "but you have to promise me that you won't try to keep me in once McKenzie comes to town."

"Done," said Kale. "I promise."

CHAPTER X

THE NEXT TUESDAY, AFTER ALISEN had talked to her parents, they obtained a pass for her to the Air Force base and signed her up to join the Civil Air Patrol.

She was very nervous when they arrived. It was a totally new environment to her, since the Patrol was organized similarly to the military and kept the customs rigidly. Kale arrived in jeans and a sweatshirt, and both of them made an odd contrast to the sea of carefully starched blue uniforms.

The cadets were all very nice. Both Kale and Alisen were welcomed enthusiastically into the group, and everyone was eager to meet them.

Alisen, looking around, saw no one that she recognized. She looked for the particular cadet who had given the speech in her last dream, as well as Jay, the secretary. But neither of them made an appearance, much to her annoyance.

As the cadets sat loosely in their chairs chattering about the school day, an anxious voice from the back shouted something unintelligible. The cadets shot up from their seats and stood at attention. Alisen slowly and hesitantly did likewise.

"As you were," said another, much quieter voice. The cadets relaxed into their former indifference.

Alisen, however, did not. She would have known that voice anywhere on earth. She twisted her head to look behind her, and there, standing with her back to the classroom, was Jay.

Jay turned around. Alisen swiveled back toward her desk. "Don't forget," said Jay, quietly yet clearly, "that there will be a mission this Saturday for anyone interested. You must arrive at the airport by eight o'clock sharp, or you'll get left behind. Anyone interested, sign up on this sheet I'm passing out." She handed the white sheet to Alisen.

Alisen tried not to show her curiosity, but her eyes took in a great deal of Jay's physical appearance. She was tall, with black hair, and something Alisen had not noticed in her dream—startlingly blue eyes. Everything else matched perfectly. This was certainly Jaylis, and she was not at all imaginary.

The rest of the evening passed in a blur. The cadets, including Kale, moved through the formalities as though they were perfectly familiar with them, but Alisen sat nearby and watched quietly. She could not take her eyes off Jay.

At the end of the meeting, Jay approached her and introduced herself. "My name is Jay Jennison. Welcome to the Civil Air Patrol. How did you like this evening?"

It was obvious that Jay was trying to be friendly. "I've enjoyed it very much," Alisen replied. "I hope we'll be able to come back soon."

Kale, who was standing behind Jay, shot her a glance of surprise.

"Excellent," said Jay. "If you should decide to join, you'll need to attend five meetings before you can do so. When you have, I'll email you an online application to fill out and return."

"Thanks," said Alisen. "I look forward to it."

Jay nodded. "Hope to see you next week."

Alisen and Kale escaped to the parking lot, where they waited for their parents. "Well? What did you think?" demanded Kale. "I heard you telling Jay that you wanted to come back!"

"I enjoyed it," repeated Alisen, seeming to have no other verbs. "But I couldn't stop staring at Jay. I hope she didn't notice."

"She notices everything." Kale shrugged. "But you probably shouldn't worry about it." After a pause he said, "Think you could get to know her so we could talk to her?"

Alisen thought for a moment. "Well," she said at last, "I think I could get to know her. I think she would tell me simple things about herself, but, Kale, there is a wall between her and everyone else. I can't say exactly what it is. It's not shyness, certainly. It's like she's sad about something, and I don't know what it is."

"And you're saying that you think she won't ever tell you?"

"Yes, and if I was her and I was going to be sad about anything, it would be the death of a certain best friend named Nathan." Alisen sighed. "I think she'll never give up the one piece of information we're looking for."

A silver van drove up to the side of the curb. "That's my mother's car," said Kale. "See you tomorrow at school."

"Right," said Alisen. "Bye, Kale."

It was nearly ten o'clock when she arrived home that night. Her phone, which she had accidentally left on her nightstand, had a new notification. Idly she clicked on it and saw a message from McKenzie: "BIG NEWS!!!! We're coming sooner than we thought. It'll only be a week now, two weeks at most. The company really wants Dad to start work as soon as possible."

Alisen sent back a half-hearted note of congratulations, but for once she was not excited to see her friend. It might move up the timetable of terrible events much faster.

*****   *****   *****

"Well, at least, nothing can happen until after the election," said Kale. He bit into a school sandwich and winced at its unexpected crunchiness. "And it can only happen then if Diane gets elected."

"It's already November first," said Alisen. "How did we miss this?"

"That gives us a week." Kale paused and dropped his fork. "That's right when your friend is supposed to be here, isn't it?"

"Exactly," said Alisen. She felt suddenly chilled. "Kale, we have to do something. Something drastic."

"Why drastic?" asked Kale, hiding a smile at Alisen's dramatic words; but she was not finished.

"We have to talk to Jay again."

*****   *****   *****

"What are you going to do?" Kale followed Alisen to the tray station. "You just said last night that you don't think she's going to tell you anything!"

"Then I'm going to tell her something," said Alisen. "Our dreams."

"What? Are you crazy?" Kale stepped in front of her. "She's not going to believe you."

"Probably not." Alisen brushed past him. "But it's our last chance."

"Fine." Kale took the tray from her and set it down with a thump. "Then I'm going with you."

"You don't have to," said Alisen, secretly pleased with his offer and hoping he would not withdraw it. "Seriously, Kale—"

"I'm the one who has her contact information," he persisted. "I'll give her a call and ask her to meet us somewhere."

"Saturday maybe?"

Kale nodded. "I'll text you the information. What's your number?"

Alisen gave it to him, and he put it in his phone. "Alright," he said. "I still think this is crazy, but whatever. I'll set up a meeting."

"Thanks," said Alisen. He nodded gloomily, and they parted to go their separate ways to class.

The school day seemed longer than ever to Alisen, who began to wonder if it had been a good idea to set up an immediate interrogation with Jay. But it was too late. When she arrived home, Kale called her and set up a meeting for lunch on Saturday, without giving a reason for the conference.

McKenzie had not texted her back. Alisen wondered absently where she was and what she was doing. Her phone rang, and McKenzie's face appeared on the screen.

Alisen answered. "Hey, McKenzie!" she cried. "How are you? And *where* are you?"

"I'm just fine. Excited to see you!" she replied. "We're in a little hotel in the middle of nowhere right now. Dad's car got a flat tire on the way, so we spent about three hours on the side of the road and finally made it here. We've got a long way to go cross-country."

"That's too bad," said Alisen. "But you'll make it. Did the tire get fixed?"

"Sure did," said McKenzie. "We'll be back on the road tomorrow. You know, it's tough business driving all the way from Washington to Ohio with two cats in the car. Hadrian—that's the brown one, you'll remember him—howled the entire way. We couldn't figure out what was wrong with him. Mittens just crawled all around the car looking puzzled and miserable. I think they were both carsick." She giggled heartlessly at the memory.

"That's too bad," said Alisen. "I can't wait to see them again. I've been trying to convince my parents to get us a cat, but so far it hasn't worked."

"Keep trying," laughed McKenzie. "So, what's going on there? Anything new with you?"

Alisen hesitated. If their dreams come true, McKenzie would be deeply involved and they would have to tell her everything, but so far none of this had happened. Somehow Alisen didn't feel like telling her.

"Not much," she said. "Made a friend at school named Kale. He's—"

"Kale," said McKenzie, "like the vegetable?"

Alisen rolled her eyes. "Yes, like the vegetable. Anyway, we went to a Civil Air Patrol meeting last night. They—"

"I love C.A.P.!" interrupted McKenzie. "Didn't I tell you? I've been a member for over a year now. We were going to find a squadron there when we arrived. Maybe we can go to yours."

"Oh!" said Alisen. McKenzie stared at her curiously through the screen. "Yes, of course," she added hastily. "That would be such fun! Only, neither of us has joined this squadron yet. We're just going to see what all's happening."

"I see," said McKenzie, who still looked rather confused. "Well, I can't wait to see you. I guess I'd better go help unpack."

"I miss you," said Alisen. "We're going to have so much fun when you get here!"

"Yes!" agreed McKenzie. "Maybe talk to you tomorrow?"

"Right," said Alisen. "Good luck with the drive."

"Thanks. Bye!"

Alisen ended the video call and put the phone on her nightstand, deep in thought. McKenzie had inadvertently solved yet another piece of the puzzle.

CHAPTER XI

ALISEN PUT ON A NICE blouse over her jeans and surveyed herself in the mirror. Saturday had come quicker than she bargained for, and she was already rather nervous. Kale was going to meet her at the sport court in fifteen minutes, and she had to hurry. She added a last touch of mascara to her long eyelashes and ran down the driveway.

As usual, Kale was already waiting for her. He sat on his bicycle, and she did not bother to dismount when she saw him. Together they rode down the street and down the hill, neither of them saying a word.

"Are you okay?" asked Alisen at last.

"Yes," Kale shot her a surprised look. "Oh, I guess I never told you, did I? My father died a few weeks ago. It's been hard without him. Today's just a worse than usual day."

"No, you never told me." Alisen paused. "I'm sorry. I can't even imagine that."

He shrugged. "It was some kind of overdose. That's all Mom will tell me."

"That's terrible." Alisen couldn't think of anything else to say.

"But," continued Kale, trying to look cheerful again, "I'm alright. I'm looking forward to hearing your questions for Jaylis."

"I'm rather nervous, to tell the truth," said Alisen. "I'm afraid she's going to think we're crazy and not tell us anything."

"What I was thinking," said Kale, "is that, supposing she was ever associated with the I.P., she's not going to tell anyone that."

"Why would she have anything to do with the I.P.?" asked Alisen.

"I was just thinking," said Kale, "that maybe the trial had something to do with them."

"Possibly," said Alisen. "Oh, whatever. We'll see how this goes. The worst she can say is nothing at all, right?"

They arrived at the coffee shop where Kale had arranged to meet Jay. After parking their bikes in the back, she and Jay slipped through the back door, which led into a dark paneled hallway.

Alisen held Kale back. "Do you see her?"

Kale scanned the room. "There she is." He pointed to a small table in the corner, where Jay sat by herself, reading a book.

"Take a deep breath," said Kale. "You'll do fine. It's her choice what she tells us."

Alisen nodded, and they both stepped out into the middle of the dining room.

Jay did not seem to see them until they were nearly by her table. She quickly closed her book and put it in her backpack. "Hello," she said, looking up. "It's good to see you again."

"You, too," said Alisen, through an inexplicably dry mouth.

Jay looked back and forth between them without making a sound, obviously waiting for them to say something.

Kale cleared his throat and shot an irreverent glance at Alisen. "We came here to ask you about something that's going to happen."

Jay still did not say anything but waited for them to continue.

"It's the I.P.," said Alisen desperately. "They're coming here."

"What are you talking about?" She seemed suddenly interested.

Alisen and Kale stammered and talked over each other.

"What do you know about the I.P.?" interrupted Jay, her voice once again quiet. "Why did you come to me?"

"We came to you because you know them," said Alisen, her thoughts finally clear. "We know—Kale and I—that the presidential candidate Diane

Schultz is going to help the I.P. plan an invasion of the United States. We also think that you have a connection with the I.P. from the past. So, we—"

Jay's face had gone white, and she interrupted. "How do you know this? What makes you think I know the International Policy?"

"Nevermind how," said Kale. "We just know. We wanted you to know what their plans are, so you can take precautions."

"What do you think I can do?" Jay laughed humorlessly. "I am the secretary for a squadron of unruly Civil Air Patrol cadets. There is the limit of my official authority."

Alisen was trying to frame a reply when Kale spoke up quickly. "Official authority? What we want is the unofficial."

Jay picked up her cup of coffee and took a long drink. "My unofficial authority is not to be made use of in this way," she said, after a pause. "It does not extend as far as you think."

"People trust you," said Kale. "I know it. You must have friends on the base."

"They trust me because nothing I tell them has ever been untrue, and because I have seen a great deal of the world. I have no way of verifying what you tell me, so I cannot pass on this information."

"Perhaps you could at least tell them that it's possible?" pleaded Alisen. "Maybe they could put on some extra security?"

There was a long pause, during which Jay stared at the table in front of her, as if she was thinking deeply. "Alright," she said. "Tell me what's going to happen."

"The I.P. is going to launch an attack on this city," said Alisen. "In particular, on the Air Force Base. They're going to hit while Civil Air Patrol is in session."

"And what day is this going to happen?"

Alisen and Kale looked at each other. "We don't know," Kale said at last. "Sometime within the next six years."

"That's rather a wide timetable," said Jay. She seemed calm again, and almost nonchalant, as if she didn't believe them. "Any more particulars?"

"It's in *your* best interest to prevent this from happening," said Kale.

"I don't quite see what you think I can do," said Jay. "If you have concrete proof, you should talk to the FBI. As I have said, there is little I can tell my so-called 'friends on base'."

"I think you can," said Alisen. Then she made a daring guess. "You were once a member of the I.P., weren't you?"

"If I had been, do you really think I would tell you that?" Jay stood up. "I cannot help you, I assure you. You'll have to talk to someone else."

"And what if what we're telling you is true?"

"I'll believe it when I see it," said Jay. She nodded her head in a stately but cold fashion. "See you next week at Civil Air Patrol."

The door slammed shut behind her, and a little bell jingled against the glass. Everybody in the shop looked over curiously.

"Wait!" cried Alisen. "You forgot your backpack—"

But Jay had gone.

Alisen picked up the backpack and turned to Kale. "I guess I'll give this back to her next time we meet. Maybe we should just go for now."

They left the coffee shop and returned to their bicycles.

"Did you think there was anything strange about the way she acted?" asked Kale as he mounted his bike.

"I'm sure we hit a nerve," said Alisen. "But what was it? Was it the I.P.?"

"It was what we said about them coming here." Kale thought. "That seemed to alarm her."

"Anyway, that didn't work out the way I thought it would. Oh, well, maybe we'll figure this out eventually."

They pedaled up the hill in silence.

"I guess this is where we separate," said Kale, when they arrived at the sport court. "Unless you'd like me to walk home with you."

"I'm good," said Alisen. "See you at school, Kale."

"Right." He waved and set off back down the hill.

*****   *****   *****

The next day, Alisen woke up to her phone buzzing in her ear. It was a text from Kale. "I gave Jay your number," he said, "because she called and wanted to know what had become of her backpack. She seemed to be in a bad mood."

Alisen sighed. She had wanted very much to know what was in there, especially what was contained in the pages of Jay's book. But she had known better than to look. Now she could at least tell Jay she hadn't looked inside.

Her phone rang a few minutes later, with an unfamiliar number. Alisen answered and heard Jay's voice, tense and unfriendly.

"Can I come see you today and pick up my things?"

"Of course," said Alisen. "Any time. We're home all day."

"Thanks," said Jay. Without any further speech she hung up.

Alisen shrugged and threw her phone onto the bed. It was not the time to be worrying about how Jay felt.

Jay arrived within the hour. Alisen answered the door to Jay looking anything but civil.

But with an effort to be friendly Alisen handed her the bag. "There you go," said Alisen.

"Thank you," said Jay, rather stiffly. Then she added, "You didn't read the book or anything?"

"Of course not," said Alisen. "I didn't open anything."

"Thank you," repeated Jay. "I'm sorry for asking. I suppose I just wanted to be sure."

"That's okay," said Alisen. "See you at Civil Air Patrol."

Jay nodded and turned away.

*****   *****   *****

They met again at Civil Air Patrol, but neither had a chance to speak to the other. Alisen knew that there would have to be time for trust to build between them, and she did not see the need to hurry matters.

The next day was Election Day. She met Kale at the sport court as soon as school was over, and they watched the news on her phone.

"Diane is winning by a huge margin," said Kale. "Look at those numbers."

"Why only 200?" asked Alisen, feeling rather ignorant. "Why not, well, lots more than that?"

"Those are the electors," said Kale. "You have to have 270 to win . . . and look . . ."

The numbers beside Diane's name steadily climbed. The sun went down, and Kale sighed. "They won't be finished for hours, and I should probably go home now."

"Alright." Alisen reluctantly turned her phone off and put it in her pocket. "Will you be awake when they finish?"

"I doubt it," said Kale, picking up his bike from the sidewalk. "They won't be done until about midnight, but if I do happen to see the results before you, I'll text you and let you know."

"If not, tell me tomorrow." Alisen stood up and stretched. "See you then."

"Goodnight." Kale waved and headed down the street on his bicycle.

Alisen watched him for a few moments before turning and walking slowly back toward her house. She knew exactly how many hours of sleep she had to get in order to wake up on time for school, and she intended to spend every minute she could spare watching the election polls.

Her mother had dinner ready when she got home, and she made herself a tray and carried it to her room. She propped up her phone against her lamp and watched the news. Diane's numbers were still climbing.

At last Alisen glanced at her clock and realized that it was nearly ten-thirty. It was time for bed. With a sigh she turned her phone off, put her pajamas on, and curled up in bed. For a very long time she lay still and stared up at the ceiling, a mental image of the polls dancing in front of her eyes. The largest number was always by Diane's name.

Suddenly she was jerked awake. She sat up quickly. What was that noise? There was a funny white light coming from her night stand. It was her phone. She picked it up and stared sleepily at the message on the screen:

Diane won by a huge margin. Talk to you tomorrow at school.

CHAPTER XII

ALISEN AND HER PARENTS THREW a housewarming party for McKenzie's family.

The whole thing was an enormous success. Their new house had a large, wooded yard, which Alisen and McKenzie thoroughly explored that night, while the parents stood on the deck. It was a lovely house, and a big one. McKenzie was thrilled that it was theirs.

"You'll have to come over often," she told Alisen. "There's plenty of room for sleepovers, too. Dad said that I could have the half of the basement nearest the theatre for my own use. That would be great!"

"Agreed," said Alisen. "What movie shall we start with? We've got to test out that projector."

"*The Hunt for Red October,* of course," laughed McKenzie, who was easily predictable. But suddenly she grew serious again. "Alisen, something's not right about you. It's nothing bad, or personal or anything, but you've been awfully quiet lately. Is anything going on?"

"No, not really," said Alisen. "I feel sort of tired right now."

McKenzie frowned. "Is there anything we should talk about?"

"No," said Alisen. "I'm fine, really. But thanks for checking." She grinned at her friend and poked her in the ribs. "Race you back to the house so we can get some more cookies."

"Deal!" McKenzie ran toward the house, Alisen following close behind.

"By the way," said McKenzie, after winning the race with Alisen and installing herself on the porch with cookies, "how are you liking Civil Air Patrol? I'd love to be in the same squadron as you."

"I've been to only two meetings," said Alisen, truthfully enough. "I must say, I don't really understand everything."

"Neither did I, when I first started. But Dad was in the military for a while, so that helped. I should be able to explain some."

"Great," said Alisen. "But I'm really not planning on joining. I was just going because . . . because . . . "

McKenzie waited expectantly.

"Well, I wanted to see what it was like," said Alisen, feeling slightly confused. "There's another meeting tomorrow night. How about you come with me?"

"Sure thing," said McKenzie. "Could I get a ride?"

"'Course," said Alisen. "We'll pick you up tomorrow."

*****   *****   *****

"What are you doing?" hissed Kale, when he discovered who McKenzie was. "We can't take chances like this! Now that Diane is the President Elect . . . "

"Relax," said Alisen. "None of us have joined yet, and so—"

"Where do you think I got this uniform?" said Kale.

Alisen hadn't noticed that he was dressed in blues like the rest of the cadets. "You joined?" Her voice was horrified. "How could you?"

"My mother made me," said Kale, shrugging his shoulders. "I guess she thought it would be good for me to make some more friends."

"Well, I can't join now," said Alisen. "I know McKenzie will want to, but if I don't . . . "

" . . . then maybe the dreams won't come true." Kale finished her sentence. "Maybe. But we're cutting an awfully fine line here."

Instead of replying to that statement, Alisen asked, "Is Jay here tonight?"

"Yes," said Kale. "She's already inside. Apparently, they had some paperwork to do or something."

Just then, McKenzie came over and joined them. "Hello," she smiled. "Alisen, who's your friend?"

Alisen introduced Kale. He seemed wary at first, but slowly he relaxed under McKenzie's friendliness. By the end of the evening, they were fast friends.

McKenzie's mother picked her up early, just before the meeting ended. Alisen lingered behind with Kale. "What are we going to do?"

"You can't join," Kale, with emphasis on the 'can't'. "Especially now that Diane has been elected president."

"That would certainly hurry things along a bit." Alisen sighed. "See you at school tomorrow."

Alisen spent the rest of the evening regretting her decision to take McKenzie to the Civil Air Patrol meeting. It put tremendous pressure on her, since one decision on her part might start the chain of events that would lead to the fulfillment of her dreams. The thought frightened her. Finding that homework was impossible, she picked up a book and began to idly flip the pages.

A knock sounded at her door. "Come in," she called, and her father's face appeared at the door.

He sat down on the end of her bed. "How have you been liking Civil Air Patrol?" he asked.

"I like it." Alisen wondered what was coming next.

"I'm glad," he said. "Your mother and I would really like you to join as soon as you've attended five meetings. We think it would be a good experience for you."

Dry-mouthed, Alisen stammered, "Why?"

"There are several reasons. One is simply that it looks good on a transcript. I know, you're a little young to be thinking about college, but it's about time to start. Secondly, you can make plenty of friends there. Thirdly, a little exposure to the military is a good idea. It will get you used to leadership roles, respect, and those sorts of things."

"I can't." Alisen was near tears. "I can't join."

"Why not?" Her father was obviously surprised. "If you like it, then why not?"

"No, you don't understand." Alisen tried to get her thoughts clear. "I—I don't want to give up that night. You know the teachers always give a lot of homework on Tuesdays."

"You don't want to go because of school?" He looked mildly puzzled. "Well, you can think about it, of course. But this is something we'd really like you to do. It won't take too much of your time, and you don't have to go on any of the flying missions if you don't want to."

"Right. I will." Her voice did not leave much room for hope.

Her father got up. "Are you almost done with your homework?"

Alisen looked down in surprise at the novel in her hands. "Well, yes."

"Good." He smiled. "There are pizza and a movie downstairs. We'll wait for you."

"Thanks."

As soon as the door closed behind him Alisen reached for her phone. Hastily, with many typos, she texted Kale: "Myy parens are gong to mke m join te CAP!"

*****   *****   *****

Four weeks later, after Alisen had attended her quota of meetings, she arrived attired in a sleek blue uniform. McKenzie did not understand why she was nervous and kept promising her that she would help with the drills; none of which helped allay any of Alisen's anxiety in the least.

She sat through the meeting in misery. The worst part of the evening was when Kale saw her in uniform. He whistled and shrugged his shoulders but spoke no other words to her the whole evening. Was he angry with her?

The meeting came and went without any sign of the I.P. army coming to attack. Alisen had half expected that it would happen right then and there, but nothing seemed to have changed. She was only half relieved, but still nervous on the inside.

Kale met her in the lunchroom at school the next day. "What happened? I thought we had decided about this!"

"You and I had," said Alisen miserably. "But we didn't take my parents into account. They made me join up even though I said I didn't want to."

"What are we going to do?"

"I don't believe there is much we can do," said Alisen. "After all, the damage is done. Neither of our parents are going to let us quit like that, and without telling her everything McKenzie won't quit either. We've got to stick to it."

"But how?" insisted Kale.

"Warn people," said Alisen. "That's all we can do."

"And look how well that worked with Jay."

"Stop getting angry with me! This isn't my fault!" cried Alisen. Everyone in the lunchroom turned around to look at them.

"Fine, I'm sorry," said Kale softly. "I'm just worried."

"So am I," said Alisen. "I think we're in for it. There's nothing we can do."

"Just wait and see is the policy, right?" said Kale. "I don't like it, but you're right. We have to wait."

CHAPTER XIII

ALISEN RECEIVED HER FIRST PROMOTION about a month later. She was very proud of it and pleased to have Jay oversee the ceremonies. Jay even sought Alisen out afterwards and congratulated her on the distinction, which to Alisen was the crowning glory of the evening.

Alisen found herself, rather to her own surprise, forgetting the apprehensions she had when she first joined. It was just as well, she reflected, since she had now been attending regularly for nearly two months and nothing had happened. She was beginning to enjoy the meetings more than she had thought possible. The drills were becoming fluid like a dance, the exercises were hardening her muscles and increasing her endurance, and the comradeship between the cadets was unlike anything she had seen before. There were many reasons for her to be happy.

Kale, too, seemed much less worried as the weeks went by. At first, he was always tense, but all that was gone now. They were good friends as they had been before, and there was the added element of McKenzie.

McKenzie, never having been affected with the suspicions of Kale and Alisen, was enjoying herself supremely. She was happy to be close to Alisen again, and she was happy to be in Civil Air Patrol. Nearly everything made McKenzie happy. It was hard to ruffle her temperament, and in this case, it seemed to Alisen that McKenzie had everything she desired in one place—airplanes, friends, and Alisen.

*****   *****   *****

It was Tuesday afternoon again, and Alisen was getting ready to leave for a C.A.P. meeting. She finished braiding her hair and wound it into a bun. She admired herself in the mirror for a moment before giving a last twitch to her bun and starting down the stairs.

A car pulled up in front of her house. Alisen saw it from the window; with a brief farewell to her mother she was out the door and knocking on the car's window.

McKenzie laughed and unlocked the door. Alisen clambered inside, taking care not to wrinkle a fold in her uniform. Her friend smiled at her and said, "You'll get a good rating on the inspection today. You always do. I wish I had half as much care as you."

"Right," said Alisen. "You're a neat freak, McKenzie, and you know it."

McKenzie poked her slyly. "I'm neat, but not so careful," she cautioned. "You wait and see. Before inspection, I'll have fallen on the stairs, fought with one of the boys, or rolled in a mud puddle. It always happens."

McKenzie's mother looked back at them. "It's true," she said. "Last time it was the mud puddle. That was the end of her starched uniform."

McKenzie and her mother laughed. Alisen crossed her arms and rolled her eyes.

"Tired today?" asked McKenzie.

"No," snapped Alisen. "Just . . . well . . . what can I blame it on? Everything went wrong today. Before school, I tried to curl my hair, and ended up with a big frizzy mess. At lunch, I tried to put it up, so no one would tease me, and it fell out in PE class. While we were waiting for the bus, some stupid kid was chasing me, grabbed my sweater, and tore it from top to bottom. And—yeah, the whole day was like that."

"At least nothing happened to your precious cell phone," teased McKenzie. "Then what would you do?"

"Probably pulverize whoever did it," Alisen smiled ruefully. "I still don't know how you manage to exist with that flip phone of yours."

"Better than the colonists did," said McKenzie. "They didn't even have GPS. Now you have to wonder how they got here at all."

"They were smarter. Who cares anyway?" said Alisen. "I bet it was dirty on board the ship."

"Probably true," agreed McKenzie.

They pulled up to the guard shack. The tired-looking Air Force guard looked at their IDs, then saluted wearily.

Mrs. Roth let her daughter and Alisen off in front of a hangar, with the last words: "I'll meet you out here as soon as you're done. Have fun!"

Alisen and McKenzie waved and started toward the hangar.

McKenzie paused in front of the door to stare up at the sky. "That's where I want to be," she said. "You know, I'm going to get my pilot's license soon. Two years . . . "

"Flying is so . . . " Alisen searched for a word that would convey her feelings and not offend her friend. " . . . unnecessary. Why would you want to?"

McKenzie stared at her. "Have you ever even been flying?"

Alisen shrugged. "No," she admitted. "Don't see a need for it."

McKenzie laughed cheerfully and opened the door. "Some time I'll take you," she said. "My family owns the best little plane—a Stearman. Dad is so proud of it."

Alisen attempted to smile and went inside the hangar.

Jay stood at check-in.

"Good evening," said Jay quietly. "Write your names here."

Alisen lifted the pen and smiled up at her. "Thanks, Jay," she said. "I'll see you later this evening."

Jay nodded gravely.

McKenzie followed Alisen into the middle of the hangar, where chairs and desks had been set up in front of a whiteboard. "I don't see how you can be nice to her," she whispered. "She's no kind of a leader!"

Alisen looked at her in surprise. "Really?" she said. "Nearly everyone I know has expressed the opposite opinion. She's considered the best role model in the squadron, though she doesn't really like to talk."

"That's just it," complained McKenzie. "She won't talk to me."

"That doesn't mean she doesn't like you," said Alisen. "That's just the way she is."

Someone behind McKenzie tapped her on the shoulder and started talking to her. Alisen turned away and focused her attention on the rest of the group.

Across from her, a group of boys were talking about computer science. In the first row, two girls were whispering secrets to each other, and Kale was sitting by himself. He turned around and waved to her, and Alisen waved back.

A cheerful voice behind her made her turn. "Where'd you go, Alisen?" It was McKenzie, resurrected from her conversation and seeking entertainment.

"ATT'N HUT!!" came from the back of the room. She bounced up with the rest of the class and remained standing until a friendly but quiet voice bid everyone recover.

Jay stood in front of the class and said briefly, "As you all should know, we will be having inspections today. Everybody out to the parking lot."

All the cadets stood, teasing each other, talking, and enjoying themselves, making their way leisurely out to the parking lot. Jay walked at the back of the group, pressing her clipboard to her chest and apparently looking around for someone. Alisen noticed that she looked slightly annoyed, so she sidled up to her and asked who she was looking for.

"I'm not usually in charge of inspections," Jay replied. "I was looking for Ethan. He should have been here by now."

When everyone had left the hangar and was milling around in the parking lot, Jay shut the hangar door with a loud slam that made everyone jump. "Fall in!" she ordered, and the cadets scrambled to their positions.

Jay and Kale, who was her acting secretary, inspected each cadet carefully and wrote the result on Jay's clipboard. It was important to have a good showing at each inspection if one hoped to get a promotion.

When the inspection was finished, Jay allowed the cadets to recover and return inside to their desks. It was leadership night. Alisen watched McKenzie's face fall. It was McKenzie's least favorite night and Jay was to make the first appearance.

"Why did it have to be Jay?" complained McKenzie under her breath.

"I told you," whispered Alisen in reply, "she's the best leader. Why do you think she takes care of all the paper and drills and PT?"

"I don't know," said McKenzie. "I'd much rather it was somebody else. Lisel, for example."

"Lisel!" scoffed Alisen, after looking around to ensure that the girl in question could not hear them. "She's so stuck up, all she thinks about is making friends with some of the airmen! Surely you wouldn't want to follow her lead?"

"If she was really the leader, we wouldn't have to," said McKenzie. "She would lose her marbles." Both laughed quietly.

"ATT'N HUT!" The familiar cry brought them to their feet until a voice bid them recover. It was a senior lieutenant colonel, who usually had good things to say that were well masked under a veil of silliness. It was impossible not to like him. Alisen was sure McKenzie was relieved that Jay was not speaking after all.

"I'm here to replace Jay tonight," he began, turning to face his audience. "She's on the phone with someone in the office, and she's a much better secretary than I am. So, let us begin with—"

"Sir," said a voice from the back. It was Jay, standing with a strange expression on her face. "I think you'd better listen to this."

"Can it wait?" said the lieutenant colonel. "I'm rather busy, at the moment."

"No sir, I'm afraid not," said Jay. "I think you need to hear this."

Suddenly the hangar door opened, and a young man walked inside.

The lieutenant colonel glanced hastily up at him. "Ah, there you are, Ethan," he said. "Say something about leadership, will you? I was supposed to give the seminar tonight, but Jay is calling me away on urgent business." And with that, he followed Jay into the rear office.

Ethan looked puzzled for a moment, then he walked up to the front and stood in front of the whiteboard.

"Leadership," he began, "is being able to step up and accomplish a task even when you think you're not prepared . . . "

*****   *****   *****

McKenzie appeared to grow weary of Ethan's lecture. Alisen clearly thought it was interesting, and she listened carefully while her friend sat back in her seat and counted the old, dry cup rings on the desk in front of her.

All at once Ethan was interrupted by a loud slam from the back. "Everybody out!" cried the lieutenant colonel. "Out! Quickly!"

"Sir," protested Jay, who was right behind him, "what are we going to do with them? Where are they going to go?"

The lieutenant colonel turned to Jay and said something in a low voice. Then to the cadets he added, "You heard me! Move out of this hangar!"

"Find shelter outside," yelled Jay. "It doesn't matter where you go, just go somewhere! Hurry! And when this is over, meet back here. Go, now!"

The cadets had looked confused at first, but when Jay spoke they moved. Her voice carried with it an undertone of fear. Everyone ran for the door.

Alisen stood still, her thoughts in turmoil, her muscles tightening as her eyes grew wide.

"Kale!" she screamed, looking wildly where he stood in the front row. "The dreams! The dreams!"

His face drained instantly of color. "No," he mouthed.

Alisen pulled McKenzie to her feet, her eyes wide with fear. "Hurry up, McKenzie!" she cried.

McKenzie shrugged. "You know the C.A.P. does drills," she said. "This is probably just another one. No need to hurry."

Alisen turned to face her. She put her hands on her shoulders and stared straight into her eyes. "Maybe I'd believe you if it wasn't for Jay," she said. "She's serious if ever anyone was."

McKenzie darted a glance at Jay, who stood ushering the cadets out the door.

"Right," she said wearily. "Come on then."

Jay stood watching them as they ran outside. McKenzie stopped. "Where do we go? Why are we doing this?"

"You're going to find out soon if this is real," said Jay, replying to her thoughts rather than to her question. "Make sure you cannot be seen either from the sky or from the ground. And hurry."

"Jay!" Alisen couldn't think of words. She stammered for a moment, then realized that she had Jay's full attention and that she was waiting for her to speak.

"You seem to have an uncommon amount of foresight," said Jay. "Tell me what you know."

Alisen was speechless.

"Tell me what you know!"

Suddenly a loud siren shattered the still air and made their ears ring. Jay motioned them to hurry on, and then returned inside the hangar.

McKenzie clung to Alisen, who dragged her away from the hangar. "Hurry! Hurry!" she kept repeating; and McKenzie had to follow her.

Jay, Ethan, and the lieutenant colonel were the last to leave the hangar. Alisen looked back at them. A few yards from the door Jay paused and looked up at the sky. Over the siren Alisen could not hear what she said, but she distinctly saw her lips form the word: "Planes."

Alisen stared upwards. "McKenzie! Wait!" she screamed; and McKenzie paused.

Louder and louder, a slight vibration of the atmosphere grew and increased until the ground seemed to shiver and the noise was overpowering.

Both girls turned their eyes upwards and saw military jets speeding towards them.

"Whose?" shouted McKenzie over the noise.

"I don't know, but they're not ours, or they'd be flying higher," said Jay,
appearing suddenly behind them. "You two are the slowest cadets I've ever
seen. Get moving."

She ran behind them, spurring them onward to a low building up ahead.
The door was opened by a dusty airman and shut behind them with a click.

Alisen and McKenzie stopped short. The hall was guarded by several rows
of men with machine guns

"Jaylis!" said one of them. "What did you find out? What's going on?"

"Nothing much," she said, looking at Alisen and McKenzie.

Alisen had the distinct impression that there was something she wanted
to say where they couldn't hear. "Jay, what's going on?" she whispered.

Jay looked gravely down at her. "The Civil Air Patrol received a phone call,"
she said. "I'm guessing everyone else on the base did, too. The man on the
phone said only four words: 'An attack is coming.' Then he added the name
of the organization."

"Which was?" interrupted the airman.

"The I.P."

The name sent a shiver of dread down Alisen's spine. She remembered
the dreams, she remembered everything they had learned about the I.P. Now
she could not think of what had happened. It was a strange effect. Now that
she needed it, she could not remember. Something terrible was about to happen—something, something . . . what was it?

Everything around her seemed indistinct somehow—Jay's white face,
McKenzie's frightened squeak—and there was no longer a connection between her and them. All she heard was the planes overhead and . . .

Jay's hand on her shoulder snapped her back to consciousness. "Alisen?
Are you alright?"

Alisen found herself nearly crying. "What is happening?" she whispered, looking up fearfully at Jay.

"God is on our side," said Jay, without answering her question. "Our God . . . He will save us."

McKenzie took her friend's arm. "Come on," her voice wavered. "The airmen want us in the basement, where we'll be out of the way."

The last thing Alisen saw before beginning the descent of the stairs was Jaylis taking a heavy black machine gun from the airman nearest her.

CHAPTER XIV

ALISEN AND MCKENZIE HUDDLED TOGETHER in the corner listening to the strange noises upstairs. She thought she had heard some explosions, but the noise was so loud and sharp that it might have been the soldiers' machine guns.

McKenzie was whimpering, and Alisen did not know how to comfort her. There was nothing either of them could do but wait.

McKenzie suddenly stood and stamped her foot on the dirt floor. "I can't stand this!" she cried. "Jaylis, those airmen—they're all up there doing something, and we're in this dirty basement sitting and hoping they succeed in keeping the I.P. out! This is stupidity."

"What are you thinking?" asked Alisen, pulling McKenzie back by the hem of her sweater. "You can't shoot a gun!"

"Whoever said I couldn't?" said McKenzie. "I spent hours at the shooting range with my father. My—oh!"

There was a moment of silence between the two as they remembered with horror about their parents and wondered what had happened to them.

"Where could they have gone?" Alisen finally asked. "Do they know about this?"

"My mother had a gun," whispered McKenzie. "She could defend herself."

What good was one weapon in the hands of a woman going to do against the entire army of the I.P.?

"My mom and dad stayed at home today," Alisen said aloud. "We live pretty close to the base. I'm sure they know at least a little of what's going on."

McKenzie's eyes widened. "Do you have your cell phone?"

"Of course!" said Alisen. "Why didn't I think of that sooner!"

She pulled it out of her pocket and turned it on. "Should I call my parents first, or yours?"

"Call yours," said McKenzie. "Hurry, please!"

Alisen tapped in the numbers. Both girls waited anxiously while it rang . . . and eventually went to voicemail.

"No!" cried Alisen, and was about to hang up, but McKenzie stopped her.

"Wait! Listen!"

They listened to the voicemail message.

"If it's Alisen, stay somewhere safe!" said the voice of Alisen's mother. "If it's anyone else . . . I'm sorry, I can't help."

"Try my mother!" cried McKenzie.

The ceiling above them shook and plaster fell on their heads. A moment later a deafening explosion rent the air above them.

"Bombs!" shrieked McKenzie. "Jaylis. The airmen!"

"The ceiling!" Alisen grabbed McKenzie and pulled her under a nearby desk. The ceiling shook again, cracked, and began to fall.

"This is the end!" shouted Alisen, beginning to believe her own words. "Hold on, McKenzie!"

The ceiling cracked audibly. The side opposite them fell inward with a loud crash.

"Look!" screamed McKenzie, pointing. Alisen tried to see over the wall of fallen plaster and concrete. At last she saw the still body of an airman lying atop the rubble.

McKenzie tried to climb out from under the desk to reach him, but Alisen restrained her. "Back, you idiot!" she shouted above the noise. "You can't help him now!"

With one final, terrifying split, the entire ceiling gave way and fell on top of them, burying them and the desk beneath the rubble.

Alisen felt something soft slipped over her mouth. McKenzie had torn a piece of dark blue cloth from her long military pants and covered both their faces.

"Breathe through it," she said, her voice strangely muffled.

"How are we going to get out of here?"

"We can't get out of here," said McKenzie. "Either we suffocate, or the I.P. finds us, or—"

"Or?" Alisen interrupted her.

"Or, somebody digs us out, I suppose . . . "

"How long must we wait? Can't we make a noise?"

"I suppose so," said McKenzie. They were about to raise their voices and call for help, when a sound from above halted them.

At first Alisen could not tell what it was, but in a moment, she realized that it was a voice—speaking an odd and very guttural language that neither of them understood or recognized. Then it switched to English.

"That was a good job they did with the bombs," it said. "Cleared nearly everything out for us."

Someone else said something that Alisen did not catch.

"It must be some sort of acoustic effect," whispered McKenzie. "Otherwise we would be too far down to hear them."

"Right," said the first voice. "Say, there's somebody over there. Let's see if they're still alive."

"If they are?" asked another.

"Then we have one more prisoner. The more the better, you see."

There was the sound of feet crunching on rubble.

Alisen slipped her hand over McKenzie's mouth. Both of them were frozen in terror.

"They must be I.P.," whispered Alisen. "Keep still, or we're finished!"

McKenzie nodded, her eyes wide with fear.

"Looks like a girl," said the first voice. "Living?"

"Yes," said a third voice, female this time. Alisen recognized it as Jay's. "What was the plan, anyway? Concerted attack across the country, or was there something deeper?"

The first voice laughed. "Acquainted with the ways of the I.P., are you?"

"To my regret," said Jay. She added something else, in the same language the first voice had been speaking earlier.

The conversation continued incomprehensible to Alisen for a few moments. Then they heard Jay's voice raised. "That cannot be true! It is well known that the S.P., which sponsors your army, has not the resources for such an expedition!"

The first voice coldly cut her off. "The S.P. organization sponsors our army," it said. "True. But we have another, much greater assistant than them. They are—well, you might call them our aide-de-camp. It was not the S.P. who funded this attack. They refused to have anything to do with it, for they said it was sure to fail." He laughed bitterly.

"Who was it?" demanded Jay.

"You seem to know the policies well. You know who it was."

There was a moment of silence.

"We should have seen this coming," said Jay at last.

"What?" The voice was insolent and sneering.

"Your support comes from the country you have attacked, the United States itself. Traitors! All along you planned this so—"

"You do know!" cried the voice. "No one was supposed to know—not yet!"

"What do you hide?" Jay's voice was sharp and bitter. "Who could look, and not see what you intended? You wanted only one thing, to annihilate the people who believe what I do."

"You," said the voice, slowly, "you are an ex-agent. You could not know what you do, unless you were once I.P."

"What I have done in the past does not enter into this discussion. Only what you are doing now matters."

"I don't think so," said the voice. Then, after a moment's pause, "I begin to recall to my mind the story of a certain female agent, who was nearly executed for abandoning the I.P."

"Abandoning? Strange choice of words."

"Perhaps it is time for justice to be served."

"God forbid your kind of justice is the right one," said Jay. "But so be it. Death has no terrors for me, any more than it did then."

"You would have made a brave agent," said the voice. "There is still that choice."

"I have seen who you are. I know you, and I will never go back."

"That choice will cost you your life."

"So be it!" said Jay.

There was a loud explosion, and then sudden, forbidding silence.

"The rest of you, take heed!" cried the voice wildly. "This is what becomes of the I.P.'s enemies! They shall all die!"

There were more footsteps, and then silence again.

McKenzie and Alisen looked at each other in horror. "Jay!" they both whispered at the same moment.

"How did this happen?" Alisen wiped at the tears running down her face. "We left our house to just be around friends, and now . . . "

"Now," finished McKenzie, "now they're all dead. And we're about to suffer the same fate."

"Poor Jay!" cried Alisen. "I should have spoken more to her."

"What happened to this world?" whispered McKenzie. "What did Jay mean when she said that our own country was supporting the I.P.?"

"I don't know," said Alisen. "One thing I do know. We found the safest place on the entire base, and we'd better stay here."

"Except that we're going to suffocate if we don't get out," said McKenzie. "One way or the other, we're going to end up where Jay is."

Alisen squinted at her. "What?"

McKenzie shrugged.

"That doesn't sound like you."

McKenzie burst out, "Where's God now? Why are we here? Why did Jaylis have to die?"

"McKenzie . . . "

"What?" The word came out as a strangled shriek. "Isn't He supposed to help us when we're in trouble?" said McKenzie. "We're under a building, Jay is dead, and the I.P. is taking over our country! What is happening? Where is He?"

"God?"

McKenzie stared at her.

"Maybe this is supposed to happen," Alisen offered weakly. "Maybe there's some purpose in this."

"What could it be?" McKenzie had lowered her voice as if it was an effort to speak. "Why?"

"I'm not God!" exclaimed Alisen angrily. "I don't have any answers! Stop asking me!"

"What's the point?" sighed McKenzie.

"I swear, I don't know!"

"And how are we going to get out of here?"

McKenzie had raised an important point. They had to escape as soon as possible before they ran out of air. McKenzie, holding her cloth over her mouth, started scratching at the back of the desk. Alisen watched her for a moment, then started on the other side.

After a few moments they gave up in exhaustion. It was like trying to dig out of a rock. The weight of the entire building held them trapped and pinned beneath it. They made no headway at all except to disturb the delicate balance of the plaster and send it crashing on their heads.

"At this point I don't care if it's the I.P. that finds us," said McKenzie. "Better them than nobody. I say we yell."

"Agreed," said Alisen, her dread of being trapped under the building beginning to outweigh her fear of the I.P.

They started to call for help again.

"I'm coming," said a muffled voice above them. "Stay where you are. Don't move, and don't make any more noise."

Alisen and McKenzie looked at each other with hope. "Doesn't sound like the I.P.," said McKenzie.

"I'm not I.P.," said the voice. "Stay where you are." There was a strange cough, and then the sound of rubble being moved.

Alisen grabbed McKenzie's arm and said, "What about the airman? Maybe whoever this is can help him, too."

McKenzie nodded. "Say," she called up, "there's another man trapped about ten feet away from us on the other side. Can you help him, too?"

There was a moment of silence above. "Wait," said the voice.

The girls could hear digging being resumed on the other side of the basement. Then the footsteps came back to them, and the voice said, "He's dead."

Alisen dropped her head.

The digging continued above them, occasionally interspersed with a loud, hacking cough. At last, not directly above them, but a little to one side, McKenzie and Alisen could see a speck of light. They cheered and started climbing up to meet it.

"Stay where you are," cautioned the voice, more hoarse now than muffled. "You move, and the entire pile comes back down on you."

Alisen and McKenzie immediately froze.

The coughing and the digging recommenced. Alisen hadn't seen their rescuer's face through the hole, but, as McKenzie pointed out, they would owe whoever it was an enormous debt of gratitude when they got out. Between the two of them they amused themselves by thinking what they would do for them.

"We could take them somewhere for lunch sometime," suggested Alisen; but McKenzie scoffed at the idea and said, "During a war?"

"Well, perhaps we should just ask them what they want. I'm sure our parents would help us get it."

"Probably," said McKenzie. "I can't wait to know who it is!"

"Likely it's one of the airmen," said Alisen. "Somebody from another building who happened to make it out."

"But the cough?"

"Could be the hospital. It's not far from here."

Alisen's cell phone rang.

"You have a cell phone?" said their rescuer's voice. "Answer the call and then get rid of it. That's how they can track you."

Alisen put the phone to her ear and answered. "Mom?"

"Alisen!" said a male voice on the other end. "It's Lieutenant Colonel Krakoff. I'm calling all the C.A.P. members to meet at the wreckage of the hangar as soon as you can get here without being spotted. I.P. patrols are all around."

"I'm trapped under a building, sir," said Alisen. "Only McKenzie is with me, but someone is helping dig us out. Where is everyone else? What's happening outside?"

Krakoff paused. "I don't know where everyone else is," he said. "You're the only one who's answered my phone call."

Alisen shivered. "I'll be there as soon as I can. Thank you."

"Right," said Krakoff. "And let me say it again—don't let yourself get caught by a patrol. Better to stay under that building for all eternity than to be caught. You hear me?"

Alisen and McKenzie looked at each other. "Yes, sir. We'll be very careful."

"Right," he repeated. "Hurry, then, if you can."

Alisen hung up the phone and stared at it. "What could he have meant about the patrols being so dangerous?" she said. "Surely . . ."

"I don't know," said McKenzie. "But I do know that if the I.P. hacks the cell providers, they'll be able to track you by your phone. Let's see. We want the phone to work without the tracking systems, so let me see it."

Alisen gave her the phone.

McKenzie took off the back cover and removed the battery. She pulled out another grey chip and waved it in front of Alisen's eyes. "See this?" she said. "That is your GPS receiver. Now your phone will still do everything but receive GPS. And we will go into the phone and turn off mobile data and cellular, and then you'll be invisible."

Alisen blinked. "How did you know all that?"

"Just because I don't have a big, fancy phone doesn't mean I don't know how they work," said McKenzie. "There. The ideal phone for wartime."

"Is this really a war?" Alisen wondered. "After all, if they only attacked this state, then surely the army will come, and we'll be saved—somehow?"

"The I.P. won't have made that mistake," said their rescuer's voice breathlessly. "I can't say what they've done, but they're out for victory this time."

"Do you know very much about the I.P.?" questioned McKenzie.

There was a brief pause. "Yes," said the voice above. "Yes, I do."

"Then can you tell us what the lieutenant colonel meant when he said it's better to stay under this building for eternity than to fall into the hands of one of their patrols?"

Again silence. "No," said the voice. "I know the answer, but I will not tell you. Knowing it would do you no good under the present circumstances."

There was another round of coughing from above, then the voice said faintly, "All right. You can try climbing out now. Be careful."

"Go ahead," said McKenzie, pushing Alisen forward.

Alisen got a grip on a pile of bricks and pulled herself up. She froze.

"What are you doing?" complained McKenzie. "Let me out!"

Alisen moved out of the way. "You'd better come see this," she said.

McKenzie climbed out and stared. "Jaylis!"

CHAPTER XV

FROM HER SITTING POSITION ON the ground, Jay smiled up at her.

"How'd you dig us out?" asked McKenzie. "We thought you were killed!"

Jay coughed and put a hand to her side. "The building was built on a hill," she explained, her voice faint and distant. "I was able to get to you from the back side." She put her hands on the ground beside her and seemed to be trying to hold herself up.

"Are you okay?" asked McKenzie. "Jay?"

Alisen pointed to Jay's side. "Look!"

It was covered in blood, which poured out from the deep wound and stained the plaster beneath them.

Now she understood everything that had happened. Now Alisen remembered the last dream, now she knew the tragedy that she could have prevented. It was her fault that Jay was dying. She knew, too, that there was no possible way her life could be saved now. It was far too late.

Alisen cried.

Jay fell back heavily, her head on McKenzie's lap. Her eyes closed, and Alisen could see where they were marked with dark rings that had not been present a few hours earlier. Her face was pale from loss of blood, and her hands twitched convulsively by her side, as if she was trying to fight her weakness for a few minutes longer.

Tears ran down McKenzie's face. "Why did you do it for us?" she whispered. "You could have gone to the hospital."

Jay shivered and coughed again. "No," she said. "I had to save you."

Alisen was terrified. This was her friend, the one person she knew who could protect them.

"I'm sorry for being such a prig," McKenzie said. "I was so hateful to you! I didn't mean to be. I'm so sorry."

Jay smiled. "You weren't," she said. "I didn't give you a chance."

She tried to sit up, but fell back, coughing. A thin stream of blood trickled from her lips. "Go meet Krakoff," she said. "Leave me behind."

"We won't leave you," said Alisen. "Come with us. We'll help you get there."

Jay's eyes closed for a moment, then fluttered open again. "No," she whispered. "I would never make it all the way there."

"We have to try!" said McKenzie, struggling to stand and help Jay to her feet.

"Stop!" gasped Jay, stifling a cry of pain. "You have to go without me. You cannot move me."

"You're going to be fine," said McKenzie. "We'll get you to the hospital or something."

"I'm sorry, McKenzie." She paused to try and control her spasmodic shivers. "You have to let me go."

McKenzie abandoned all efforts at keeping back her tears and turned away so that Jay would not see her crying.

"You dug us out," said Alisen through her muffled sobs, "with that wound in your side. You gave your life for ours. Why? You should have been saved, not us!"

Jay's breathing had become hoarse and strangled. With a great effort she said, "It was only justice."

"What?" asked Alisen. "What do you mean, justice?"

Jay did not reply. Instead she whispered, "The book—in the backpack—take it. It may help you . . ."

After a moment's intense inward struggle for breath, her head fell back and rested against McKenzie's shoulder. Her dark eyes were wide and sightless, staring up at the clouded sky where jets crossed back and forth.

McKenzie looked up at Alisen, her face wet and fearful. "I think she's dead, Alisen."

Alisen reached for her wrist, soaked in blood from her wound, but drew her hand back before she touched it. "Why did it have to be her," she whispered. "Why Jay?"

McKenzie gently stood up and let Jay's body slide to the ground. "I don't know. Her courage, her knowledge. It would have helped us so much. She deserved life!"

"What did she mean," said Alisen, "when she said that it was only justice for her to help us?"

"I don't know," said McKenzie again. Then she wildly shouted, "The I.P. will pay for this!"

"Shut up!" said Alisen, terrified. "You're going to get us killed!"

McKenzie savagely pointed to Jay's still form. "Look at what they left behind!"

"But you can't stop them all by yourself. Jay would never have wanted you to do something stupid like this. She said to go meet Krakoff. And if we have to defy the entire I.P., then we'll honor her last request."

McKenzie stared at her coldly. "You try to sound all courageous," she said. "We'll honor her last request, all right. We'll avenge her death."

"McKenzie! What's got into you?"

For a moment McKenzie was silent. Then she fell to her knees and wept without restraint. "I've never seen anybody die before," she said. "Not even in movies. We never watched anything."

"I'm so sorry," said Alisen. There was nothing else she could have said. Nothing and nobody could ever bring Jaylis back.

She stood on top of a pile of rubble and looked around. She was on the highest visible point on the horizon. She could see where the bomb had made an immense hole in the ground, hardly two hundred yards away. Anyone who had been there was beyond their help. Nowhere could she see an entire building still standing; all were like the hangar, or the barracks they had taken shelter in.

A bright speck caught her eye. The red stripes of the American flag fluttered nearby on top of a loudspeaker system. The flag had been hauled down, replaced by a green and white canvas, the I.P.'s signature.

McKenzie, still kneeling, looked past Alisen at the flagpole. "At least Jay didn't live to see the American flag replaced by the I.P. flag."

Alisen wanted to tell her to stop talking about Jay, to stop reminding her of the pitiful sight behind her. But she couldn't bring herself to do it. She knew that McKenzie was deeply wounded by what she had seen, more so even than Alisen was herself.

"Hurry," said Alisen, "before we sight another patrol. We've got to get to the hangar." She crawled over the rubble and retrieved Jay's backpack, which felt light and almost empty.

"Right," said McKenzie. "I'm coming. Let's go."

They grabbed hold of each other's hands, took a mutual deep breath, and began to run across the road.

Every moment Alisen expected to hear shouts behind them. Once she thought she heard gunfire, and nearly overturned McKenzie trying to look back. "Come on!" cried McKenzie breathlessly. "We have to make it there!"

Alisen turned back around and tried to keep up with McKenzie. She pulled too hard, and their hands separated.

An I.P. patrol rounded the ruins of the barracks and came into the road, not thirty feet from where McKenzie and Alisen were.

McKenzie saw them first. "Look out!" she screamed. "Run!"

The patrol seemed so surprised to see anyone alive that they did not immediately react. It gave Alisen and McKenzie time to scatter and dive away from the road.

Sweat dripped down Alisen's face. Never had she run for her life before, and she was surprised at how slowly she seemed to move. The trees flitted by, what few of them there were, and Alisen thought she heard pursuit. A moment later she was sure of it. She looked around in desperation, searching for a place to hide, until she spotted a ruined building she thought she could crawl under. She darted towards it and slid underneath.

A hand slipped over her mouth.

She tried to scream, but no sound came out. A voice quieted her frantic struggle. "Quiet, it's me, Kale." He removed his hand from her mouth. "Are they following you?"

"I don't know," said Alisen. "I think so."

"Did they see you come under here?"

"I hope not," said Alisen. "Kale? It is you, right? I can't see you."

"Yes, it's me," he whispered back. "Are you okay? Hurt or anything?"

"I'm fine," said Alisen. "But I lost McKenzie, and Jay—"

"Jay?" repeated Kale. "Where's Jay?"

"Dead," said Alisen briefly.

Kale took a deep breath. "We knew it would be like this."

They held their breaths as the sound of rapid pursuit came closer and closer.

A voice began to speak in the mysterious language that Alisen did not recognize.

"That's Arabic," whispered Kale.

"You speak Arabic?" Alisen hissed.

"Not a word. But I do know that it's the national language of the I.P."

"What's he saying?"

Kale raised a finger.

"Quit talking like that," said another voice in accented but precise English. "You know the orders, *assimilate*. It's why you were chosen. You all speak English, so do it."

"Where could this girl have gone? You know the patrol leader is going to be angry if we don't find her."

"He won't," said the other voice. "He knows as well as I do that one small girl or another isn't going to make much of a difference. After all, when one takes over a country, there still have to be people to rule over and to work the land, wouldn't you say? She'll learn to her cost what it's like to meddle with the I.P."

The footsteps grew more faint, and at last passed out of hearing.

Alisen turned to look at Kale. "Why me?" she whispered nervously. "Where am I going to hide?"

"You're going to get rid of your cell phone if you've got it," he replied. "There's a GPS chip in the back."

"Was," corrected Alisen. "McKenzie took it out."

"Good," said Kale. "They can't track you. Anything else electronic? Fitbit, watch—anything?"

Alisen felt in her pockets to be sure. "Nothing," she said. "Why?"

"They can track the Bluetooth signal," said Kale.

"Why are you so calm?"

"I'm not," he said. "Inside, I'm cursing this day and wondering about my family and my school and my house. But that's not going to help me, so I'm trying not to focus on it."

"You have such strength," sighed Alisen wearily. "I wish I was like you."

Kale did not reply.

"Must I leave?" said Alisen. "Where will I go?"

"We can't very well stay under this building," said Kale. He paused to think. "I know my way around this base. If the bombs haven't levelled it, we might be able to get to the commissary for supplies. Then . . . "

"Supplies?" asked Alisen.

"How long do you think it'll be before we make it to a grocery store again?"

"I haven't thought that far ahead," said Alisen, hiding her face in her hands so that Kale would not see her cry. "The commander told me to try to get back to the hangar. I was on the way there with McKenzie when the patrol found us."

"Then we'll go there first," said Kale. "Follow me."

He darted out from under the building and into the shelter of some trees. He turned back to look for her, and she had no choice but to follow.

"Keep your head down," cautioned Kale in a whisper. "I'm going ahead to see if the road is clear. We can't afford to mess this up. When you see me wave, you follow."

Alisen shivered too hard to reply, but she nodded her head vigorously, and Kale started off.

He was halfway down the slope before he waved to Alisen. She came down with a tumble and nearly fell into the road.

"Careful!" said Kale, steadying her. "I think we are safe to cross. There are no patrols in sight either direction."

Alisen followed him as they cautiously descended the rest of the slope. They were nearly to the road when Kale said suddenly, "Somebody's coming!"

"McKenzie!" shrieked Alisen, louder than she had intended. The forlorn figure limping toward them sped up its progress and embraced Alisen vigorously.

Alisen held her friend at arm's length and scanned her curiously. "What happened to you?"

Kale broke in, "This isn't the time for reunions. Someone could come along any minute. Hadn't we better save this for the hangar?"

"Kale's right," said McKenzie. "I'll tell you later. You owe me a good story too, seeing that you found one of the missing C.A.P. airmen."

"Hurry!" said Kale.

They crossed the road at a trot and observed the state of the hangar. The rear part had collapsed burying the planes, but the front part was intact and looked safe to enter.

Kale held the door open, and they slipped inside.

It was eerily empty. The whiteboard had been overturned as if by an earthquake, and various items belonging to the members were scattered around the floor where they had been suddenly abandoned. There was no sign of the lieutenant colonel.

Kale said his name in a fierce whisper: "Lieutenant Colonel Krakoff?" There was no reply.

He tried again, this time a little louder. "Lieutenant Colonel Krakoff?"

One of the closet doors opened, and an unfamiliar man stepped out, dressed in a light brown uniform. He smiled in a friendly manner, then picked up a machine gun that had been lying unobserved at his feet and slung it over his shoulder.

"You did not really think that your commander would tell you to come back here," he said. "Apparently you have never heard his voice over the phone. I did rather a good job counterfeiting it."

"Who are you?" McKenzie's voice shook.

"My name is Dalek, and I am the equivalent of a commander in the I.P. army. I have come here to see how many of you I could round up."

"Us?"

"You, precisely, my lady," said Dalek. "As you can see that it would be useless to resist, perhaps you had better come single-file into this closet. Hurry up now."

There really was nothing they could do. Dalek was armed, and they could not hope to gain anything by storming him. One by one they entered the closet.

Dalek waved to them before he closed the door. "Goodbye," he said. "I hope we shan't meet again."

The door slammed shut and darkness enveloped them.

"Now what?" asked Alisen as she looked around the room.

"Now," said Kale, "now, we wait and hope the lieutenant colonel is around here somewhere."

"Kale, that's exactly what we did in the dream, and it didn't work! Can we depend on him? For all we know, they may have caught him!"

"Well, Jay did say to return to the hangar after . . . oh." Kale paused awkwardly. "I'm sorry. Well, we have to wait for the commander," he added, after an uncomfortable few seconds. "We can't get out of here by ourselves."

"Dreams?" interrupted McKenzie, obviously confused. "What are you talking about?"

There was a long pause.

"You mean you knew this was going to happen?"

Alisen looked at her. "Kale and I were having strange dreams about an event just like this," she said, her voice low and uncertain. "I dreamed about this very night, about two months ago. So far everything, down to the sequence of events and very nearly the exact words, has been exactly as I dreamed."

"Then why didn't you do something?" McKenzie asked, her voice growing higher in pitch. "I would have helped you!"

"I don't know," said Alisen miserably. "We did try to tell Jay, but she didn't believe us. I guess I was afraid you wouldn't either."

"What's going to happen next?" asked McKenzie.

"Something happens to the hangar." Alisen tried to remember. "Oh, it's no use! I don't remember—I can't think!"

Suddenly Kale noticed the backpack she was wearing. "Where did you get that?" he said. "That's Jay's, isn't it?"

"She gave me her journal. You remember, the book she had when we met her at the coffee shop," replied Alisen.

"Her story?"

"I don't know. She didn't say."

McKenzie, who had been scratching in the corner, entered into the conversation. "We can't wait for the commander."

"What do you propose we do?" said Alisen sharply. Tempers were running short.

"Do you smell that?" asked McKenzie.

Alisen sniffed, and suddenly fear took hold of her.

Kale was the first to say it aloud. "Fire."

"Then we have to get out of here," said McKenzie. "There has to be a way out!"

Kale put his hand to the metal door and drew it back quickly. "The fire's inside the hangar," he said. "If we're going to get out, it won't be through that door."

Alisen ran into McKenzie as she was crossing the room to feel at the door. She stumbled back, fell against the wall, and crashed through.

McKenzie and Kale rushed to look at her, eyes wide. "That's what we need! A battering ram!" said Kale. "Is there a door in there?"

Alisen turned to look and saw that she had gone through the drywall and into the next room. There was a door on the back wall.

McKenzie helped to her feet. "Come on!"

She pulled Alisen through the opening and ran toward the door. It opened, and they hurried outside, then froze suddenly while still standing on the doorstep.

Dalek stood there, a machine gun pointed at them.

*****   *****   *****

There was no point in wasting energy by screaming for help. Everything seemed to go into slow motion: Dalek's leering face, the end of the gun, and suddenly—

Kale jumped on him. The gun went off pointed at the sky, and Dalek's head hit the pavement hard. He lay motionless, without a sign of life.

"The kickboxing my parents made me do last year came in handy," said Kale. "Let's get out of here."

They ran. None of them knew where they were going. There was no object to their flight, other than to escape the patrols and Dalek's mortal vengeance. They ran until they could run no further. They were thirsty, and tired, and lost.

They took shelter under what had once been a jet, now twisted and broken far beyond repair.

Alisen took off Jay's backpack and pulled out the journal. "Jay said we might find answers in here," she said. "We'll need all the help we can."

"Read it out loud, from the beginning," said Kale.

Alisen looked at the page and shook her head. Tears dripped from her eyes. "I can't," she sniffled. "Kale, you read it."

Kale took up the book and began reading at the first page.

CHAPTER XVI

"WHY WOULD ANYONE WHO HAS seen the terrible things I have write them down? One would think that it would only make me remember the past that for so many years I tried to forget, all alone. And so it does. But I am really writing this so that anyone who may come after me will know—will understand the full implications of our international enemy, the I.P.

"My story begins when I was fifteen years old. My parents had died; I was living alone in the woods, hoping that nobody would find me until I was old enough to get an ID and prove my independence. I would eat only what I could find, for I refused even then to steal—out of ignorance probably, and a desire not to be caught.

"A recruiter for the International Policy came to town. His words were both sweet and bitter, for the mention of any kind of military reminded me of my Marine father. On the other hand, I might be able to follow in his legacy if I had an ideal to fight for. Without giving away my age, I came to town to see what the recruiter was doing. I found him giving a speech about how International Policy was planning world union and endless peace. We were to be the soldiers who would fight for it, who would take up arms— literal arms—to make peace. Two things I forgot then, in my inexperience and distraction—one was very simple. It was the question, 'How can one use arms to force peace?' And secondly, the fact that world union is a very dangerous thing.

"But I joined. The recruiter didn't care how old I was, nor whether my parents approved or not, which should have been a warning to me. But nothing was going to stop me now, and I joined and caught a flight overseas to Syria, with money the recruiter had given me—"

Alisen interrupted. "We were right!" she cried. "She was I.P!"

"She would never have told us anything," said Kale. "No wonder." And he continued reading.

"At first my life was bearable. The training was strict, but they fed us well at least, and so far I had no cause to regret my life at home. Later, though, I began to notice very strange things happening. You might eat breakfast next to someone one day and never see them again, and what was stranger, no mention was made of their names. They simply vanished into thin air. Then, too, there were certain subjects of conversation that were *verboten*; 'where,' for example, was a question that nobody was allowed to ask. 'Whom,' also, was a dangerous question.

"I worked hard, despite this, and rose up in rank until finally I graduated from training and became an officer. Here I met a friend. His name was Nathan Miller. He was very quiet at first—and so was I—but gradually as we came to know each other better we spoke more freely in each other's company. We became very good friends.

"I asked him about the disappearing people. His face became furtive— hesitating and secretive—and he led me away to a place where we could be alone. Then he said, 'There was something wrong with those people.'

"I didn't understand him at first, so I asked for more details.

"'They may have been traitors of some sort, or they may have asked the wrong question, seen something they shouldn't have, or professed an ideal that the I.P. doesn't agree with. Do you know what happened to them?'

"I didn't, but his words frightened me. And my guesses were as horrible as the reality.

"'They were shot, every one of them. I know, because I was the second guard at the executions one day.'

"In horror I asked him why.

"'For no reason at all,' he replied. 'Usually because they owned a book—a small black book—something like this.' He held up a Bible in his hand.

"'They were executed for that?' I asked. 'Why? What does it say?'

"'Because the Bible teaches the opposite of everything the I.P. believes in,' he replied. He handed me the book. 'Take this and read it. When you do, you'll understand.'

"I took the book as if he had handed me a dynamite bomb. 'Keep it secret,' he said, 'or they'll catch you and charge you with treason.'

"It did not seem like a very safe idea to read the book, so for a long time I did nothing with it and evaded Nathan's questions about it. But then, one day, something happened that changed everything.

"The commander called together the recruits and asked for volunteers for special duty. I wanted to get my name out and known to the higher officials, so I volunteered, without knowing where we were going or what we were doing. I soon found out. We were assigned to be witnesses to a court trial. At least, it had the marks of a trial, but that was not what it was, and I could easily tell.

"There were several defendants. One was a girl no older than me. She looked frightened, and the expression was mirrored on the faces of her companions. Yet there was something else there too, something I could not define. It was something almost peaceful.

"The judge began by telling the court that they were former members of the I.P. and that they had been arrested for embracing the wrong ideals. That was how he put it. When the jury—that is, the I.P. members who were acting as a jury—asked him to say specifically what the ideals were, he only said, 'Christianity.'

"I could tell from the faces of the jury that this information sealed the fate of the defendants. One by one they were sentenced to immediate execution—death for embracing an idea. Then myself and five other of the witnesses were called up to perform the duty.

"They lined up the victims in front of our guns. There were four of them, I remember—one for each of the four I.P. soldiers and two left to guard. I stood in front of the young girl, my gun pointed at her head, my finger on the trigger. She looked me straight in the eye, and her emotions were plainly visible to me—fear, almost amounting to terror, and the innocence that comes with little experience of the world. I pitied her.

"The commander gave the order to fire. Three guns went off, but mine did not. I couldn't have pulled the trigger any more than I could have flown to the moon. I dropped the gun from nerveless fingers and said, my voice trembling, 'The trigger is jammed.'

"To my surprise they didn't make me come back and finish the job. I took my weapon to the armory and had it looked at; of course, nothing was found amiss with it, but apparently my testimony was believed, because nothing happened to me just then.

"Now I had to know. Why would the I.P. be so cruel to so impotent an enemy as that little girl? What were they afraid of? And I knew that the answers were in the book Nathan had given me.

"That night I stayed up late and read where he had marked for me to begin. I read and read until nearly three in the morning, by which time I had read from the beginning of Matthew to Revelations. And then I spent the rest of the night deep in thought.

"The message of the book was clear: God himself had sent His Son—His only Son—to die for me, to keep my sins from overcoming me and dooming me to hell that was worse than this hell on earth I had created for myself. I had questions; oh, so many questions. The first and hardest was simply: Why? Why me? I had done nothing to deserve it. I had only been very fuzzily taught about morals before my parents died, but I knew I had done and stood party to some terrible things, especially in company with the I.P. How did I deserve such a sacrifice? And what made it even harder to understand was the fact that I had never known the love of my parents—they had died before it could become familiar to me.

"Another thing that I still did not understand was why the I.P. hated this book so much. But after some thought, I came to the bottom of it. The answer was very simple. This book commanded men to sacrifice themselves for others and to give up power; the I.P. wanted to keep their power and share it with no one. It was possible, also, that the power of evil spoken of distinctly in the book had something to do with it; I did not know, for I had never studied such a thing.

"But one thing was very clear; if someone really had given his life for me, I wanted to be able to acknowledge it. I had read the verse that says to believe; I knew a little about prayer, and I wanted to give my thanks to God and His Son. So, before my roommate awoke, I fell to my knees in the middle of the floor and silently poured out all the pain and grief that until then had found no outlet. I cried, too. I cried for my parents, I cried for myself, I cried for the people who had been executed, and most of all I cried with remorse, for at last I understood now that I had been wrong to come here. I understood what had happened to those people who had disappeared; I understood the subtle feeling of dislike and discomfort that ran among the I.P members, and most of all I understood the terrible danger I had just placed myself in. I did not know what I should do. At first, I tried to reason it out by my own mind; then I remembered that I was supposed to ask for help; so I went to my knees again and prayed for an answer.

"It came immediately and clearly: Talk to Nathan.

"I went and found him; he was outside walking in the cadet's enclosure before breakfast. I cornered him as far from the guard as we could get and told him everything.

"He looked straight into my eyes, red and shining from my tears, and embraced me. I hadn't ever thought of him doing that, and it came as a surprise—and in a way a relief. I had found a friend in Nathan, but until then I had not known how close we had really been. Now we both knew.

"'The I.P. will not let you resign until you have served your term—fifteen years,' said Nathan. 'Unless you are determined to escape—'

"'I want to help my friends,' I said. 'They need to know about this, too.'

"'That will be difficult,' said Nathan. 'You must be careful who you tell. If you are not, you will become one of those members who mysteriously vanishes in the night.'

"'You told me,' I said. 'You didn't care about the penalty.'

"Nathan smiled. 'I trusted you,' he said. 'I still trust you. You can do this.'

"Just then, the guard called to us and told us that breakfast was ready. We separated and went to our separate mess halls, neither of us glancing back at the other.

"Right before our first class of the day, a recruit brought me a summons to the commander's office. He did not give a reason, and I had no cause to suspect anything unusual.

"I went as quickly as possible. The commander was waiting for me; his name was Dalek, and he was a strange man. Laughing, incorrigible, cheerful—and as hard as stone and crueler than iron. I hated him deeply, but did not know why then.

"'Sit down, Jaylis,' he said; and when I expressed my desire to remain standing, he continued quickly. 'There is a report of a traitor in our midst, you know. An old friend of yours.'

"My heart began to beat quickly with evil premonition. 'Who, sir?'

"'Nathan Miller.' He paused, to let the words sink in. 'He has been distributing illegal propaganda.'

"'Who has brought the charges?' I said, trying to sound cool. 'I am sure I can speak for his character—'

"'Ave Genine, if you must know,' said Dalek. 'I am afraid we cannot take the time to test your word against hers. The I.P. is much too busy for that.

That is what I called you in here for—you are to take your weapon and make an end of this.'

"I stood frozen, not knowing what to say or where to look. Finally I cleared my throat and said carefully, 'You want me to kill him? Without a trial, Ave's word against—against nobody's?'

"'As I said, the I.P. has time neither for pity nor for formalities,' said Dalek, and his face hardened. 'Will you do it, or will you not?'

"Slowly I left the room. I went to the armory and retrieved my weapon, then continued slowly to Nathan's apartment. I knew well that he would be there, for this was the usual time that we met together for fellowship and talks. Sometimes other people came, too.

"I found him there as I had expected. He was sitting on his bed, poring over the 'illegal literature' that was to be his death. I simply stood in front of him, staring down alternately at him and at the book.

"He looked up at me, and immediately his face broke into a smile. 'I was hoping you'd come,' he said. 'I have something for you.'

"Without thinking about anything at all I sat down beside him. He fumbled with his pocket, then pulled out a little white box and gave it to me.

"I opened it and saw a beautiful white diamond ring sparkling against a velvet backing.

"'I love you,' said Nathan softly. 'I want us to be together forever, if you're willing. Please, Jaylis, will you marry me, when finally we have escaped from this place?'

"I looked at him. I looked at him for a single moment and then I burst into wild, hysteric tears.

"He pressed my head to his shoulder very gently and asked me what was wrong.

"'The commander sent me in here to kill you,' I wailed. 'Somehow they found out what you were doing from Ave, and—and—' I was too choked to continue.

"He pulled away and stared me in the face. 'And you were going to do it?'

"'No,' I sobbed, and I knew I was sincere. 'No, never. I would rather die first, and—and'—I sniffled pathetically—'I want to tell you yes, I want to tell you I'll be with you forever. But it doesn't look like we're going to get the chance.'

"He sat back down and held me to his side. 'I'm sorry,' he said. 'I wish—I wish you hadn't been involved.'

"I couldn't bear his needless remorse. So I looked at him, steadied my voice, and said, 'This isn't over yet. And whatever happens, you taught me a truth that I will never forget. I love you, Nathan. And thank you for everything you've done.'

"He smiled at me, but immediately his face grew grave. 'We must get you away from here,' he said. 'They'll book you as soon as they find out you disobeyed. Let's see, what can we do.'

"His face was anxious, and I understood why; there was no way to escape the I.P. in a desert controlled entirely by their soldiers.

"In the end, we decided that there was nothing to do; the commander would find out all too soon and there would be an end of both of us. That seemed to be our only option.

"During the intervening two days we spent a great deal of secret time together, studying the Bible and possible plans of escape. But nothing presented itself.

"It was the third day that the end finally came. The commander—"

"Shh!" interrupted McKenzie. "I hear something!"

Kale paused and looked up at the sky. The sound was familiar to all of them, and they stared at one another other, dismayed.

"Planes!"

"Fighters, nonetheless," muttered Kale.

"Where can we go?" cried McKenzie, fear in her voice.

"Nowhere," said Kale. "Hopefully they will see that the land here is already destroyed and spare us another bombing. If they don't . . . "

The likelihood was that the bombers would aim for the smoke of previous bombs to hit their target. And if they did, Kale, Alisen, and McKenzie would be caught in the middle of the devastation.

Alisen took Jay's journal from Kale and put it back in the backpack. "Let's see what else is in here," she tried to keep her voice steady over the roar of the planes approaching. "Maybe something here can help us." She dug around in the bag and produced a series of odd-looking, soft grey tubes. "What are these?"

Kale took one and studied it. Suddenly he said, "These are flares! Quick, see if there are any matches in there!"

Alisen obediently dug around in the bag and handed him a box of matches.

Kale seized them with a yelp and ran out from under the jet.

"What are you doing?" cried McKenzie and Alisen in terror, but Kale only continued running. They watched him run several hundred yards to a deserted building, light the flare, throw it as hard as he could, and run back toward them. He signaled frantically.

Alisen suddenly understood his plan. "Come on, McKenzie, run!"

They ran away from the jet and away from the direction of the flare as fast as they could. Kale caught up with them and together they pounded over the tarmac and dived for cover under a destroyed trailer.

The three cadets covered their ears as the bombs dropped and exploded, but they were just barely far enough away to be safe.

A wall of fire erupted from the building, and they watched in awe as it grew and consumed the structures all around it.

At last they fled from it across the runway and through the surrounding fields.

"We have to stop," panted Kale, slowing down behind Alisen and McKenzie, "until we figure out where we're going."

It was against immediate instinct to stop, but Alisen could see the reason in his words. It was madness to run with no destination and no plan, especially when they did not know the location of the I.P. patrols. They returned to where Kale was kneeling and paused, breathing heavily from the run and the acrid smoke.

He looked up at them. "The Commissary isn't far from here," he said. "We can get supplies there if the I.P. hasn't sacked it. By then it will be dark, and we'll have to find a place to hide."

"And if they keep bombing?" McKenzie shivered despite the heat of their run.

Kale shrugged. "We try to stay out of the way."

Alisen had been looking over his shoulder. "A patrol's coming!" she cried, suddenly pointing behind him.

Kale turned quickly. "They've seen us!"

"Run!"

They all took off running in the opposite direction. The patrol followed with all speed. Alisen's breath grew short, and she was terrified she would fall.

Kale was in the rear, looking back every few seconds to note the patrol's progress. "They're gaining," he panted. "Hurry!"

"Must—find—rest," gasped McKenzie. "Have to hide!"

"I know," replied Kale, glancing anxiously back. "A building, a smashed plane—anything. Come on!"

"I know where," Alisen gasped through shortened breaths. "Follow me."

She led them in a wide circle around the airfield, the patrol ever following and ever getting closer. The sun cast their shadows deeply on the concrete behind them, adding to the eeriness of the chase. It also made them clearly visible to the pursuit.

Kale and McKenzie followed Alisen. She led them back the direction they had come from, back around the Civil Air Patrol's hangar, which had burned out slowly, like a torch, and subsided to a dull flame here and there, and to the building which had collapsed over herself and McKenzie. Jay's body, cold and still, lay atop the rubble. And beside her was the hole through which they had crawled.

"Hurry," Alisen panted, "get inside, before they come."

When they were all inside, crammed into the tiny space under the desk, she pulled a piece of plaster over the hole and hid them from sight.

Everyone breathed deeply, trying to catch their breaths as softly as possible.

"This is a wonderful hiding place," said Kale in a low whisper, as soon as they could speak. "They'll never dream of looking in here."

McKenzie was sniffling. Alisen put an arm around her, and the two girls lowered their heads to each other and cried. They wept for Jay; they wept for their families, their parents, their friends, and the terrible danger that assailed them from every side. There was nothing they could do, nothing more they could have done; still Alisen felt that Jay's death was her fault, and the sight of her lying among the rubble had reawakened these thoughts.

Kale sat silently watching, without interrupting. At last he spoke softly. "It's Jay, isn't it?"

"I was hateful to her," sobbed McKenzie. "I never understood her until she was dying. It was so unfair of me!"

"And I," added Alisen tearfully, "I should have warned her in time. Jay didn't deserve to die!"

Kale was silent for a moment. "You know," he said gently, "that if she believed what she said she did in her journal, she wasn't afraid of dying."

They looked up at him.

"People who believe in the Bible—who truly believed in it—were supposed to believe they went to heaven or something after they died. They had no fear. And Jay wasn't unhappy," he added, "but her life here was far from joyful. She believed a reward was coming . . . she believed it would be better this way."

"You're saying," sniffled Alisen, "that she died believing in a lie?"

"No-o," said Kale. "I haven't investigated this yet. None of us have. All I'm saying is, she didn't feel that death was some kind of punishment. For her it was merely a transition to something she had been waiting for."

Alisen pulled out the black journal, stained with blood, and looked at it. Finally, she whispered, "Why can't I have the same kind of peace as Jay did?"

She flipped the pages until she came to the words, "The message of the book was clear: God himself had sent His Son—His only Son—to die for me, to keep my sins from overcoming me and dooming me to hell that was worse than this hell on earth I had created for myself. I had questions; oh, so many questions. The first and hardest was simply: Why? Why me? I had done nothing to deserve it. I had only been very fuzzily taught about morals before my parents died, but I knew I had done and stood party to some terrible things, especially in company with the I.P. How did I deserve such a sacrifice? And what made it harder even to understand was the fact that I had never known the love of my parents—they had died before it could become familiar and safe to me."

"Is there really a God?" Alisen cried. "Why is He letting this happen? Where is He now?"

Out of that dark hole came the age-old question of misery and faith that everybody must ask at some desperate moment in their lives. It was uttered in tones of despair and pleading, as if willing the answer to be 'yes'.

McKenzie struggled to her knees and said hoarsely, "No! I will never give my allegiance to someone who lets us suffer like this!"

Alisen stared at her.

"I agree with McKenzie," said Kale. "A crumbled building in the middle of a war zone is no place to find religion. Religion belongs to churches and whitewashed steeples. We have more to think about than that right now."

"But if something happens to us . . . ?" Alisen was reluctant to give up the point. "And remember, the disappearances were predicted in the Bible."

"I guess we'll know when they happen, won't we?"

Alisen did not feel it worth pointing out that by then it would be too late. She relented so far as to find herself wondering if Kale was right.

CHAPTER XVII

AFTER RESTING FOR A LITTLE while, Kale asked Alisen for Jay's journal to finish reading. She gave it to him, and he began where he had left off.

" . . . The commander caught me in an ambush while I was on my way to visit Nathan. Without a word to me I was placed in captivity under strict guard. Nathan was nowhere to be found.

"Our trial came in two days. At least, they called it a trial; but it was not, it was a pretended justification to take our lives. Ave was there. Once we had been friends, but now we both knew there was no more chance of that. She was cool toward both of us, with no more pity than the judges themselves.

"I will spare myself the remembrance of that trial. Suffice it to say that they did not even wait to execute Nathan properly, but shot him as he stood in the courtroom, covered with bruises and blood and showing signs of the ill treatment he had received at their hands. Me they let go, and I will never know why. Perhaps they intended to take the most terrible revenge by forcing me to live the rest of my life with the memory of what I had seen.

"But if that was their intention, it failed. The pain comes back, the fear and the terror and the helpless anger, but because I believe that I will see Nathan again I can still hope. Because of that and because I am rescued by God . . . miraculously, hope still exists for me.

"Now for the I.P. I heard rumors in my service that they were planning a massive attack, though I never did know exactly where they got the weapons. It will hit first of all on their own government, to ensure their dominion over their own land, but next on the United States. Then the attack will spread the world over, if successful, and then they will set up a one-world government.

"I don't know how much of this is true, nor do I know what the implications will be or how the attacks will come. But I do know this. Many people are going to die, and perhaps I am one of them. If so, I want whoever reads this to know one thing about the future. But they can't learn it from me. Mark 13:19 says:

"For in those days there will be such tribulation as has not been from the beginning of the creation that God created until now, and never will be.

"And Revelation 3:10 says:

"Because you have kept my word about patient endurance, I will keep you from the hour of trial that is coming on the whole world, to try those who dwell on the earth—"

"Just like my dream!" Alisen interrupted Kale. She turned excitedly to face him, unable to keep still. "This is exactly what that pastor told me when I talked to him about it. He said that the people would disappear and—"

"This passage says nothing about disappearances," said Kale pointedly. "It only says that certain people who keep God's word won't have to go through this."

"But the rest of it! The tribulation—I think that's what he called it—and all the other predictions!"

"Would somebody fill me in?" asked McKenzie.

After a rather awkward pause, Kale explained to her about their final dream and the disappearance of the Civil Air Patrol members.

"I see," said McKenzie. "And the pastor told you that it was a sign of the end times?"

"Right," said Alisen.

"But in order to believe the pastor's words," continued McKenzie, "you'd have to believe in God, also correct?"

"Of course."

"What reason do we have to believe in God right now? He let Nathan and Jay die. He let our country get attacked. He let all this happen!"

"That's aside from the point," said Kale quickly. "None of that matters right now."

"I think it does," said Alisen. "When that dream comes true, we're out of time. We'll be too late."

"We're about out of time anyway," said McKenzie. "This attack will claim thousands and millions of lives. Why shouldn't our own be among them?"

Kale and Alisen remained silent, not knowing what to say to comfort their friend's despair.

"Remember that Jay said hope still existed—"

"For her, to finish the quote," interrupted McKenzie. "With some delusion of God—"

"Shut up!" cried Kale. "Just shut up, be quiet. There's no point to this discussion. What we have to focus on now is saving our lives and our friends' lives. Religion can come later."

McKenzie and Alisen turned to face him, silenced by his outburst of anger and passion.

"First, we have to find food," continued Kale, "and water. The only place we can get that is at an abandoned house or the Commissary. The first would be better, as the Commissary is five or six miles from here. The housing's just around the corner. We need to hurry, before it gets dark and we can't see our way."

"Kale—" Alisen began to protest.

"We have to do this." His voice was hoarse, but resolute and determined. "We can't do anything for ourselves or for anyone else until we get provisions. Shelter will be our next affair."

"Don't be stupid," McKenzie glared at him. "If we go out now, we'll be caught for sure. For all we know, that patrol could still be on our tail."

"I know you're hurting," said Kale. "And I know that you're regretting the way you treated Jay. But we have to—"

"Who said I treated her badly?" cried McKenzie.

"You did," said Kale and Alisen together.

McKenzie scrunched in the corner, her head on her knees. Alisen could see her shoulders trembling, and finally she burst into wild, high-pitched sobs. "I'm so sorry," she gasped, between breaths. "I know I'm an idiot, but I can't take this! I don't understand it, and there's no one I can ask for help!"

Alisen silently put an arm around her. "We're here," she said.

"But you don't understand any more than I do!" wailed McKenzie. After a pause she added in a whisper, "No offense . . . "

"None taken," said Alisen, "and you're right. But we have the dreams, and we have Jay's journal. We can make sense of this."

"On our own," continued Kale, "without any help. Certainly, without God, for goodness' sake. First, we have to save ourselves, and then we must help other people."

McKenzie lifted her tear-stained face up to look at him. "How can we help others if we can't even help ourselves?"

"We're in this together," began Kale.

"That is the most overused movie cliché ever," said Alisen, with a strangled laugh. "Let's give up on the propaganda. It's not going to do anybody any good. We have to do this thing; we have to stay alive, we have to follow the dreams, and Jay's journal. And I think we have to seriously consider the last message of the dreams."

"God again?" asked Kale incredulously.

There was a long pause, broken only by the muffled sounds that came from above.

"I'm alright," said McKenzie at last, wiping her eyes. "I'm ready to follow you."

"Then let's go," said Kale. "We have time to get to the housing and back—if we are coming back—before it gets dark."

With a scuffle and some difficulty, they succeeded in climbing out of the hole. The sun hung low on the horizon, but there was plenty of light for them to see in every direction. No patrols were in sight. The only noise that broke the deathly stillness was the sound of distant flames crackling.

"The base housing is that way," said Kale, pointing west, in the direction of the lowering sun. "Follow me and keep a look out."

With a cautious glance around, they climbed down from the shattered building and into what used to be a road. There was no one in sight. Across the field, the I.P. flag hung limply on the flagpole.

The road led them to what had once been a neighborhood, providing housing for the military families. Now they were almost all flat. It was no easy task to walk down what had once been the road. It was cracked and upheaved in places. Occasionally there were rifts in the ground that seemed to go infinitely deep. These could not be jumped over and had to be gone around. By the end of the detours Alisen lost all sense of direction, but Kale did his best to keep them on the right roads.

Finally, they reached a house that was still partially standing. It half leaned over the road but looked fairly safe to enter. At least it was higher than everything else nearby.

Kale swung open the door and looked carefully inside. A cloud of dust for a moment obscured the view, but when he could see again he announced that it was safe. "Come on," he whispered, "let's see what we can find. Stay together."

He stepped inside. The floorboards creaked with terrifying volume. Alisen felt for McKenzie's hand, and they gripped each other tightly before entering. Inside it was dark, a deep, velvety dark that could not be penetrated because of the dust. Kale rubbed his finger across the wall. It came away white with plaster.

"Look for the kitchen," he whispered. "Find food, anything. I'm going upstairs to find something to carry it in."

"I thought you said stay together!" hissed Alisen, but he had already departed for the stairs.

She and McKenzie tiptoed gingerly around the house looking for the kitchen. Everything was eerily silent. Not a sound, not a whisper broke the perfect silence except for the soft tread of their shoes in the dust and debris.

For a single moment Alisen let go of McKenzie's hand and peered around the corner into a long hallway. A scream—a loud, horrible scream—petrified her and broke her nerve. She dared not look around. Something soft blundered back against her.

McKenzie sobbed. "It's them, it's the people!"

Slowly Alisen turned to look. At first, she could make out nothing distinct, but then she saw two still forms lying on the floor—two people, motionless and indistinct. She drew her breath in sharply and tried to keep from screaming.

McKenzie was in a paralysis of fear. She clutched Alisen tightly around the middle, gasping and sobbing and unable to say a word. Alisen herself was half terrified, but she held McKenzie's wrists and tried to calm her, drawing her eyes away from the pathetic sight.

A thumping sound came from upstairs. A moment later Kale was at their side asking what had happened.

Alisen pointed across the room.

Kale looked silently. "I'm sorry, McKenzie," he said at last. "I should never have brought you here. I should have come alone."

"She'll be alright," said Alisen. "She's never seen anything like this." She tried to still her shaking hands to hold McKenzie tighter.

"As if any of us have," muttered Kale. "When will this end?" He sat down limply in the middle of the floor. "Go back to the front room," he said at last. "I'll ransack the kitchen, and when I'm back we can find a place to sleep."

Alisen nodded, finding no words, and half-carried McKenzie back to the front of the house.

McKenzie slid down against the wall, still crying bitterly. "Why? Why?" she repeated over and over. "Oh, why is this happening?"

"McKenzie," Alisen shook her by the shoulders. "Stop! You have to stop crying! If someone hears us, they'll kill us!"

"Who cares?" shrieked McKenzie. "If only I could get away from here!"

"No! You can't think that way!" cried Alisen. "Think about your parents. Think about your friends. Think about me, and Kale!"

"Leave me alone," whimpered McKenzie.

"I won't leave you alone," said Alisen resolutely. "I care about you, McKenzie. We'll get out of this somehow."

McKenzie dropped her head to her knees.

"This won't last forever," continued Alisen, sitting down beside her. "Don't you remember reading books like this? When the characters were pursued by—"

McKenzie raised her head and said listlessly, "When have we ever read a book like this?"

Alisen thought about the United States; how everyone had believed it was strong and perfect and could never be invaded. She remembered Jay's words about how treason had been involved, and about the cruelty of their attackers. And she knew that McKenzie was right. Nothing like this had ever been or ever would be again.

Kale came out of the kitchen, loaded with a backpack full of cans. "This should be enough for a couple of days, if we're careful," he said. "Now the question is, where do we go from here?" He glanced with a shudder back to the living room. "We can't stay here."

"You're the one who knows the base," said Alisen. "What buildings could be standing?"

Kale shrugged. "Any buildings that are standing will be occupied by the I.P."

"Well, then?"

"It's warm outside, for now anyway."

Alisen opened her mouth to protest, then realized that Kale was making a feeble attempt at a joke. "Right," she said saucily. "Any better ideas?"

"I was just kidding," said Kale, with a half-smile. "It's getting dark, or I'd say we should look around a bit. What if we stayed upstairs tonight? Just tonight," he added hastily, looking down at McKenzie. "There's nothing . . . nothing up there."

"I guess it's the best we can do," said Alisen. "By the way, do you think there's a computer up there?"

"A computer?"

"So we can look at the news. Maybe we can figure out how much damage has been done."

Kale nodded slowly. "I did see a computer," he said. "It's a long shot how long the battery will last, since there can't possibly be any electricity. But I'll go get it."

Alisen helped McKenzie to her feet. Slowly they trailed across the living room and up the stairs. They creaked ominously as Kale walked ahead of them. Alisen wondered if they were safe to climb.

Kale installed the two girls in a comfortable bedroom with two twin beds side-by-side. There was a computer on the desk in the corner, the blinking light of which showed that its battery was still charged. Alisen helped McKenzie, who was still sobbing quietly, to the bed, and then sat down in front of the computer.

Kale peered over her shoulder. "Is it connected to the internet?"

Alisen typed in the search engine. "No," she said with a sigh, "I had forgotten. Of course, none of the modems are working."

Kale uttered a curse, and then smiled shamefacedly. "I'm sorry," he said. "Sometimes I forget . . . "

"You're under horrible pressure," Alisen said. "I wish I could help you more. You're really the leader of this group, you're strong, and you have the skill."

"I wish," said Kale, sitting on the side of the bed. "I hate myself right now. I'm not worthy to lead you and McKenzie. I'm not worthy to lead anybody."

Alisen shrugged. "I don't believe you. I think you can lead us better than anyone else could." There was a long silence. "You know," added Alisen, "that if you ask God—"

"Please stop," said Kale wearily. "I know, I know, God's stronger than me and all that, but if He was He could have just stopped all this from happening."

"I don't understand," said Alisen. She put her head down on her chest and tried not to cry.

Kale put an arm around her. Gingerly at first, but then he squeezed her tightly by her shoulders. "Don't be ashamed to cry. I would if I could, but every time I try—"

"—you think of Jay," sniffled Alisen. "Maybe that's it, maybe it's not, but I know I do. What a day, Kale! How could this have happened?"

"I don't know," said Kale. "I don't know."

They sat silently for a few minutes, thinking and listening to the quiet night sounds.

"We had better go to bed," said Kale at last. "I'm sleeping across the hall if you need me. I'll try not to wake you up in the morning."

Alisen smiled sadly. "Alright," she said. "Thanks for talking to me."

"Any time," he said. "Thank you for your encouragement. It's nice to feel that at least someone believes in me."

Alisen remained sitting on the side of the bed after he left. She knew she could never sleep, and she knew that the dreams she would have if she did sleep would only frighten her into wakefulness again. So many horrors had happened in a single day. The attack of the I.P., Jay's death, their flight from enemy pursuers, their shelter under a wrecked aircraft, their foraging in this old house, and now this. Alisen could hardly believe it was all real. But it was real, most horribly real.

At last Alisen got under the bed covers and tried to sleep even though she didn't feel tired. She could hear McKenzie's deep, even breathing beside her. Perhaps just a little bit of sleep, just a little . . .

A tremendous crash awakened her. For a moment she lay shivering in bed, terrified, until Kale's steady voice came through the door: "Are you okay?"

She got up and went into the hallway where Kale was standing. "What was that?" she half-whispered.

Kale peered through the gloom. It seemed that a new cloud of dust had been raised, but neither could tell where it had come from. "I don't know," he said. "Let's look around. Where's McKenzie?"

"Right here," said a faint voice from behind them. "I'll look over here."

Alisen rounded the corner of the stair rail. She was just about to put her foot on the top step when Kale shouted and ran toward her. She nearly over-balanced and fell in her effort to stop herself, but Kale put an arm around her and dragged her back.

"Look," he said hoarsely.

There was nothing but empty space beyond the top two steps.

He drew Alisen back until she was safe. "We have to be careful," he gasped. "Somebody must have heard that."

McKenzie came flying toward them, a horrified look on her face. "Alisen! Are you alright?"

Alisen nodded, too dazed to speak.

They sat in the hallway for nearly a half an hour, listening intently to all the sounds that came their way. Finally, hearing nothing suspicious, they felt sure they were safe, and they all went back to bed.

*****   *****   *****

In the morning, Kale was up long before the two girls. He pondered how it would be possible to descend from the second floor of the house now that the stair was gone. Jumping was always an option, but the ceilings had been very tall, and the fall would be a long and dangerous one. There were no trees anywhere near the windows that might be used as ladders, and as far as Kale searched he could find nothing resembling a rope. He experimented with the bedroom sheets but found that it was completely impossible to make them into any sort of a ladder. Finally, he gave up wandering around the top floor and sat down to think.

He decided he could occupy himself with another problem, the problem of internet. Kale was fairly good with electronics. Maybe he could somehow use a small battery to power the modem. It might only work for a little while, but if he could find the battery and some wire, he might be able to at least check the news.

He found some batteries in a television remote and was able to pull some wire from the back of the television itself. He stripped them carefully and linked the batteries together. Then he carefully touched the two ends of the wire to the end of the modem's plug.

Rather to his surprise, it powered on, but only for a moment. The current was not strong enough to turn it on all the way.

Reluctantly he put his contraption down on the floor and went back into the hallway. A noise behind him startled him. Alisen stood with a blanket around her shoulders as if she was waiting for him.

"I was sort of worried," she explained, "that we wouldn't be able to get downstairs now. Besides, anyone could come into this house any minute and find us here. So, I thought that if you were up, you could help me pull the bannister down . . . "

"The bannister!" exclaimed Kale. "Of course! It runs along the edge here, and if we pull it apart and put it back together end-to-end—"

"—we can use it as a ladder," finished Alisen. "Exactly what I was thinking."

"An excellent idea," said Kale. "Let's give it a try."

It worked, though it was much harder to remove the bannisters than they had thought. It also made a great deal of noise, which they feared could easily be heard from the street. When they had finished their construction, they waited for a while to see if anyone came, but no one did.

McKenzie appeared in the hallway shortly after they had finished. "This looks like a good job. I apologize for sleeping late and not helping."

"Well, should we go down?" asked Alisen. "We have to find out what's going on around here, don't we?"

"I think," said Kale as he studied their makeshift ladder. "I think, maybe, that we should send just one person down at first. They could have a look around, sort of see what's going on, then come back and report what places are safe and how far the damage goes."

"I agree," said Alisen. McKenzie nodded.

"And since I know the base . . . " continued Kale.

"No," said Alisen and McKenzie together. "We need you here."

"You wouldn't know your way around!" protested Kale. "It's settled. I'm going."

"Stop!" cried McKenzie, trying to catch hold of his ragged blue uniform.

He descended the makeshift ladder, smiled up at them, and slipped outside.

***** ***** *****

"Well, now what?" said McKenzie. "Are we supposed to just wait until he gets back here?"

Alisen smiled wearily. "Your long sleep apparently changed your thinking," she said. "I don't think you want to go downstairs. Maybe we should just wait."

"But, Alisen," protested McKenzie. "I've been thinking. What happened to the people in these houses? They can't all be dead. Maybe we could help some of them."

Alisen looked at her in surprise and whole-hearted admiration. "That's a good idea," she said. "Let's try it."

"What kinds of tools will we need?" asked McKenzie.

"Shovels," said Alisen. "And some water for the people. Hopefully that will be enough, because I don't think we can carry much more."

"We can find those things downstairs," said McKenzie. "I hope we can help someone."

"So do I," said Alisen. "Hurry up, let's go look."

They descended the bannister ladder and went into what had once been the house's garage. There they found a heavy metal shovel and a plastic snow shovel which they took along with some bottles of water packed into a small plastic cooler.

It took some courage to walk the desolate streets. There was an unnatural stillness compared to the proceeding day. More frightening still was the thought that there might be people somewhere, people who needed help and who had no chance for life unless Alisen and McKenzie came to their rescue. They set out from the house after looking carefully around for I.P. patrols walking down the street.

The first house they came to, or rather the first pile of rubble that had once been a house, was only a few yards from where they had spent the night. It was flat—so incredibly flat—that it was hard to believe it had ever been a three-dimensional structure. A light pole had fallen on it and bored a horizontal line through the wreckage. There was no sign of anything moving.

"I think," said McKenzie hesitantly, as they stood staring at the wreckage, "I think that if there was anyone in this house, they're probably . . . probably . . ."

"I agree," said Alisen hastily. "Let's keep moving."

They continued further down the street, pausing at every house or ruin of a house before continuing past in despair. If there had been anyone on this street, they were surely dead by now. One of the bombs must have fallen very near here, and the flying debris from its impact had not helped matters. It was a strange feeling, a feeling of loneliness and indistinct terror that could not be ignored.

"This isn't doing any good," complained McKenzie, dropping her shovel and sitting down on a cardboard box. "It's like looking for—"

"Watch out!" cried Alisen, but it was too late. The cardboard box collapsed inward and McKenzie fell through.

Alisen laughed hysterically, despite McKenzie's wrathful face which was upturned from the bottom of the box. "You're probably right," she said, tears in her eyes from her unnatural laughter. "We should go back."

"Somehow, I didn't find any of this as funny as you," growled McKenzie as she climbed out of the box. "You seem to forget that we're the only people left alive on this street."

Alisen took a deep breath. "Sorry," she said. "I haven't forgotten. It's just . . . if you're dark all the time, what's left for you? I mean, it was pretty funny, the way your legs stuck out of that box and—"

"Shh!" whispered McKenzie. "What was that?"

Alisen froze in place. Terror rooted her to the ground, fear of the I.P. or possibly of something worse. Then she laughed unsteadily and said, "I didn't hear anything."

"Yes," said McKenzie, listening intently. "There it is again!"

This time Alisen heard it. A voice, a very remote or else very quiet voice that seemed to be talking.

She looked at McKenzie with wide eyes. "The I.P.?" she said. "Do you think?"

"Keep listening," said McKenzie. "Let's see if we can tell what he's saying."

"Alright," said the voice, "here goes. I have to decide to cry for help, or I have to stay here with this thing on my arm and die that way. Which is better? The I.P. or this cursed column?" The expression changed to one of deep fear. "The I.P., of course, of course. Ah, the pain! Somebody must help me!"

"Where do you think it's coming from?" said Alisen, looking around. "He must be very close."

"Maybe in that house," suggested McKenzie, pointing to the nearest ruin. "In the basement, I should think, if he's still alive." Her eyes glowed with mingled excitement and fear. "We have to help him."

"Of course." Alisen tried to speak calmly despite her own emotions. "But suppose it's some sort of trick? Maybe the I.P. wants to lure us and then—"

"If he really is under that building," said McKenzie, "there's no way he could have gotten in from the outside. Look, you can see for yourself that there's no opening."

That was certainly a good reason for supposing that the cries were genuine. Alisen and McKenzie picked up their shovels and bottles of water and hastened to the ruined structure.

The house was in slightly better condition than the others. Its second floor had collapsed in onto the first floor, but the foundation had suffered very little damage. Oddly enough, its front door was still standing, even though the walls had collapsed in on either side. An eerie place, and the high-pitched cries had done nothing to make it less so.

Alisen marched to the door and called out in an unsteady voice, "Hello? Is anyone there?"

A wild, inhuman scream drifted up from beneath her feet, a sound that animals make in the last moments of their lives. Alisen leapt back. McKenzie dropped her shovel and turned to run.

The scream was followed by the voice, which cried, in a frenzy of terror, "The I.P.? The I.P.? Oh, have mercy on me, please heaven! Don't take me back to bondage there. I'd rather die here! Leave me, leave me. Or if you be of a compassionate nature then put a bullet through my head."

Alisen and McKenzie looked at each other, horror-stricken by these words.

"I'm not going to hurt you," said Alisen, recovering her voice. She inched gingerly closer to the door. "We're here to help. We're not the I.P."

"Not the I.P.?" The voice seemed to hesitate. "You must be I.P., because nobody but the I.P. can be out right now. All dead, everything ruined!" Then it continued into a nonsensical and inaudible mumbling.

"Where are you?" shouted Alisen, plucking up courage again.

There was a long pause—a very long pause—during which Alisen was afraid he would refuse to answer. But after a bit the voice said, "Down here."

"Down where?"

"In the basement."

"Alright, we're coming," said Alisen, turning to McKenzie. "You have the shovels?"

"I don't like this, Alisen," said McKenzie, her teeth chattering. "This person, whoever he is, seems a little disturbed. What are we going to do with him after we get him out? I'm beginning to think this person, whoever they are, might be better off here, since he wants to die anyway."

"What are you saying?" cried Alisen. "We have to help him. He was begging for our help. Besides, that's what we came for, isn't it? Now come on. Whatever he may be, he can't do anything if, as he says, his arm is trapped under a column." She plunged into the house.

McKenzie followed gingerly, carrying a shovel and two bottles of water in her pockets.

"Good," said Alisen, attempting to show that she was not afraid. "Now we have to look for a basement door or something."

"It's right here," McKenzie pointed to a door that was surprisingly intact. "Looks like the stairs and everything are—"

She was interrupted by the renewal of the voice's plaintive cries, which seemed to come from beneath their feet. "You found the door," it said. "If it's I.P.—oh, I don't suppose it can get much worse than it already is. They'll come and—"

"We're not the I.P.!" shouted Alisen. "Can't you tell by our voices? Now be still, wherever you are, and we'll come get you. You can see that, can't you? Right. Don't move, now."

"The stairs look steady," said McKenzie, after a single nervous glance in the direction of the floorboards. "Shall we try them?"

Alisen nodded. "Here goes." She stepped onto the top stair and took hold of the rail.

There was a sickening crack, and the rail gave way. Alisen screamed and lost her balance, falling backward into McKenzie's arms. The stair shook, crumbled, and gave way, and McKenzie was unable to hold Alisen. With a final scream she fell with the stairs and lay silent at the bottom.

"Alisen!" shrieked McKenzie. "Alisen, are you alright?"

"I've always wanted to be a gymnast," Alisen picked herself up from the wreckage and peered up. "McKenzie? You up there?"

"Of course," she said. "Are you hurt?"

"Twisted ankle," said Alisen, biting her lip between words. "I think I'll be alright if we find something to wrap it with. But McKenzie—"

"Cold steel! I have to get out of here. Have to get out!" The mysterious voice laughed wildly.

And Alisen saw a faint glimmer of metal moving down across the room. "Stop!" she cried. "What are you doing? Stop! You have to stop!"

"It's paradoxical, really," continued the voice, still at a wild pitch. "To get out I must leave a part of myself behind. No doctor, no nurses, no clean white sheets smelling of bleach. I'm on my own this time, and I WILL GET FREE!"

"What are you doing?" cried Alisen. "We're here to help you! What are you—for heaven's sake stop! McKenzie!"

"What's going on?" cried McKenzie desperately. "Where . . . what's that? What's he doing?"

"He's got a knife in his hand," panted Alisen. From somewhere below there came a rustling and then a crash. "His arm, it's trapped, under a beam of some sort, and I think . . . I think he's trying to cut—"

"Freedom at last!" cried the voice.

"Stop!" screamed Alisen again, and she struggled over the floor to him. "Put it down!" She tried to open his hand, clenched on the handle of the knife. "Don't do this! There has to be another way!"

There was a long pause—a very long pause. "Don't do what?" said the voice, very normally and without any of the terrific emotions it had shown earlier. "What have I been saying?"

Alisen took the knife from his loosened hand and threw it across the room. "You were trying to use this knife to amputate your arm, so you could get free from this beam. Brave, but idiotic. We are here to help you. What's wrong with you, anyway?" She collapsed into a sitting position a few feet away from him, her injured ankle stretched out in front of her.

"I don't know," said the man, pushing his dark hair behind his ear with his free hand and closing his eyes. "I suppose it's PTSD of some sort."

"Does this happen often?" asked McKenzie.

"No."

"Sorry," Alisen said. "It's just most people don't try to perform self-surgery in the basement of a house."

"Also, you were talking some nonsense about the I.P.," said McKenzie from above. "Are you familiar with them?"

"As much as most, or possibly more. But really, I'd rather not talk about that right now. I don't feel so well. I should like to be freed."

"I don't know how," said Alisen. "I fell down the stairs while we were trying to get down here, so I'm afraid I'm not of much use. But at the top of the stairs is my friend McKenzie, and she might be able to help us."

"Of course, I'll help," said McKenzie, "but at the moment I don't know what to do. If we had some rope—"

"That only works in the movies," interrupted the man. "We'll need something a little more stable."

"Right," said Alisen. "And I happen to know just the thing. I saw one of those aluminum ladders as we were coming in."

"I was using it to paint the side of the house." He grimaced.

"I think it will be long enough. Can you find it, McKenzie?"

"I'll have to get free first," said the man "I still can't move. My arm is trapped under something."

Alisen shook her head. "I don't think I can help you," she said. "Just try moving a little. Can you shift whatever is on top of you?" She rolled onto her knees and reached toward the beam. "It doesn't feel very heavy. It's worth trying to move it."

There were a few seconds of silence and then a soft thump. "Well," said the stranger, obviously startled, "I wonder why I didn't try that sooner?"

"What happened?"

"It wasn't a beam at all. It was a two-by-four from the ceiling." He paused. "I'm sorry. I don't know what I was talking about. I'm free now."

McKenzie disappeared from the head of the stairs. It seemed to Alisen that she was gone for a long time, but when she reappeared she had the ladder. Carefully McKenzie balanced it on the edge of what had once been the stairs, and it was just long enough to reach the floor below. Alisen struggled to get up the ladder without further injuring her twisted ankle. After a few moments' work they were all three safely on the main floor, and a few moments after that they had gone outside.

"Thank you," said their mysterious homeowner, dusting himself off, "both for getting me out of that hole and for keeping me from doing anything stupid. Might I ask your names?"

"My name is Alisen, and this is McKenzie," explained Alisen. "And you?"

He nodded. "My name is Naorin," he said. "It's an Arabic name in case you were wondering." His face was serious, but there was a twinkle in his eyes which made Alisen guess that he was only a few years older than they.

"Do you speak Arabic?" asked McKenzie curiously.

"Of course," said Naorin, "If you have shelter, I would like to accompany you there. I might be of service carrying Alisen since it must be painful for her to walk. Or, if you had rather part company here, I shall say thanks again and stop bothering you."

"We don't have any proper shelter," said McKenzie. "We are living in a—"

"A badly damaged house not far from here," finished Alisen hastily. "But we will be leaving soon. I don't know where we will go after that."

"I see," said Naorin. "I understand why you would not wish to trust me. But I will tell you, those words spoken in the darkness of that empty, deathly basement were true. I hate the I.P., and whatever it takes to keep myself out of their hands I will do, even if it means my own death. And whatever it takes to bring about their ruin, that also I will do, though it should cost my life or my neighbor's." His face contracted, and his eyes darkened as he spoke those words. There was no doubt he meant them. No acting of any kind could ever have put such an expression of deep hatred on his contorted face. It was almost more than Alisen could bear to look at. She turned away from Naorin.

"But if you don't trust me," he continued, as though nothing had happened, "that's alright. I entirely understand. I will be on my way, and perhaps if you ever need a favor I will be on hand to repay my debt to you. My arm isn't nearly as bad as I thought while I was trapped down there, and I don't believe it's broken."

"Hold on just a moment," said Alisen. "Would you mind letting me and McKenzie talk this through? No offense to you, of course, but we're bound to be cautious about this."

"I understand, and there is no offense taken. I'll go see what items might be of use." Naorin disappeared into the house.

"That Naorin is not loyal to the I.P. is pretty obvious," said Alisen quietly. "That he's kind of crazy is also fairly obvious. If he has a fit like that when the I.P. is on our tail . . . "

"But aren't we supposed to take care of people like that?" said McKenzie. "I mean, he can help us out when he's not acting all weird. He might be a good companion to have. He's nice, and he's not lying."

"No," said Alisen. "No, he's definitely not lying, at least not about the I.P. I've never seen such a look of hatred in my life. Well, I suppose we could take

Naorin with us. He does seem nice, and friendly, and strong, too. I wouldn't mind some help getting back to that house anyway."

"I think that's fine," said McKenzie. "We can always change our quarters and kick him out if we need to."

"Right," said Alisen with a half-smile. "Let's go find him."

Almost as if by magic Naorin appeared out the door. "Persimmons," he said, holding out his arms full of big orange fruits resembling tomatoes. "Can you believe it? Nothing edible in the house except this fruit. And dozens of them, at that." He handed one to Alisen. "Here. You'll enjoy these. One bright spot in a decidedly cloudy future."

Alisen took a deep bite of the fruit. It was unexpectedly delicious, tasting rather of a pear or mango or melon, or all of those combined into one.

"Thank you so much," she said. "This is like . . . like . . . "

"Like a change from all the darkness and horror," finished Naorin. "I know. I know because, well, because I've tried it before."

Alisen looked at McKenzie and handed her the rest of the persimmon. "Here," she said, "try this, while I fill Naorin in on our plans."

"I should be delighted," said Naorin in a quaint, polite way.

"We're living in a half-ruined house at the end of the street here," said Alisen, pointing back the way they had come. "We aren't planning to stay there for too much longer, since the I.P. could come along any day and we have to keep moving. But such as it is, and for as long as it lasts, you are welcome to stay there with us. That is, with us and with our friend, Kale."

"That is very kind of you," said Naorin. He hesitated. "But I've been thinking . . . maybe it isn't such a good idea for me to stay with you after all. It is a kind offer, but I might—I might bring danger on anyone I am with, should we be discovered . . . "

Alisen paused. "Would you mind telling me how so?"

"I'm sorry," said Naorin, "but I really can't right now. Or rather, I could, but I prefer not to think about it. You will have to take me at my word. I can't stay with you, because if you were caught it might have serious consequences. However, we may still be able to help each other. I'll come late at night to your refuge, and I'll tell you where mine is, so that we can keep in touch with each other and possibly receive aid if we need it. Would that be agreeable?"

"Of course," said Alisen, "but really, you don't have to be afraid of staying with us. We'll help you if you need it."

"No," he said, shaking his head in decision. "I cannot. But I will carry you to your house, and then I will depart to find one of my own."

"Thank you," said Alisen. "That's very kind. But I think I can make it all right with McKenzie to lean on. Come see us tonight and look for the old grey house with dark blue shutters. It's right down this road."

Naorin bowed gracefully. "Until tonight," he said. "Best wishes."

Alisen put an arm around McKenzie and limped down the street. "Naorin was awfully nice," she said. "But seriously, what century is he from? I could see him in one of those old-fashioned king's suits."

"My thoughts exactly," said McKenzie. "He's ridiculously formal, but at least he's funny."

"I think he might be a useful ally, whatever all that rubbish was about him putting us in danger. We're in danger enough as it is."

"I've been thinking," said McKenzie slowly, "you know, if we were still with Jay, she would have put us in danger."

Alisen paused and looked at her.

"The I.P. knew her and hated her, so if she had been found with us, they would have thought we knew her and knew her story, even though we didn't at the time. Maybe it's like that with Naorin."

"I don't see that it matters," said Alisen, after some reflection. "What matters is that he hates the I.P. as much as we do, and more probably, and there's no danger of him turning us in. He'll tell us his story when he's ready."

"Right, right," said McKenzie. "Well, let's get you back home. Kale is probably freaking out, and I can't say I blame him."

Kale had already arrived at the house and was frantically searching for them. When he saw them coming through the door, he looked relieved but rather annoyed.

"You crazy lunatics," he said, "don't you know the danger of being out alone? You could have been caught by a patrol, and I could never have found you!"

"I'm sorry, Kale," said Alisen. "It was my idea. And we were able to help someone, a man named Naorin."

"Who hates the I.P. as much as we do" volunteered McKenzie. "He would be a good companion to have in case of any difficulties."

"I'm glad you're both back," said Kale. "But I think you should stay here for now. The patrols are getting more and more numerous. I think the army will arrive shortly, and when that happens there won't be any safe places left. We have to get moving."

"And where are we going to go?" McKenzie asked. "Where can we go that the I.P. won't follow?"

"I think I have an answer for that," said Kale slowly. "I found a computer at the library today that still worked, and I was able to check the news. These attacks have occurred all across the country, from east coast to west coast. They centered on major cities and military bases and are moving outwards quickly. The I.P. soldiers were trained in the desert, where the visibility is almost hundreds of miles and where there are no obstacles in the way. If we can find a landscape that is entirely different, I think we could hide there."

Alisen and McKenzie looked at each other. "I think it's a good idea," Alisen said. "Anything's a good idea that gets us away from here."

"How did the I.P. get to the United States anyway?" asked McKenzie. "Did they just fly over the ocean on airplanes, or did they take a boat, or what? How did they surprise us?"

"There was an article about that," said Kale. "I didn't get to read the whole thing before the computer died, but I think it said that the I.P. soldiers are mostly legalized citizens of the United States, and that they were just waiting for their cue. They did everything they could to avoid suspicion, and they acted like ordinary citizens, but underneath they were always waiting for something to happen."

"And somehow," said Alisen, "the I.P. headquarters in Syria got them a message, and all these people just rose up and went crazy?"

"Exactly," said Kale.

"How horrible," said McKenzie. "We let this happen. These people must have been coming in for decades, and we never knew about it."

There was a long pause.

"We can't stay here," said Kale at last. "We need to find a place to go."

"What about Naorin?" asked McKenzie. "Should we take him with us?"

"Who is this Naorin person anyway?" asked Kale.

"We rescued him out from under a building," said Alisen. "He was raving about how much he hated the I.P. and how terrified of them he was. He was about to do some damage with a knife until we pulled him out. That's why you don't see me standing, I twisted my ankle in the rescue process."

Kale's face lengthened. "Then we won't be going anywhere tonight," he said. "Is Naorin coming here? Are you sure that's safe?"

"If you had heard him and seen the look on his face, you wouldn't doubt it for a second," said McKenzie.

"Alright. Well, I guess we'll have to wait until he comes. Is your ankle all right, Alisen? Have you bandaged it?"

"No," said Alisen, "and it does hurt. Maybe we could get some sort of makeshift compression wrap. Then I might be able to stand on it."

"I think we can do that," said Kale. "Let me see it first, though, so we can see if it's swollen."

Alisen took off her shoe and sock, and Kale examined her ankle. "It's swollen a little, but it could have been worse," he said. "I'll get a sheet from the beds upstairs, and we'll wrap it up for you."

Alisen felt a great deal better when her ankle was bandaged and stable. She even ventured to walk around a little, and to climb the makeshift ladder back upstairs. It was while she was resting on the bed that she had an idea.

"McKenzie," she said, "these C.A.P. uniforms weren't meant for wilderness living. Maybe the people who lived here have something that would fit us."

"I don't know if I could wear their clothes," said McKenzie hesitantly, "after seeing them like that."

"We have to find clothes somehow," Alisen waved away McKenzie's reluctance. "I'll go look, if you help me out of bed. I'm sure we can find something."

McKenzie reluctantly agreed, and together they crossed the landing and went into the main bedroom. The closet was full of clothes, belonging probably to the older members of the family. But all the clothes were too large, and they found nothing that would suit them.

"Let's try down the hall," said Alisen. "I remember seeing some girls' bedrooms down there. Maybe they had teenagers."

They found the closets in those bedrooms filled with clothes just their sizes. Alisen changed into loose blue jeans and a soft cotton sweater, while McKenzie put on the most comfortable clothes she could find: sweats and a T-shirt from a local church. Then they returned to their bedroom.

"You know," said McKenzie suddenly, sitting down on the bed next to Alisen, "I've been thinking . . . "

"What?" Alisen yawned and lay back on the bed.

"You remember . . . what Jay said, in her journal? And how Kale said that, for her, death was merely a transition and not something to be afraid of? I think, if I could figure out how that could possibly be true, I would face death or anything else willingly enough."

Alisen sat up slowly. "I wish I could be as brave as Jay, at least," she said. "You saw her. In horrible pain, yet giving her last breath to save two stupid, terrified teenagers when in all probability she would have lived if she had gone for help. People read books, and people write books, where the characters do such things, but in real life it's a cruelly different story."

"Maybe people are afraid of death because they don't know what is beyond," suggested McKenzie, tears in her eyes. "But Jay didn't fear anything, death least of all, so she must have known what was coming."

"Are you talking about God?"

McKenzie nodded silently.

"But I thought you were the one who so very passionately denied His existence when we were reading Jay's journal."

"You know," said McKenzie, ignoring Alisen's comment, "that we never did finish reading Jay's journal. Maybe we could do that now?"

"Sure," said Alisen, "if you think you can."

"I think so." McKenzie took a deep breath. "I need to know about this."

Alisen went into Kale's room and brought back the black journal.

"Are you ready?" she asked, glancing at McKenzie.

"I suppose," she replied, resting her chin on her hands.

Alisen began, "Revelation 3:10 says:

"Because you have kept my word about patient endurance, I will keep you from the hour of trial that is coming on the whole world, to try those who dwell on the earth.

"I think this verse has a lot to say about the future, and I think that whoever reads this should be prepared. Times are not going to get easier, and people are going to die. Indeed, as this journal is my closest guarded possession, it is safe to surmise that if anyone but myself is reading it, my own life has been given up for some reason or another. If the reader is a friend of mine, I would tell them not to despair. The only thing that can give them hope is the message of the Bible. If you are lost and alone, you will find a friend there. If you are facing death yourself, know that the courage to do so comes from God Himself.

"Every word I have written is from my deepest heart, and not one is untrue. I beg that the reader will take the deepest consideration of it, for it is a matter of eternal consequence.

-Jaylis Jennison

"*P.S. The I.P. is here. The attacks have come as I knew they would. They have used us as puppets, and we have deserved the ill treatment. The only person who knows the true secret is Diane, who has become the President of what was once the greatest nation on earth. Shame on us! It will be the undoing and ruin of—*"

"And that," said Alisen, "is the end."

"There is nothing more on all those empty pages?"

Alisen flipped through them. "Nothing more," she said. "She must have intended to write more. I guess that last part was written as soon as she got the phone call."

McKenzie did not reply.

"Did that answer your question?" ventured Alisen.

"Did it answer yours?" she replied shortly.

"Well, I should think it came close," Alisen said. "You asked, how could death be a transition instead of an ending? She answered, courage to face death comes from God. I think that means you have to look. Well, to look in the Bible would be a good start."

"Did she have one of those in her backpack?" asked McKenzie.

"I don't know, but the backpack is in Kale's room. Could you go look for me?" Alisen sat back against the headboard. "My ankle hurts a lot right now."

McKenzie paused and then nodded. "Of course," she said. "Hold tight."

She came back in a few moments empty-handed. "I couldn't find one," she said. "Maybe later I'll look downstairs."

"Are you sure you want to wait?" asked Alisen. "Maybe you should go now."

"I don't need you telling me when to do things!" she snapped. Then she dropped her head in her hands and sighed. "I'm sorry, Alisen. That wasn't fair at all."

"It's okay," replied Alisen gently. "We're all on edge."

McKenzie stood up. "I feel like I should be doing something, something to save the world I guess." She laughed drily. "And I look outside, and there's no world left to save."

"You're looking for a reason to go on living," said Alisen. "There's nothing you can do, there's nothing I can do, but maybe now you know where to find the answer."

"Do you believe in it yourself?" asked McKenzie.

"I don't know. I've never seen it before. Who knows what kinds of things are in the Bible, the book of lies and good morality? Maybe it isn't lies after all. And McKenzie," she paused, and stared at the ceiling. "I surely have to hope it's not."

"Yeah. That's right." There was a long pause.

"Where's Kale?" asked Alisen suddenly.

McKenzie looked surprised. "Isn't he downstairs?"

"What would he be doing down there?"

"I suppose I could go look," said McKenzie. "I'll be back."

Alisen sat on the bed and wished she had someone to talk to. She felt the same loneliness as McKenzie did, and talking helped, but there was so much more to say. She wanted to talk about her parents, about her friend from school, Sadie, and now Kale had disappeared, and she had someone else to fear for. And she wished something good would happen to break the monotony of horrors they had seen since the last meeting of the Civil Air Patrol.

She heard McKenzie's footsteps in the hall. "I didn't find Kale. He left a note on the counter, with paper he found goodness-knows-where," McKenzie said, beginning to speak while she was still on the makeshift ladder outside. "Says he's gone to look for some supplies and will be back before dark. If he isn't, don't go looking. That's all he said. But I did find Naorin! He was prowling around like he was completely lost." She rounded the corner into Alisen's room, followed immediately by Naorin.

Naorin made another graceful bow. "It is my pleasure to be here. You have it quite comfortable, I see."

"I suppose so," said Alisen. "It's rather like living in our own house, sort of, anyway."

He nodded. "Well, is there anything I can do to help out? I was hoping to meet your companion, Kale, but I see I shall have to wait. Perhaps, in the meantime," he gestured toward the stairs and showed the first signs of embarrassment that either of the girls had seen in him, "you would like me to take care of the remains of . . . of the family that once lived here, which are downstairs."

Alisen and McKenzie looked at each other. "We'd like that," said Alisen. "We might have done it ourselves, only . . . "

"I understand," said Naorin, "and that is why I offered. Wait up here, and I will be back in a half hour or so."

He was back sooner than Alisen had expected. Neither she nor McKenzie had moved in his absence. They sat sitting side-by-side on the bed, staring out the window, and saying nothing.

"Well," said Naorin, "I owe you my thanks for your rescue this morning, and an apology for my behavior."

Alisen looked up from the window. "What happened? If, that is, you want to talk about it."

Naorin leaned against the doorframe and thought. "It's difficult to explain, from my point of view," he said hesitantly. "You know what PTSD is? I have that, and sometimes it makes me go crazy." There was a long pause. "You see," continued Naorin very quietly and with uncanny calm, "I was once a member of the I.P. The things I saw there will not bear telling, so I will not try. But it was there that I lost the innocence of my childhood, and it was there that I learned to kill and to hate and to destroy. And in the process," he laughed bitterly, "I learned that man is not made to hate. So, I fell into a sort of fever, and ever since then I have had these fits of insanity when anything reminds me of it. I destroyed many people's lives, and in the process destroyed my own."

"Did you," asked McKenzie hesitantly, after a period of silence, "did you know Jaylis?"

Naorin hid his head in his hands. "Jaylis Jennison?"

"That's her."

"I knew her," he said. "Yes, I knew her. Everyone knew her. But she was executed at a mock trial for insubordination, years ago."

"No," said Alisen. "She was set free."

Naorin looked up. "How is that possible? Do you know her?"

"We did," Alisen replied.

"She was killed yesterday by an I.P. patrol," said McKenzie softly. "She saved our lives."

Naorin was silent. "That was like her," he said eventually. "After she changed, anyway. But why did you ask if I knew her?"

McKenzie shrugged. "Just curious."

"Were you expecting me to?"

"I don't know," said McKenzie. "But you know, it bears out your story of being in the I.P. Not that we ever doubted you," she added hastily.

Naorin smiled. "This is a time for doubt," he said. "Right now, you should doubt everyone and everything you see, because the I.P. has many tricks. You never can be too careful."

"Naorin," interjected Alisen, "do you have enough supplies? And if you're hungry, why don't you stay and eat with us? We have plenty, and maybe it will keep you here long enough to meet our friend Kale."

"Thank you for the offer," he replied. "I shall certainly stay. Provisions are running short in my locality."

"Do you know where Kale put everything?" asked McKenzie.

"He left it where he found it, in the pantry," said Alisen. "I'd do a lot for some buttered pasta."

There was a strangled snicker from Naorin's corner, but by the time the girls could look at him his face had relaxed to perfect composure.

"I'll go down and look," said McKenzie. "Would you mind helping Alisen downstairs?" she added, turning to Naorin.

"Certainly," he replied, and before Alisen could move he had lifted her as easily as a kitten and carried her into the hall. He followed McKenzie down the ladder, and deposited Alisen gently on the remains of a sofa.

"I'm going to help McKenzie," he said. "We'll be right back with a status report."

Alisen heard some clattering in the kitchen and a few words that she could not distinguish. Then McKenzie entered the living room and sat down beside her on the sofa. "Naorin is a good cook," she said. "He's making pasta. No butter, unfortunately, since it went bad with the power outage, but with salt and powdered cheese and other nice things. He also found a few bottles of water."

"Excellent," said Alisen. "All we have to do is wait then, I suppose."

"You know," said McKenzie, "I'm getting a little worried about Kale. He's been gone for nearly three hours."

Alisen sat up straight. "So he has," she said. "But he did say not to worry if he wasn't back by dark . . . "

"He didn't say not to worry," corrected McKenzie. "He said not to come looking for him."

"Where could he have gone?" Alisen frowned. "The Commissary is a long way from here, from what he said. There isn't anything but houses and offices for miles."

"Maybe he was trying to raid one of those," said McKenzie. "Or . . . " She was suddenly silent.

"Or what?"

She looked all around as if she was afraid someone would hear her, and when she spoke, it was with a very soft voice. "Naorin showed up not too long after he left."

"Where's the connection?" said Alisen, puzzled. "There's still a good hour left before dark."

"It's a possibility," said McKenzie. "Maybe Naorin had something to do with his disappearance."

Alisen shook her head doubtfully. "Either he's the best actor I've ever seen, and anybody's ever seen, or he's dead serious about hating the I.P. I don't think he would give anyone up to them."

McKenzie shrugged. "I guess you're right," she said. "It's just, I was sort of thinking about what he said when he told us to test everything."

"Right," said Alisen. "I think he checks out. And I smell—"

"Onions and peppers," Naorin's voice finished from the kitchen. "And pasta and cheese."

Alisen and McKenzie looked at each other and laughed.

The dinner was ready in about a half an hour. Naorin had made excellent pasta which was covered in thick cheese and onions and peppers, and had brought some persimmons from the house he had been trapped in. It was a good feast, and only one thing was missing, Kale.

As the evening went on, Alisen's worry increased as Naorin talked steadily into the night. It grew steadily dark, and still there was no sign of Kale. Soon Alisen found herself sitting in silence and left to her own thoughts. She wondered if McKenzie worried about Kale, too.

CHAPTER XVIII

NAORIN LEFT ABOUT NINE O'CLOCK. And McKenzie and Alisen went to bed, but neither of them slept very well. Every noise that came from outside woke them at once and they started up, hoping that the noise was caused by the return of their friend. It never was.

Morning came. McKenzie was red-eyed and Alisen was sure her gritty eyes looked as bad. Kale had not come back. Neither Alisen nor McKenzie spoke of his absence until after they had breakfast. They sat in the living room, waiting.

"Surely, he would be back by now if everything was alright," said Alisen. "I wish Naorin was here to advise us."

"He would tell us to stay put," said McKenzie with a sigh. "He's so almighty terrified of the I.P."

"I beg your pardon," said a voice from the front door, "I am not almighty terrified of anything, save perhaps in my ravings when I say something I soon forget. But I would certainly advise that you stay put, or rather, that you come to the door and let me in."

"Naorin!" McKenzie blushed. "I . . . I didn't mean it that way."

"No offense taken," He crawled in through the wreckage of the front and entered the living room where the girls were sitting. "How is your ankle, Alisen?" he asked.

"Better," she replied. "I can walk a little bit today."

He nodded at her reply. "The I.P. is coming. Hurry upstairs and get anything you'll need. I'll pack the food, and then we must leave at once."

Alisen looked at McKenzie, then back at Naorin. "Are you sure?"

"As sure as I have ever been of anything in my life. Now hurry, we haven't much time. Go upstairs and get only what you need." Naorin went to the window and looked out. "Hurry!"

With one quick glance at McKenzie's terrified face, Alisen got up from the sofa and scurried upstairs. McKenzie followed closely behind. They filled Jay's backpack with extra clothes and a few random but possibly useful items they found, including two loose jackets from the girls' closets, a Swiss army knife, and a candle in a jar. They carried it downstairs and found Naorin near the door, carrying another large bag full of cans from the pantry and bottles of water. He cast an anxious glance around the horizon and led them outside into the street.

Naorin led them almost at a run down the street and deeper into the neighborhood. He spoke breathlessly. "It is the I.P.'s habit to make a systematic search of an area after they take it over to ensure that there are no refugees in hiding. I thought we had a few days, but I saw their patrols not half a mile from here yesterday and knew that time was short."

"What about Kale?" panted Alisen. "Where will he go?"

"He will have to find that out for himself," said Naorin, "which shouldn't be difficult if he is careful."

They spoke no more after that. Out of breath, Alisen and McKenzie could do nothing but follow him. Naorin made a wide circle around the center of the neighborhood before coming back to the street opposite their house. He pushed the girls under a fallen roof, and there they lay hidden, with a clear view of the entire street.

It seemed they had been there for an hour when a patrol came in sight. Alisen watched in horror as the patrol applied gasoline to the exterior wall and set it afire. In a few moments their entire house was lit up like a huge bonfire, and the intense heat compelled the patrol to move back several yards. They cheered and shouted like madmen as the house slowly but surely sank to a pile of ashes. Within an hour the fire had died out, leaving where there had been a house a nameless heap of burned material.

The patrol moved on as soon as the fire was over. Alisen sighed with relief. "Naorin, we owe you more than we could ever repay. If they had come along before we got out of the house—"

"—we would have been fried to a crisp," said McKenzie with a very white face. "We owe you our lives."

"Well, then," said Naorin cheerfully, "the score is even. Now follow me and be careful. Make no noise if possible."

He crawled out from their shelter, looking right and left before stepping into the road. It was not hard to walk quietly. The flying ash covered everything for a long distance around and padded their footsteps. The girls followed him down the street, past innumerable piles of ash where the patrols had fired a house, around corners, and through monotonous, dry fields until it was nearly dark outside. Alisen's ankle was sore, but she dared not stop to rest it.

They reached Naorin's shelter just after dusk. It was the remains of an old gas station that had somehow escaped the bombs.

"You're welcome to stay here tonight, and tomorrow, if you wish," said Naorin, leading Alisen and McKenzie inside. "And for as long as you want after that. Tomorrow I will go and look for Kale, and if I find him, perhaps this can be our shelter for a long time to come."

"Where will you even look?" asked McKenzie. "Why didn't he come home on time? What could have kept him?"

"Many things could have kept him," Naorin looked between her and Alisen, concern etched into his face. "You will have to wait until I can find answers. For now, come inside, and let's see what I can find in the nature of beds."

They partitioned the back corner of the large, single room for them, and helped Naorin pile a mound of pillows and blankets to cover the floor. The gas station had been a nice one of its kind, and there were plenty of provisions for dinner. Naorin tried to convince them to eat, but neither Alisen nor McKenzie felt hungry. Alisen fell into bed out of sheer exhaustion and fear. Naorin and McKenzie followed suit.

***** ***** *****

With some difficulty Alisen climbed out of the mound of pillows without waking McKenzie and went into the center of the room. Naorin was nowhere to be seen. She peered around the aisles a bit until she found some peanuts, sat down on the counter, and waited while she ate.

After a few minutes McKenzie woke up and inquired sleepily about Naorin. "He's gone already," said Alisen, opening a peanut. "I haven't seen him this morning."

McKenzie pushed aside the sheet and stood wavering in the opening. Alisen glanced at her and began to giggle, slowly at first and then hard enough to drop peanut shells all over the floor. McKenzie's hair stood nearly straight up and frizzed all about her face.

"What are you laughing at?" demanded McKenzie.

"Nothing," choked Alisen, "nothing, only, when you haven't brushed your hair in days . . ."

"Who's talking," said McKenzie derisively. "You look like a . . . like one of those fuzzy caterpillars!"

It was a momentary relief from their struggles. Alisen jumped off the counter and pulled McKenzie into the bathroom, where they looked at each other in the mirror.

"I'll bet they sold hairbrushes here," said McKenzie. "Let me go out and look . . ."

She returned in a moment in triumph with two pink hair brushes. They doused them in water and brushed their tangled masses of hair.

"We're so dirty, too." Alisen rubbed at a black smudge on her forehead. "Let's wash up a little bit. I guess we have plenty of time."

"Good idea." McKenzie splashed some water from the sink on her face and winced at its coldness. "I'd give anything for a shower."

"Me too," agreed Alisen. She rinsed her face and then admired herself in the mirror. "At least we can clean our faces a little."

She sighed. It felt much more like a normal day. Normal?! When would anything ever be normal again?

"Let's go see if we can find anything better than peanuts for breakfast," Alisen suggested as they cleaned themselves up. "I saw some granola bars on the shelves last night."

"Good idea," said McKenzie.

They searched the shelves until they found enough for a good meal: four granola bars, two tiny boxes of cereal, and a bottle of water. They piled the items on the floor and sat down beside the pile to eat.

While she ate, Alisen let her thoughts roam. Shadowy at first, and vaguely taking shape, she remembered. She gasped. "Jay's journal!"

"What about it?" McKenzie asked around a mouth full of granola.

"We left it behind! It was burned with the house!"

McKenzie stopped mid-bite. She shook her head slowly. "We lost Jay's journal."

With the book lost the sting and pain of her friend's death again returned. If only they had had more time to think about what they took with them, but it was too late to wonder. The journal had been burned, and now they had nothing of Jay's but a soiled backpack and a painfully clear memory.

McKenzie sighed and rubbed her shoulder. "That's not the worst thing we've lost. Kale is still missing, too. And now Naorin is gone."

"He won't get caught," said Alisen. "He would die first."

McKenzie shrugged. "I hope not." She stared vacantly out the window for a moment. "Oh, look! There he comes now."

Naorin swung open the front door with an expression of frustration and fatigue. He sat down on the counter above the girls, and the first thing he did was to seize an unopened bottle of water and drain it to the bottom.

"That's better," he said, water dripping from his lips. "I have traveled many miles today."

"And Kale?" Alisen asked.

Naorin's face hardened. "No sign of him. In fact, you two are the only living beings, human or animal, that I have seen all day."

There was a long moment of silence.

"However," continued Naorin, starting on a granola bar, "I merely stopped by here to get a drink and some breakfast. I will be going out again in an hour."

"And what should we do?" asked McKenzie.

"Stay here," said Naorin. "You must not leave this place under any circumstances. It is the best hiding place around, and there is plenty of food and supplies. To be seen going out would be to jeopardize the future, even if you were not caught."

Alisen nodded slowly. Much as she hated the inactivity, she understood Naorin's reasoning.

Naorin put down the empty bottle and granola wrapper and took a deep breath. "Wake me in forty-five minutes," he said, curling up on the counter. "There's a clock over the door."

Alisen glanced up at it. It read 9:21.

"Will do," she said. "C'mon, McKenzie, let's go search the store and see what we can find."

McKenzie deposited the last of her granola in her mouth and jumped up from the floor. "We'll have to find bedding for Kale when he gets here."

Alisen looked back at her, pressed her lips together, but did not reply.

McKenzie immediately dropped her eyes. "I'm sorry, Alisen," she said. "I keep forgetting. It all seems too terrible to be real. And I seem to think that Kale is just on his way home."

"It's okay," said Alisen. "I know how you feel." She walked back to McKenzie and put her hands on her shoulders. "For now, we must believe that Kale will come back."

McKenzie smiled faintly and wrapped her arms around Alisen in a bear hug.

They stood together, each taking in the other's emotions and feeling again the pain of losing, all in a few days, their parents and their school friends, their Civil Air Patrol classmates and their captains, and most of all, the only one who had been left to them—Kale. He had been their leader, he had been the one to give orders when orders were needed, and now he had vanished. Even Naorin could not quite take his place.

The girls separated. Finally, Alisen shrugged. "Now you know everything I have thought of these last few days. It's like telepathy."

"Shall we search the store?" asked McKenzie, looking away from Alisen.

"I'll search the right side and you search the left. Get a basket and bring back anything you think we might need."

Alisen took a basket from a rack in the front of the store and departed to the right side to look around. She found several useful items in the toiletries section, including two boxes of painkillers, a box of gauze and a roll of tape, some antibiotic spray, a pack of toilet paper, and three pairs of nail scissors. With these in her basket, she returned to the front of the store to wait for McKenzie.

*****   *****   *****

McKenzie unloaded her basket: a pair of scissors, a box of thumbtacks, a box of pencils, a notepad, a spool of twine, and a black volume that Alisen could not identify.

"What is that?" Alisen asked curiously, pointing to it.

McKenzie reddened, and seemed to be searching for something to say. She pointed to the pack of toilet paper in front of Alisen and said, "What's that?"

"That," said Alisen in a dignified manner, "is toilet paper, which is going to be very useful to us when we have to leave this place."

McKenzie stifled a laugh, which turned into a sort of sputtered choke, and quickly recovered herself. Then she picked up the black book and said reverently, "I just thought, since we were talking about Jay's journal, you know, I picked up a Bible to study while we wait for Naorin."

"Who, by the way, we ought to wake up," said Alisen, with a glance at the clock. Then, looking at the Bible, she added, "I don't blame you. I'd like to know more about what it says. Maybe it has some information for people like us."

With a quick smile in her direction, McKenzie stood up and shook Naorin awake. He responded with a few sleepy blinks, eyed the clock, and got up reluctantly off the counter.

He motioned towards their pile, "What's all that?"

"Stuff we found in the store that might be useful," said Alisen. "We thought it would be a good idea to gather it together in case we had to leave suddenly or something."

"Good idea," said Naorin. He picked up McKenzie's Bible and said, "Where did you find this?"

"Over on the left side of the store," said McKenzie, pointing. "The store is surprisingly well stocked."

He flipped through its pages with great care, as though handling a book made delicate by hundreds of years of wear. "That is where you should look, in times like these. What hope is left is in those pages." He put the book down and moved toward the door. "I'll be back before dark. Don't leave this place for any reason, alright? See you later."

"What is it with this book?" said Alisen, looking at the Bible. "Everyone says it has life-saving information in it, and I'd hardly ever considered it before I started having these strange dreams. What could be the deal with it?"

"Perhaps we should look," said McKenzie. "Where does one begin in a thick book like this?"

"At the beginning?" suggested Alisen doubtfully.

McKenzie shook her head. "It's a little late to be hearing about how the world got made."

"What did Jay say?" said Alisen thoughtfully. "Romans something? Is there a chapter in it called Romans?"

McKenzie scanned the table of contents. "Romans. Right here."

"Now what? Is it a long chapter?"

McKenzie flipped a few pages. "Fairly long. Let me start at the beginning. I'll read to you anything that sticks out at me."

"Right," said Alisen, and curled up against the counter to wait.

There was a long pause while McKenzie read. Then her voice broke the stillness. "The wrath of God is being revealed from heaven against all the godlessness and wickedness of people, who suppress the truth by their wickedness, since what may be known about God is plain to them, because God has made it plain to them. For since the creation of the world God's invisible qualities—his eternal power and divine nature—have been clearly seen, being understood from what has been made, so that people are without excuse.

"For although they knew God, they neither glorified him as God nor gave thanks to him."

Alisen interrupted. "That means we should give thanks to God?" she said. "That doesn't sound like a complete set of instructions."

"No," said McKenzie. "But the first paragraph really describes the world now, doesn't it? 'Suppress truth'? 'Godlessness and wickedness of people'?"

"You're right." Alisen thought of the question of abortion she had so carefully investigated not long before McKenzie had returned to the state, and she remembered how one side had hidden the truth, while the other had made it plain to her.

"'Therefore,'" continued McKenzie, "'no one will be declared righteous in God's sight by the law . . .'"

"Which means," said Alisen, "that we can't be, I don't know, acceptable to God just by obeying the law?"

"I guess," said McKenzie. "I suppose it's not enough. Besides, we all know that nobody keeps the law all the time."

"True," said Alisen. "So, if you can't come to God by the law, what do we do?"

McKenzie read silently for a moment. "I've got it!" she said suddenly. "'But now apart from the law the righteousness of God has been made known, to which the Law and the prophets'—who are they, I wonder?—'testify. This righteousness is given through faith in Jesus Christ to all who believe. There is no difference between Jew and Gentile, for all have sinned and fall short of the glory of God, and all are justified freely by his grace through the redemption that came by Jesus Christ.'"

"What does that mean?" Alisen asked. "'Justify?'"

"I think it means," said McKenzie, with a deeply preoccupied look on her face, "that people sinned, so they aren't worthy to be with God, who by definition has to be perfect, or He wouldn't be God, and this Jesus person somehow made it possible for us to be forgiven."

"How could that work?" said Alisen. She paused. "I remember the man I talked to about my dreams saying that people who believed that Jesus could take their sins away would be taken to heaven. But how could this man take sins away?"

"I don't know," said McKenzie. "And you know, all this raises another question. If there is a God, and He did all this work, so we could be forgiven, how come He's letting people get killed left and right by the I.P.? Isn't He powerful enough to prevent it?"

"I suppose," said Alisen, "that thinking God is allowing it to happen is better than thinking it happens just because, and there isn't really any reason for or escape from it."

"True," said McKenzie slowly. "I guess that really is true."

"So, we should look for something about Jesus."

McKenzie flipped slowly through the Bible. "Where does it talk about . . . oh, look! Here it is!"

"That was a lot quicker than I thought it would be," said Alisen, with a half-smile.

McKenzie, without looking up, began reading.

Not two minutes into the beautiful narrative of Luke Alisen was confused. The same question had to be in McKenzie's mind, too. If Jesus was God's son, why did He have to come to earth and die? Why couldn't there have been some other way to make up for the people's sins? And why, why on earth could the people not see, after all the miracles, that Jesus really wanted to help them?

The answer was discovered within minutes. Simply, it was explained that the people's sins were so black compared to God's grace that an imperfect sacrifice could not make up for them. Only something perfect could do that, and only God was perfect.

"I think I could serve somebody who did that for me," said McKenzie, setting down the book at the end of the chapter. "I never thought that God Himself would do something that hard, just because it saved me."

"If God is willing to die for us," said Alisen, "we must be pretty important."

"And He must like us an awful lot," said McKenzie hesitantly.

"I don't think either one of us would be able to die that horribly for a friend who had done something so cruel to us," said Alisen.

"But what's the result?" asked McKenzie. "I've seen Christians praying—like, talking to God, so do you think we can do that?"

"We've found out that we have to believe," said Alisen. "I don't think there's much to doubt here."

"I think you're right," said McKenzie. "So, we've believed, but we have to tell God that, right?"

"Probably," said Alisen. "Maybe He would give us some advice, too? I mean, if He knew that people were sinning on earth, He must have some connection to us. And if He loves us . . . "

" . . . it must be a personal connection."

"Exactly," Alisen nodded. "Let's tell Him."

They knelt side-by-side in silence, each waiting for the other to begin.

Finally, with a scared giggle, McKenzie whispered, "You go first."

Alisen cleared her throat. "Umm . . . God," she began. "My friend and I just read about how we could be saved from our sins by Your son Jesus, and we'd like that. I guess we'd be willing to do anything for someone who left heaven and came here and died when He could have just been happy forever. We're not really sure what to do down here, but we wanted to tell You that we believe, and we wanted to say we're sorry for all the sins we contributed to the general pile. We wanted to ask You to forgive us, and we wanted to ask You to get us out of this mess." Alisen paused and struggled for words. "I guess that's all right now . . . I'll finish off by saying thank You, again."

"We did it," said McKenzie, raising her head. "We figured out what Jay was talking about!"

"We figured out everything," echoed Alisen, "so we don't need her journal anymore. All we need is Jesus to be with us, and we'll have someone to give us advice and to keep us safe after we die."

"I remember having the wrong idea and hating God because I was so miserable," said McKenzie. "I didn't understand how people could look to God for help when He got them into difficulty in the first place. But I know better now."

"I wonder," said Alisen thoughtfully, "if the dreams I had were a kind of warning about this. I mean, obviously they were a warning, since everything came true, but maybe God was trying to get us to know Him in time for something big."

"Something big," said McKenzie thoughtfully.

"I wonder what," Alisen gazed at her friend. "I wonder what He was—oh!"

"What? What?" asked McKenzie. "What did you think of?"

"I know. I know what it's going to be!" she said breathlessly. "I remember! The very last dream. I finally remember what's going to happen! Oh, McKenzie—"

"Stop being dramatic and tell me!" McKenzie pushed Alisen into a sitting position. "What was your last dream?"

Alisen swallowed nervously and took a deep breath. "I dreamed," she said slowly, "I dreamed that after all the attacks, somehow the Civil Air Patrol managed to meet together again, and this cadet got up in front of everybody else and started talking. He was just talking about the end times and how prophecies from the Bible were coming true, when he disappeared and so did a couple of other people. The cadets who were left freaked out and ran out of the building like crazy people."

"Then what did you do?"

"I got up the next morning and went to talk to a pastor," said Alisen. "He told me that at the end times, people who believed in Jesus would be taken to heaven, and people who didn't would have to live through seven years of the most horrible punishment and judgement possible. Maybe that's what we were being prepared for. So, we won't have to survive the judgement!"

"Your dreams have been right so far," said McKenzie. "I'm not the one to doubt it. But we're safe now, you know, so all we have to do is tell as many other people as possible."

"Like Kale, when he gets back," said Alisen. "Let's think about what we are going to say to him."

For nearly an hour they buried themselves in thought, planning the exact words they would say to Kale to convince him of their own relief from the distressing puzzle of dreams and events and sacrifices. They referred to the Bible, they asked their new-found Creator, they whispered to each other in low voices. Soon they had everything beautifully planned out, but they were missing a key piece to the puzzle—Kale himself.

Alisen grew restless, and when she looked over at McKenzie, she saw that she was fidgeting and unable to keep still. Surely, they would have a better chance of finding Kale if more people were looking for him. They looked at one another.

"Are you thinking what I'm thinking?" Alisen asked.

"If you're thinking that we should be looking for Kale, then yes," said McKenzie. "I know Naorin told us not to leave, but . . . "

"We could cover so much more area this way," finished Alisen. "We'd have a better chance of finding him."

"I guess it's not such a bad idea," said McKenzie thoughtfully.

"Shall we?"

"Why not?" said McKenzie. "If we're careful we can't come to any harm."

"And if we find Kale, we won't have to go out again for a long time," said Alisen. "I think it's worth the risk."

McKenzie stood slowly and stretched. "Is there anything we should bring with us?"

"A first aid kit?" suggested Alisen. "Just in case. Not to be pessimistic, or anything."

"And some water, too," said McKenzie. "I'll get the water if you get the first aid kit."

Alisen ran to the back of the store and picked up a small first aid kit from the bottom shelf. When she returned to the door McKenzie was waiting with Jay's backpack over her shoulder.

"Put that in here," she said, holding it open.

"Maybe you should strap that backpack on under your jacket," suggested Alisen. "Just in case we have to run or anything."

"Good idea," said McKenzie, replacing the backpack under her jacket and zipping it securely. "Now let's go."

Alisen took a deep breath. "We can do this."

McKenzie was starting to look rather doubtful, but she followed Alisen out the door and into the grassy meadow beyond.

It was a clear, sunny day, without a shadow of movement anywhere except in the swaying grass and light breeze. The ground in front of them was flat and grassy for nearly a mile in every direction. Alisen noticed that she could see everything taller than three feet with crystal clarity all around. She dropped to the ground, pulling McKenzie with her.

McKenzie glared at her. "Are we sure this is a good idea?"

Alisen glanced back at her but did not reply. She began to inch forward through the thick grass, terrified that someone would see or hear them.

They had gone about a quarter of a mile when Alisen felt a panicky hand on her shoulder, and McKenzie's voice saying unsteadily, "What's that?"

Alisen paused to listen.

"Oh. Oh, no, no," she whispered, looking up at the sky.

"An airplane," said McKenzie.

"It doesn't sound like the other ones."

"It's probably going slowly enough to see us."

"They could spot us from a mile high down here anyway." Fear settled in. Alisen gripped her friend's arm. "We have to think of something, quickly!"

For a moment they remained motionless, holding tightly to each other and trying not to give in to fear. Alisen felt McKenzie's hot, uneven breath on her shoulder, and knew that her life was not the only one at stake. She grabbed McKenzie and shook her hard. "We have to get the grass to cover us," she said. "The dirt here is soft. We'll have to dig. We'll have a few minutes before it's close enough to see us."

McKenzie nodded and followed her lead. Feverishly they scratched at the soft, warm earth, piling it as carefully as they could beneath the grass a few feet away. The sound of the plane's engine grew closer and closer. The holes grew deeper and deeper, until it was possible for the girls to lie level with the ground once in them. With a final effort they got down in the holes, covered themselves as best as possible with dirt, and turned their faces to the ground to hide their pale skin.

There was a loud scream of the engine overheard, and Alisen fumbled to cover her ears. She looked up and saw a grey shape glide swiftly overhead, hardly fifty feet above the ground. The noise was overpowering. A wave of heat hit them from the plane's powerful engines.

And McKenzie was screaming, "American fighters! American fighters! The Air Force is coming to save us!!"

Alisen and McKenzie jumped up from the ground and jumped up and down in sheer excitement. The fear and pain were gone, and replaced by sheer exaltation, relief, and joy. Alisen grabbed McKenzie's hands and they laughed, cried, and nearly sang in their excitement. The ground was trampled under their feet, the grass was thrown aside. It was a beautiful moment.

But they still had to find Kale, and they still had to be careful. No one knew what might happen before the American troops recovered the territory. They gradually calmed themselves and slowly continued making their way across the field, using less caution than before in their sudden confidence.

When they reached the end of the meadow, they stood in the middle of a neatly mown soccer field, with a deep crater in the middle where a bomb had struck. Alisen looked in every direction before they left the grass, then crossed the soccer field and arrived in the colonels' neighborhood.

They were walking down the road, looking from side to side and eyeing every building warily, when they heard a sudden click of metal and heard a wild voice: "Who goes there?"

They spun around, looking up and down and all along the road, but seeing no one.

"Alisen," said McKenzie softly, "that was the cock of a rifle . . . "

"How do you know?" demanded Alisen, surprised.

"Because Dad used to take me skeet shooting on the weekends."

"Right. Well . . . "

"Who goes there?" screamed the voice again.

"It's—it's two Civil Air Patrol cadets," said Alisen hesitantly. "Who are you?"

"Civil Air Patrol?" The voice grew softer and less high-pitched. "Third house on your left."

Alisen and McKenzie looked at each other.

"Should we go?" whispered McKenzie.

"I don't think so," said Alisen. "Kind of an unnecessary risk."

"Come on! What are you waiting for?" asked the voice. There was a pause. "On second thought, maybe you would prefer I come out to you. So. Stay where you are."

There emerged, from what was left of the front door of the house, a lonely, tired-looking Air Force gate guard with a hunting rifle slung across his chest. He walked with a limp, and where his uniform had frayed away below the knee the girls could see a long, bloody line running nearly the length of his calf muscle.

Alisen's eyes flashed from the wound to his face. "Are you alright?" Fear was forgotten in her desire to help this unfortunate man. "We have some first aid materials if you want it."

"You have?" The man seemed to straighten suddenly. "What do you want for it?"

"Want for it?" Alisen was surprised. "Nothing. We—"

"C'mon," said the soldier. "That isn't how the black market works. You always want something."

"Black market?" Alisen glanced at McKenzie, confused. "I don't know what you're talking about. We just want to help."

The soldier eyed them. "The black market tries to convince you that they'll give you something, and then they take everything in return. That's how it always works."

"Where is this black market?" demanded Alisen, growing annoyed.

The soldier looked surprised. "Why, it's everywhere," he said. "So long as there is war, there's a black market. So long as there is a black market, there's disaster and heartbreak."

"But we're not the black market," said Alisen. "We just want to help you. We'll give you the kit—"

"Stop!" cried the soldier, his voice growing shrill again. "I don't want it for the price!"

"But there's no price!" cried Alisen. "Don't you see?"

"No nearer!" shrieked the soldier.

Alisen advanced a step toward him, holding out the kit. "You can have it," she said. "Just take it—"

The soldier backed up quickly and unslung his rifle. "No nearer! No nearer!" he repeated. "I want none of your gifts! All I want is to stay clear of the black market and the I.P. for as long as I can!" His voice faded to a series of breathless gasps, and he turned and ran back in the house.

Alisen and McKenzie stared after him, eyes wide with horror.

"What's his problem?" whispered McKenzie.

"I guess it wouldn't be so hard to go crazy if you had been alone all through this," said Alisen slowly. "Let's get out of here. Who knows who heard all that shouting."

They had barely traveled a quarter mile down the street when McKenzie stopped and looked back. "Alisen!" she cried. "There's a patrol behind us!"

Alisen spun around. "There!" she cried, pointing to a fallen house. "We can hide—"

"Wait!" said McKenzie. "They're going in that house. The house that gate guard came out of!"

Alisen pulled McKenzie behind a blackened bush that had once been part of a stately hedge. Safely under cover, they peered between the branches and stared back at the house.

There was a wild, terrifying scream, audible even from that distance. Alisen trembled. She knew exactly what it meant.

The patrol came back outside. Alisen squinted but could not see exactly what they did. Suddenly the house rose in flames, and the sky was filled with dark, grey smoke. There was no sound from within. The patrol watched the flames with savage pleasure for several minutes. Neither Alisen nor McKenzie moved a muscle. All they could do was stare at the house, stare at that emblem of merciless cruelty and try not to think of what was inside.

The patrol seemed to be preparing to move on, picking up backpacks they had dropped and forming back into a neat, symmetrical order. Alisen and McKenzie watched for a moment, paralyzed, and then realized that they were trapped. The patrol would see them if they moved but would surely catch them if they remained where they were.

Alisen gulped. "Run, McKenzie," she said. "It's our only chance."

"Follow me," said McKenzie unsteadily, and bolted off the left of the road.

Alisen looked back. "They've seen us!" she cried. "Run!"

She nearly tripped over a broken piece of wood, then rebalanced herself and ran after McKenzie. Even as she did so she knew that flight was hopeless. There was no cover anywhere before them, except the remains of ruined houses which were unsafe to hide in. All they could hope to do was to avoid the pursuit for a few minutes, perhaps try to reach someplace with shelter; but if they did not, they must inevitably be caught.

"Faster, faster!" shrieked McKenzie hoarsely. "They're catching up!"

Alisen searched the horizon frantically for a place to hide. Her lungs were on fire, her mind spinning, and she needed to stop for a rest. Her ankle began to throb miserably and burn with incessant pain. But she could not stop—not with the murderous patrol hot on their trail and not without a shelter to provide a refuge. So, she ran on and on following McKenzie, trying not to fall.

"Stop!" said an accented voice from behind them. "We have you covered! If you continue running you will be shot!"

Alisen collided with McKenzie. They both came to a sudden abrupt halt, looked at each other, and slowly raised their hands above their heads.

"Right," said the voice. "Turn and face us, then down on your knees."

Alisen turned and dropped to her knees. The tears that had been building overflowed. Not tears of fear, but tears of anger and frustration that they should ever have been caught.

With McKenzie kneeling next to her she waited for further instruction.

"Why, it's my little friends—two of them, anyway," said the voice, with morbid cheerfulness. "Don't you remember me?"

Alisen did, but she could not quite place his voice . . .

"Dalek," gasped McKenzie.

He laughed. "You do remember," he said. "I remind you of a lot of things, don't I? Your friend Jay, for example, who we found dead two days later on a pile of rubble. Your friend Kale. I have a score to settle with him. Where is he?"

Neither McKenzie nor Alisen replied.

"I see," he said. "Well, I am sure we will find out when we take you back to headquarters."

He made a quick motion to his men, who went behind the girls and tied their hands. "By the way, I am sure you have many questions about the I.P." Dalek smiled. "Feel free to ask me anything you want to know. Now is the time, you've got a captive audience." He laughed at his own joke.

"You knew Jay," said McKenzie, her voice breaking as she was pulled to her feet by the soldiers. "How did you know her?"

"That is an easy question to answer," said Dalek. He crossed his arms behind his back. "Are you familiar with her story?"

Before McKenzie could reply Alisen said loudly, "No, we know very little about her at all."

McKenzie's eyes did not falter.

He smiled even bigger and said, "I was her commanding officer. She only knew me as Dalek. You can call me Amar."

"You were her commanding officer?" asked McKenzie.

"Indeed, I was."

"Then it was you who—"

"—how could you have so little respect for her?" Alisen interrupted her friend, knowing that McKenzie was going to ask him about Nathan.

"Respect is not a virtue highly thought of in the I.P.," said Amar with a short laugh. "But come on now, let's get moving. Feel free to work your intellect and your tongue all the way to headquarters, if you like. It's the last chance you'll get."

During the long trek to 'headquarters', an Air Force building that had survived the bombs, Alisen was absorbed in her own bitter thoughts and asked no questions of Amar. Her thoughts centered on Kale, and Amar's assurance that his disappearance had something to do with the I.P. patrols. And she feared Naorin's response when he returned and found them missing— Naorin who had freely admitted to a passionate hatred of the I.P. and who had confirmed it in his spell of insanity.

And she feared for her parents, whom she had not seen since the day of the bombing.

CHAPTER XIX

WHEN THEY ARRIVED AT HEADQUARTERS, Amar asked no questions, but sent them away under the surveillance of a pair of guards to be imprisoned in an old office with a strong lock on the door. It was pitch black inside the room. Alisen and McKenzie stumbled into each other several times before they found their footing and stood up unsteadily to survey their surroundings.

"Who goes there?"

McKenzie jumped in terror and fell against Alisen, who tripped and stumbled backward against a desk, which crumpled beneath her weight and sent them both crashing into a heap on the floor.

"Who are you?" McKenzie's voice shook.

"The I.P.!" the voice wailed. "The I.P. will pay for this! The imprisonment of American citizens, the bombing of towns, the—"

McKenzie put a hand on Alisen's arm. "It's Naorin."

Alisen breathed a deep sigh of relief. "Let's hope there are no knives in here to give him ideas. Naorin," she said loudly, "it's us, McKenzie and Alisen. We're here, too."

There was a long pause. Alisen feared that Naorin might have injured himself in his frantic revolutions about the room, but after a few moments the voice calmly replied, "I feared it would be you. You should never have left the shelter, but I suppose I am partly to blame for that." He sighed.

"You are not to blame at all. We are," said McKenzie. "You gave us clear directions and we didn't follow them. I'm sorry, Naorin."

"And I'm sorry, too," added Alisen.

"It's too late to be angry now," he said. "Is there anyone else in here?"

Alisen listened for a few moments, but there was no sound.

"Well," said Naorin, "that desk you ran into might have some supplies with which we could make a light."

"What's it worth?" asked Alisen. "In a few hours they'll have us out of here and into the nearest quiet place to be shot."

"That's not how they work," said Naorin. "The I.P. makes a great and rather elaborate pretense of giving every victim a trial before they kill them. Of course, it ought to suggest something that a victim never escapes, but many foreign nations have congratulated them on their fairness and just resolve. We'll have a few days, at least. We might have a chance at this, but we can't do anything blind. We need a light of some sort."

"Well, I suppose we could start by looking over here." Alisen got to her knees gingerly and started feeling over the floor. "There's really nothing. Just pieces of wood that shattered when I landed on it."

There was a sound that sounded like wooden pieces being moved across the floor.

"There must have been drawers of some sort though . . . "

"I found one." The sound stopped as McKenzie spoke. "It's almost empty. There are just some little cylinders rolling around in the bottom, with bumps on the end. Big ones, and little ones."

Alisen took one from her and felt it carefully. "Batteries!"

"That could be useful, but you'd need something metal to put with it," came Naorin's voice. "What are the big ones?"

"Water bottles," said McKenzie. "That will hardly help us make a fire."

"It might keep us alive though," said Naorin. "Keep looking. I'll check this side of the room."

Alisen kept searching around the desk. "Here are some pencils," she said after a pause. "Coloring pencils, I think. There are about twenty of them, all tied together with a rubber band."

"Could be fuel, I suppose," said Naorin rather doubtfully. "Anything in your pockets?"

Alisen searched hers carefully but found nothing. "Wait!" she cried. "McKenzie, you've got Jay's backpack!"

There was a moment of silence, then McKenzie actually laughed. "I forgot," she said. "We put matches in here, didn't we?"

"And a candle!"

"You two," said Naorin disgustedly. "Making us all walk around in the dark and look for fire. You know, if you hadn't suddenly revealed that you were actually carrying matches, I probably would have short-circuited a battery and electrocuted myself trying to make a light."

"Sorry," said McKenzie. "I guess it's always good to be prepared, and it's usually even better to remember that you're prepared. I hear something."

Alisen paused and listened. "Someone's coming!" she cried.

The door swung open, and two guards appeared silhouetted against the white fluorescent lights outside. Between them they were carrying something elongated and limp, and even with the light streaming in from the hallway Alisen could not make out what it was. Then she saw an arm drooping from between them. They would have to wait until the guards left to find out who this was.

The guards deposited the person, who was limp and apparently unconscious, on the floor in the corner nearest the door. Then, without further ceremony, they shut and locked the door behind them, and all light suddenly disappeared.

"Right," came Naorin's voice, after a few seconds of tense silence. "Hand me one of those matches and the candle."

Alisen helped McKenzie unzip her jacket and retrieve the backpack. After a few moments of blind rummaging, they found the tiny box of matches and the big glass candle, which Alisen passed to Naorin. Alisen waited in suspense for a moment or two and was rewarded with the sight of a tiny flame, bright and penetrating in the absolute darkness.

"Now we can find out who they put in here with us," said Naorin. He passed the candle to Alisen. "Who is it?"

Alisen held the hot candle over the person's face, and she felt McKenzie shiver convulsively by her side.

"It's Kale," she said.

His face was covered with blood and grime and sweat. His hair seemed somehow wet and was hanging in points over his forehead, and his eyes were closed. His uniform was tattered and nonexistent below the knees, and several of his buttons were missing. It was obvious that he had endured cruel treatment, possibly from his own adventures but more likely from the ill usage of the I.P.

Naorin bent over him, then with a sigh he sat up and said, "His wounds are deep, and left untreated, may be dangerous. What can we do without water and bandages? Here, McKenzie, can you spare your jacket? Or do you have anything else in that fancy backpack of yours?"

"There's a first aid kit in here somewhere," said McKenzie. "And water. We can use that to clean off the blood."

"Good job, both of you," said Naorin. "Hand me that stuff. This wound on his arm looks serious. It's bleeding more than I would like, and we're going to have to bandage it tightly."

Alisen found the first aid kit and handed it to Naorin, who cleaned the blood from Kale's face with a piece of wet gauze. To her relief, the blood was mostly from his arm, and not from another wound. He looked much more like his usual self once the bandage was applied and the blood removed, but his eyes did not open.

"We'll try everything we can," said Naorin. "Since we only have a little water, we'll have to save it carefully to keep his wounds clean. We'll see."

McKenzie sat shivering in the corner, looking alternately between Kale's still form and Naorin's white face. Alisen crawled over beside her and put an arm around her, trying to think of what to say and unable to form the words. Kale had seemed invincible. He had made plans and he had executed them, and he had been their steadfast friend for months. To see him helpless and almost in the grip of death was more than either of them could watch.

Naorin sighed again and glanced over at them. "Let's put the candle out," he said. "There's no way to keep it lit without attracting attention, especially since it smells like a pumpkin. One of us can keep watch on Kale, while the others sleep. I expect we will soon be visited by the guards. For good or ill is hard to say. In the meantime, I will look after him."

McKenzie shrugged and remained sitting against the wall. Alisen, after a momentary look in Naorin's direction, spread herself out on the floor and folded her hands behind her head to make an effort at sleeping. The candle went out, the light disappeared, and once more the room was left in complete darkness.

***** ***** *****

It seemed like only a moment later, but suddenly Alisen found herself awake. Light streamed in from the open door. McKenzie was no longer sitting beside her. She and Naorin were leaned against the back wall, with Kale lying in front of them. A fifth figure stood before the door, the light at his back.

"Good morning, or evening, I suppose I should say," Amar said, with easy courtesy.

Nobody replied to him. Alisen sat up and rubbed her eyes sleepily.

"I see," he continued, "that Kale here has been bandaged up very nicely. I told you I had a score to settle with him, so I was delighted to hear that we had caught him." He laughed lightly and put his hand on the door handle. "Well, there is no use in beating about the bush, so here we go. I have come to bring you, one at a time, into a nearby room for questioning. No pressure, and you needn't be afraid. The I.P. delights and takes pride in justice for all, even its prisoners. But there are a few things we would like to know, and if you will tell us, you will be well rewarded. Now let's see, who's first? What's your name? Alisen? Well, come along. Follow me." He held the door for her.

Alisen struggled to her feet, half blinded with conflicting emotions. Here was Amar, assuring her that she would be well treated by her enemies, showing her simple courtesy with apparently unaffected simplicity, and this was the same man who had killed Jay only a few days before. How could the two characters be reconciled? These thoughts passed through her mind in a flash as she left the room, with a last glance at the frightened eyes of McKenzie, the stony face of Naorin, and the still form of Kale.

She nervously followed Amar out into the hallway. The guards outside straightened respectfully and touched their flat caps in a quaint manner as they passed by.

This treatment had an almost hypnotic effect on her. She was confused by the courtesy. It softened her guard a little bit. The guards they met all showed the same politeness. Perhaps she was safe after all.

As they were going along the hallway, Alisen noticed two guards coming towards them, pulling between them a thin, dark-haired girl who looked younger than Alisen. Her eyes were blank and staring, her face pale, her wrists bruised where the guards had squeezed them tightly.

"Sadie!" she screamed, pulling away from Amar and running toward her friend. "Sadie!"

Sadie looked up listlessly, but her eyes regained their sparkle when she saw Alisen. "It really is you!" she cried, trying to run towards her; but the guards held her back. Alisen shot a glance at Amar, who nodded at them. They reluctantly let go of Sadie and allowed the girls to embrace. "What happened to you?" asked Alisen. "You look—you look—"

"Like I got in a bar fight," said Sadie with a wearied smile. "Or like a hobo, or like I fell off the Empire State Building. Something like that, right?"

"I suppose I look about the same."

"Yup, I think so." Sadie laughed half-heartedly. "What's new with you?"

Alisen rolled her eyes and caught sight of the guards advancing to recapture Sadie and take her with them. "Listen," she whispered quickly, "do you know where the Civil Air Patrol hangar is?"

Sadie shook her head curiously.

"It's at the cross of Arnica and Butler Street."

"I can find that," said Sadie.

"If they let you out of here alive, then go there. We'll try to meet you, somehow or another. Maybe we can do something."

"I will." She paused. "Alisen . . . I haven't told you about your parents."

Alisen froze. "You know what happened to them?"

Sadie gulped, as if reluctant to say the words. "I think the bombs hit your house, Alisen," she stuttered. "I know they were both at home. I was just down the street, on my way to see you. I was just barely far enough away, and even then . . . it was so hot. I was almost burned."

Alisen gazed past Sadie's shoulder in shattered hope. She had tried to make herself believe that her parents were alive, especially after having nearly reached her mother on the phone while she had been trapped under the building with McKenzie, but it had apparently all been for nothing. They were dead, and Alisen would never see them again.

The guards had come up behind Sadie and taken hold of her wrists. As they were leading her away she shouted back, "I might be wrong. Keep looking! Don't give up hope!"

Alisen stood in the middle of the hallway without moving or making a sound.

There was a gentle touch on her shoulder, and Amar stood there beside her. "I'm terribly sorry," he said.

"What do you care?" cried Alisen. "It was your army!"

"We had no desire for this," said Amar. "We intended to hit the base only. Unfortunately, accidents happen in war. I really am deeply sorry."

Alisen shrugged, being unable to think of any other gesture to express her confusion.

"Follow me," said Amar, turning away.

He led her into a white-walled room, which contained no furniture except a desk with a chair on either side. He pulled back the chair closest to the door, in which Alisen gingerly sat, and then took his seat in the chair on the other side.

"So," he said, placing both wrists on the table and folding his hands, "I suppose my first question for you is very simple: of all the people in your Civil Air Patrol group, have you seen any of them, except for McKenzie and Kale, since the beginning of the war?"

"No," said Alisen, simply and truthfully.

"I see," said Amar. "Well, then, where have you been staying?"

"I don't know my way around here," said Alisen. "I don't know how to tell you where we were."

Amar prodded a little more. "Base housing? On base? Off base?"

"I really don't know."

Amar nodded. "This next question will touch on a rather sore point, and for that I am sorry," he said, and his voice lowered as if in reverence. "Your friend Jay, who met her death by such a deplorable accident, how much did you know of her story?" He leaned back in his chair. "I give you my word, if you answer this question truthfully, I will have you and your friends out of that office and into the service of the I.P., where you will be better off than anyone else for a very long time to come."

"Accident?" The word was out of Alisen's mouth before she could stop it. "But Jay—I mean, it was you who killed—"

"I am sure it seemed that way," said Amar smoothly, covering her hesitation. "I could hardly expect you, who did not see the event, to think otherwise. But the truth is, Jay was threatening the patrol with a revolver she had concealed in her clothing. She had just taken aim to fire, at point-blank range, and they were forced to defend themselves. I am sorry, for she was a beautiful girl. But her death was certainly not my fault."

Alisen's mind was reeling. She tried to think back to the event, but her mind was blank and she closed her eyes. Had Jay really been at fault? Was it that her story of her cruel treatment in the I.P. had been exaggerated? Was her story of salvation mistaken or purposely misleading?

Alisen opened her eyes, about to speak, about to tell Amar everything she knew. But before the words came out the image returned: of Jay, lying atop the mound of rubble, the life draining slowly out of her after the energy spent on their rescue. Her eyes had not been wild, fanatic, or guilty in any way. They had been full of peace, quiet satisfaction, and the beauty of those assured of their future. It had been a beauty the best actor could never imitate. Jay's death had been her own choice. She had given her life as a sacrifice to her friends. She had not given it in a wild attempt for revenge against the I.P., whom she had cause to hate. And she had made the right choice.

Alisen felt the life and energy returning to her veins. "Thank you," she whispered, hoping that somehow Jay would be listening and would be able to hear her. Then she straightened up, assumed a certain frigidity of manner modeled after Jay herself, and said, "I am afraid I cannot tell you what you wish. I am not sure what you hope to gain by it, but whatever Jay's story may be, you are sure to know it better than I."

"Very well," he said, his voice weary and pitying. "I suppose I cannot help you then. Guard, you will see Alisen to Room 13 at once."

Alisen felt her arm seized from behind and was pulled through the door. Her last look at Amar revealed a complete change of his face. His eyes were bright and malicious, anything but weary and certainly not pitying.

*****   *****   *****

Alisen found herself in an entirely bare space, about eight feet square, with a small window on one wall. She was alone for a few minutes, when

McKenzie arrived and huddled in a melancholy heap in the corner. She did not speak to Alisen about the questioning.

Alisen tried to find the words to tell McKenzie what Sadie had told her, but she could not bring them to her lips.

She expected that Naorin would appear shortly, but what seemed like an hour passed and no one entered. There was no sound outside the door except the guards' monotonous tread along the hall. Her mind wandered to the fate of her parents, her friends from school, and the fate of the entire rest of the world. Had the attacks been concerted? Would they ever know, and did it really matter? If the I.P. was strong enough to attack the United States, how could any other country in the world hope to stand against them?

She pushed closer to McKenzie, seeking the warmth of another living being. As she did so, the door opened, and Amar's face glowed in the light. "Follow me, both of you," he said shortly, then abruptly turned and left the room.

With a nervous glance at each other, they stood up and slowly followed him out the door. He did not turn to see if they were following, but merely continued down the hallway at a quick pace. He was so far ahead of them that Alisen more than once wondered if it would be possible to slip away unnoticed, but she found no chance. The halls were amply lined with I.P. guards, who, though they never moved a muscle, seemed all the more forbidding.

Amar opened an exterior door and motioned to the guards. Two of them moved from behind the door and held Alisen and McKenzie closely. Imprisoned in this fashion they were marched across a wide plain of neatly mown grass, Amar never saying a word nor looking back. He led them to a row of what appeared to be cages, fashioned crudely out of chain fence and surrounded by I.P. guards in black suits. At first Alisen could not see inside. When she could she saw several cheap office desks but no people. The ground appeared to be trampled.

Amar made another gesture, and this time the movement in response to his order was on the other side of the cages. One of the guards applied a kick to somebody standing beside him, and he tripped and fell to his knees. There was a hoarse wind of laughter from the other guards, but whoever had been kicked got up again quickly without seeming to be hurt. Alisen strained to see through the chain fence. It seemed to be a man, of medium height, with dark hair, who wore nothing but a tattered pair of what had once been khakis.

The guard opened the door to the cage and pushed the man in before him. Alisen felt rather than heard McKenzie gasp. She looked at her and saw an expression of such horror. Alisen looked back at the cage. And when her eyes focused, she froze, her eyes riveted on the scene before her.

The guard pushed the man up to the table and forced him down so that he lay face down and at full length across the table. Then he looked up at Amar, as if waiting for a signal.

The man looked up slightly, and his eyes met Alisen's.

"Naorin," whispered Alisen, her hand feeling desperately for McKenzie's in the wild fear of suspense.

Naorin dropped his head.

Amar smiled pleasantly, though the look was tinged with hatred and something far more horrible, then turned to look at the girls. "I am sorry for your friend," he said. "But he would not answer our questions, and I have reason to believe that he knows far more than he will say. We are going to get answers, or we are going to have his life. That is the justice of the I.P. I daresay it is cruel, but if you want to win the world, what better way to do it?"

His face broke out into a smile. It was more terrifying to Alisen than anything he could ever have pretended.

"I thought you said there would be a trial!" gasped McKenzie. "You can't just kill him!"

"We can," said Amar, his face hardening again, "and we will, unless he gives us the answers we require."

Naorin lifted his head again. "It's alright," he said to the girls. "Don't be afraid for me. I have been prepared for this moment for many years. And—" He was cut off by the guard, who hit him cruelly on the back of his head with a club.

"Stop!" said Amar harshly to the guard. "How can he speak when he is unconscious? One of you go now and fetch some water." There was a struggle between the guards to see who could be first to appease their annoyed leader.

"Please, no, please, stop!" cried McKenzie desperately. "What good will you get out of killing him? Let him go, and we will leave you alone! Please, please!"

"You will get nothing by bargaining, and I assure you that you cannot free this man."

McKenzie turned away, her eyes red and glittering with overflowing tears. Alisen tried to reach her, but the guard held her fast.

The guards returned and splashed water liberally over Naorin's face. He raised his head slowly, blinked, and looked around as if he could not remember where he was. Then he saw Amar and the guards and made a motion as if he would rise and assault them. But the chains that held him to the table prevented him from moving.

Amar nodded to the guards. "You may begin," he said. "Ask questions first and persuade after."

McKenzie shrieked, and Alisen closed her eyes.

Dimly, through ringing ears, she heard the voice of the guards harshly questioning Naorin. She could not tell what was said, but she knew by the tone of Naorin's voice as he replied that he had refused to answer. And then there came a horrible sound. A gleeful yelp on the part of the guards, a sort of whistling as of something being swung through the air, and several half-stifled gasps of pain from inside the enclosure.

Alisen dared not open her eyes, half afraid of what she would see, and half afraid of what she would do if she did see. She squeezed her eyelids tightly shut and tried to prevent any tears from escaping.

Suddenly the terrible monotony of noises was broken by a high, shrill voice. "It was you, Amar! You who wanted Jay dead, and all is lost! It was you! I know you, and everything you stand for!" The last word was slurred, and the 'r' sound dragged on as if it would never stop.

"Naorin! Stop! You have to stop!" Alisen heard McKenzie's voice as she tried to stifle Naorin's frenzied cries.

"You cannot repress me!" cried Naorin, regardless of the interruption. "You can torment me as you tormented Jay, but you will never escape the justice that waits you!"

Alisen snapped her eyes open. The guard stood above Naorin, the club he held bloody and grotesque, paused in a movement by Naorin's sudden screams. McKenzie was desperately pulling against her guard to run toward him. Amar was yelling orders to unresisting soldiers. But nobody was moving, in that single instant, except Naorin.

His bare, bloody back seemed to lift for an instant as he struggled against the ropes that bound him to the table. There was a moment of breathless anticipation, and they snapped, one by one, as if despair gave Naorin superhuman energy and strength. The guard standing above him seemed paralyzed, unable to move to defend himself. Naorin leaped up from the table, pulled the guard's gun from his belt, and fired it at his chest.

With a strangled cry the guard fell. Naorin stepped, or rather jumped, over him and pointed the gun toward the back of the cages. Alisen, McKenzie, and their guards watched in paralyzed horror as he fired. Every shot met its mark, and in a moment, there was no one left standing on that side but Naorin himself.

Amar was screaming at the impotent guards. The one holding Alisen began to move toward Naorin, who swung around and fixed the sight on his forehead. "Move an inch," he said, breathing heavily, "and you're dead."

The guard stopped in his tracks.

Amar stood silent.

"Let the girls go," said Naorin. "Let them go!" He held the pistol firmly pointed at the guards.

Slowly Alisen's guard relaxed his hands from her shoulders. In a moment they were free, and they darted to one side to watch.

Hidden safely behind a bush, they huddled together, terrified.

Amar cried, "Don't either of you two cowards dare? Somebody, disarm him!" He was jumping up and down like a madman.

Naorin looked at him calmly, flicked a lock of sweaty black hair off his face, and covered him with the pistol. "Now is my time, Amar," he said. "Let the girls go."

Amar lifted his hands in a gesture of submission. "Okay. Fine. Look around. Do you see them anywhere? Does it look like I tried to stop them?"

Naorin turned his head to look for them, and in that split-second Amar's hand was on his belt. Alisen screamed a warning to Naorin, who looked around just in time to see Amar's eyes, bright with malice and hate, looking at him through the sight of a black revolver. He pressed the trigger. There were three deafening explosions, drowning out Alisen and McKenzie's horrified cries for mercy, and three flashes all coming from the barrel. In an instant Amar was the only one left standing; Naorin and the two guards lay still on the ground.

"Naorin!" cried McKenzie. She ran to the cage. Alisen followed close behind, and ran through the opened door.

McKenzie held his wrist and lifted it from the ground. "Naorin, please, please, wake up," she whispered, tears running down her face.

As if in answer Naorin's eyes fluttered open wearily. He looked first at McKenzie, then at Alisen, and seemed confused. "What happened?" he murmured, with no trace of the wildness that had been in his voice only a few moments before.

"Don't ask, Naorin," said Alisen gently. "You tried to save us. You did your best . . . " Tears streamed down her cheeks.

Naorin's muscles tightened in a shudder of pain, and he tried to look around. "The guards . . . ?"

"Dead. All of them," said McKenzie, looking back at the fence.

Naorin looked at his side, where the pistol he had snatched lay covered in blood. "With that?" He struggled for breath. "I did it?"

Alisen and McKenzie looked at each other.

He exhaled roughly. "I suppose it was justice," he said. "I didn't know what I was doing . . . "

"Of course, it was justice, Naorin," said McKenzie, gently brushing his hair off his forehead. "You were trying to save us."

A swift smile crossed his lips. "I am sorry for them," he whispered.

McKenzie looked up at Alisen and let Naorin's wrist slide to the ground. "He's gone, Alisen. Naorin's gone." She ducked her head in her arms, and her shoulders shook with sobs.

Alisen put an arm over her back, and they knelt together over Naorin's body. Their tears fell on his breast, and there was no one to dry them.

Alisen looked up. Amar was still standing behind the fence, looking at them with a puzzled expression.

McKenzie staggered to her feet with Naorin's weapon in her hand. "You wretch," she said, breathing deeply with heavy emotion. "You—"

Alisen stood up. "Let us go," she said. "Don't you think you've done enough killing?" She pointed to the two guards on the ground. "They were your men."

Amar did not move, and the puzzled expression did not leave his face. "Why?" he said, after a moment's pause. "You really loved him, didn't you?"

Now it was the girls' turn to look confused.

"Running out from cover. You didn't have to do it, but you wanted to be with him," said Amar. "Why?"

McKenzie was opening her mouth to answer his question, but Alisen stopped her. "Don't listen to him!" she said. "The guards are coming up behind us. Run, McKenzie, run!"

With a rapid glance over her shoulder McKenzie took off running with Alisen. Shots were fired after them.

Amar cursed furiously, and his voice could be heard long after the girls had passed the clearing. Fear lent them wings. They could hear the sound of pursuit behind them, they could hear the voices of the men who wanted to take their lives. They did not know the ground, and the I.P. did. So, the chase was entirely one-sided from the beginning. The end came when they found themselves trapped in a clearing without cover. There was no way the I.P. could miss, and their guns were raised, aimed, and cocked. Alisen and McKenzie were forced to surrender.

CHAPTER XX

IT WAS BACK TO ROOM 13, back to confinement. Worse, perhaps, than the physical torment was the mental pain left by the death of their friend. Naorin had always seemed to strong and invincible, and a single fit of frenzy had brought about his death. Somehow Alisen had looked to him as a protector. Now he was not there to shield them.

The first day of confinement was the worst. They had grown ravenous, with nearly two days of famine, and the snacks McKenzie had packed were all gone. Water was scarce and disgustingly dirty.

Slowly the sun changed from afternoon to evening to night, and no one came in. No sound broke the deathly stillness but the guards' heavy tread outside the door. McKenzie and Alisen lay on opposite corners of the room, each absorbed in her own thoughts, neither moving or speaking for hours on end.

Finally, McKenzie looked up, a glazed and dreamy expression on her face, and said slowly, "What are we supposed to do now?"

After the prolonged quiet, her voice had startled Alisen. "What do you mean?"

"Well, aren't we supposed to ask God, or something? After all, what good is it if we read the Bible, believed in Him, and then never did anything else?"

"What's to ask?" said Alisen bitterly. "He won't bring Naorin back, it doesn't look likely that He'll get us out of here, and—"

"What about Kale?" asked McKenzie.

"I guess we could try," said Alisen. "I wish they'd bring him in here so we could know he's okay."

"Then let's ask for that," said McKenzie.

Together they knelt in the middle of the floor and put their arms over each other's shoulders. "God," began McKenzie, "we're worried about our friend Kale, and we wanted to ask if You—"

The door swung open with a grating noise behind them. They remained as if rooted in position, neither daring to look back. They heard it slam shut, they looked at each other, and suddenly swiveled their heads around. And there, sitting upright on the floor and blinking miserably, sat Kale.

"Kale!" they cried and stumbled toward him.

He smiled and hugged both of them. Despite his condition he seemed more cheerful. "I'm glad you're safe," he said. "When I heard they had taken you outside, I was afraid Naorin wouldn't be able to cover for you anymore. I had a good long talk with him after you two were taken for questioning and got to know him a little better. He fascinates me. I think he has a long and bitter history with the I.P. Where is he, by the way?"

Alisen and McKenzie looked at each other.

Kale's eyes darkened. "You mean they didn't bring him in here?"

"No-o," said Alisen hesitantly. "They took him somewhere else."

"Perhaps we can get a message to him," said Kale. "He'll be alright."

"Kale," said McKenzie, "they took him outside."

Kale looked up.

"They were going to question him . . . "

"He had a sort of spell," Alisen's voice shook. "I mean, it was like he went crazy. He escaped from the guard, took his pistol, and . . . "

There was a long pause.

"And what?"

"Amar shot him," said McKenzie, dropping her head.

"Where is he now?" Kale waited for them to answer. "Where is he?"

"He's dead, Kale," said Alisen. "We saw it happen."

Kale put his head in his hands and slowly walked to the window. "Why, why, why did it have to be Naorin," he said at last. "I never did really know him."

"He was trying to help us escape," said McKenzie.

Kale did not move.

Alisen hesitantly put a hand on his shoulder. "I miss him, too . . . "

Kale's shoulders heaved miserably, and he looked back at her, with tears in his eyes. "I wish I could have had more time with him," he said.

"We all do," said McKenzie gently. "He was a good friend to us."

With an effort Kale straightened and slowly ceased his sobs. "Now what?" he said despairingly. "You know we'll never get out of here."

"I think we will," said Alisen. She was sure of it.

Kale looked at her. "What do you mean?"

Alisen started speaking very fast. "Remember the last dream we had, about the meeting of the Civil Air Patrol where all the people disappeared? That's the only one that hasn't come true."

"But the disappearing?" said Kale. "How can that come true? Things and people don't just disappear."

"We think they will," said Alisen. She looked desperately at McKenzie for backup.

"While you were gone, and we were staying with Naorin," McKenzie said, coming to her rescue, "we read a Bible. And it said—"

"You read a what?" asked Kale.

"A Bible, Kale. Anyway, it says that people who believe in Jesus—"

Kale crossed his arms.

"—will be taken to heaven before a period of judgement—"

"I've heard all this before," said Kale. "But what does this look like? We're having a 'judgement' right now, and you're both still here. Everybody's still here. When is this supposed to happen?"

"Not yet," said Alisen. "We're going to get out of here, and when we do—"

"—then it will be time to start looking," finished McKenzie.

Kale kicked his heels restlessly against the wall. "It sounds idyllic," he said finally, "but it just can't be true. Maybe I'll believe you if we do get out of here and if we do have a meeting with the C.A.P. cadets. I don't know. But it's awfully hard to believe in God when people are dying all around you."

"I know," began Alisen, "but—"

"Please, just leave me alone," said Kale, sliding down against the wall and hugging his knees to his chest. "I don't want to talk about it right now."

Alisen and McKenzie looked regretfully at him and retired against the opposite wall.

*****   *****   *****

Alisen had curled up against the back wall to sleep. Kale had not moved from his slumped position near the door. McKenzie was sitting nearby, possibly sleeping, making no noise except for her slow, heavy breathing.

There was a gentle squeaking noise, and a thin stream of light crept into the room. Alisen opened her eyes and saw the outline of a guard standing in the doorway. He seemed to look at somebody behind him, put his finger to his lips and signal them to be silent, then he looked back into the room.

"Is there somebody named Jay here? Or a friend of hers?"

There was a long silence.

"I'm sorry," he said. "Here, I'm coming in. I'll explain myself in a minute." He cast another hesitant glance behind him, let himself in the room, and shut the door behind him. Then he fumbled in his pocket, produced a small black book, and held it up. "Does this belong to anyone here?"

"I can't see it," said McKenzie.

The guard switched on a small flashlight, careful not to shine it in their faces, and illuminated the book.

Alisen gave a half-stifled cry of surprise.

"Yes," said McKenzie cautiously, "the book does belong to us."

"Then you're Jay?"

"No," said McKenzie. "We knew her briefly a while ago."

"She gave this to you?"

Silence answered him.

"I ought to have started from the beginning." He took a deep breath. "I was outside when your friend, Naorim, Naorey, got free and shot all those guards. I was hiding behind some bushes near the building, and I had my revolver pointed at his head, about to pull the trigger, when Captain Amar shot him and those two guards. I couldn't figure why he would shoot the soldiers. One of them was my friend." His voice became unsteady, but he continued, "I've seen so many things I can't explain. People disappearing and never returning to their posts. Stuff like that, that I started to wonder if this is what happened to them." He held up the book. "I had found this in a house we fired and saved it as a curiosity. When I started reading it, I learned some things I almost wish I'd never seen. But they made me wonder if I could find the person who owned it. I coaxed some information from Captain Amar, enough to help me find you, and so here I am. And here's the book." He placed it in McKenzie's hands.

"I suggest you read it," he added, when nobody replied. "Read it very carefully, especially the end." He stood up and opened the door. "*Especially* the end. It is very important." Without a salutation of any kind, he slammed the door shut and locked it from the outside.

But he had left his flashlight.

When he had been gone for a few minutes, Alisen said, "I wonder why he was so insistent that we read it. Surely, if he knows it belongs to us, he would assume we've read it before."

"I don't know," said McKenzie. "Maybe there was something that stuck out to him."

"We could try to find out what it is," suggested Alisen. "It would give us something to do."

"Who cares," said McKenzie. "We've read it before."

"It doesn't matter," said Alisen. "Here, let me see it."

McKenzie handed it to her and curled back up against the wall.

Alisen trained the flashlight on the last page.

She read it through, wondering what had so struck the soldier about this page. But there was nothing out of the ordinary so, with a sigh, she flipped the switch on the flashlight to turn it off and go back to sleep.

To her surprise, the flashlight did not turn off, but remained on, shining a purplish glow that seemed to give no light to the room. It was a black light, and she wondered if the guard had left it there for a reason. She opened Jay's journal to the last page of writing and shone the light on it. To her astonishment and delight, several sentences appeared under Jay's last words.

She cried aloud, waking her companions.

"What? What is it?" said Kale, blinking and rubbing his eyes sleepily. "Where'd you get that?"

"It's the flashlight the guard left," said Alisen. "Look! It's a black light, and when you turn it on, it reveals words."

"Let me see," said McKenzie. Alisen spread the book on the floor and shone the light on the last page. It revealed the following message: 'Tomorrow at 0600. Stay awake. Your only hope is to trust me, and I swear everything I told you is true. -Yavuz'

"What? What's going to happen tomorrow? And what kind of a time is that?" wondered Alisen.

"It's military time, of course," said Kale. "0600 means simply six o'clock AM. What he's talking about is another matter."

"Do you think Yavuz—"

"Is the guard's name?" McKenzie interrupted in excitement. "Yes! And the only thing he can be talking about—"

"Is escape," finished Kale.

"This is our chance!" said Alisen.

"But what if that long story he told us was a lie?" asked McKenzie doubtfully.

"We can at least know for sure that he was where he said he was," said Alisen reasonably, "since no one was left alive but us and Amar, who probably wouldn't publicize such an event. Therefore, it follows that he saw it himself."

"And," added Kale, "we know that it must affect him somehow to realize that his leader killed his companions."

"You're for trusting him?" said McKenzie in surprise.

"I don't see how we could be worse off," said Kale half-humorously, shrugging his shoulders. "Why not take the risk?"

"I'm for it," said Alisen. "Remember the dreams. We knew we were going to get out."

"Alright," said McKenzie reluctantly. "I suppose it's our best chance."

"Anybody know what time it is?" said Kale.

"What time does the sun usually come up?"

"Earlier than I was ever awake, at this time of year," he said. "And I always get up at six-thirty."

"It doesn't matter, though," said McKenzie, "since he told us to stay awake."

"We can't stay awake forever," said Kale. "I'm going to guess that you, like me, haven't slept in a long time. If we're going to escape, we'll need energy."

"Suppose one of us keeps watch," suggested Alisen.

"Good idea," said McKenzie. "I'll take the first shift."

"No, let me," said Kale. "I never got to finish reading the journal, you know. Maybe I could find something in there about faith, or God, or whatever it is."

Alisen and McKenzie snuggled together against the back wall, leaving Kale awake with his eyes trained on the journal with intense concentration.

CHAPTER XXI

ALISEN WAS AWAKENED BY A rough shake. "Wake up," whispered an unfamiliar voice. "We must hurry."

She opened her eyes sleepily, wondering where she was and who was accosting her. Then she saw the face of Yavuz, the guard who had seen them last night, and became fully awake.

"Hurry," he repeated, and went to wake McKenzie.

Kale was standing in front of the door, anxiously scanning the hallway. Alisen stood up quickly and went to his side. There was nobody in sight except the other guard, who was a friend of Yavuz's, and there was no sound coming from anywhere else in the building. The coast was, for the moment, clear.

Yavuz and McKenzie came to the door. The guards looked both ways, exchanged some words in a low, anxious tone, and pointed to the back door. Finally, Yavuz said, "I think it will be safer if we go around back and try to escape through the cages. There's plenty of cover in the woods there."

They merely nodded, indicating their readiness to follow him.

"Come then," he said, with one last glance up and down the hallway. "Follow me and be very quiet."

"Where are we going?" asked Alisen.

"Out back by the cages," said Yavuz shortly. "You can get to the woods from there."

"And once we get to the woods?" prodded Kale.

Yavuz turned to face him. "Once you get there, you'll have to be on your own. I can't come with you. I have to be back in the building by seven-thirty. That leaves us about an hour to get there."

"It's only a few hundred yards," said Alisen. "It shouldn't take that long."

"So you'd think." Yavuz stopped, held open the door for her and McKenzie, and cast an anxious glance around the dimly lit hallway. "But we have to be extraordinarily careful. If anybody sees us, we might as well not have come."

For a few minutes nobody said anything. Yavuz was leading them in a very roundabout circuit through the building. And then, when Alisen had entirely lost track of her location, Yavuz opened the last door and a pale morning sun streamed onto their faces. They had accomplished the first step. They had gotten out of the building without being noticed.

They crouched behind a set of stunted bushes, which barely afforded room for all of them. Yavuz appeared to be expecting somebody. After about five minutes of discomfort, an I.P. guard strolled leisurely around the corner on his beat. Yavuz signed to them to be silent, and they watched anxiously for what seemed an unbearably long time before at last he continued on his way and disappeared around the corner.

Yavuz stood up immediately. "We're short on time," he said, with a muttered curse. "I would rather have waited and made sure that nobody was following us, but there's no help for it. We'll have to run to the woods."

"Why are we so short on time?" began McKenzie, but Yavuz cut her off.

"There's less danger going this direction," he said, "but once I'm on my way back, I'll have to be more careful. My friends will be out after breakfast, and they will want to know where I've gone when I'm supposed to be on duty."

He looked right, then left, then right again, and with a shrug as if to express his doubt, set off running in the direction of the woods.

"Come on," said Kale. "We have to keep up." He took off after Yavuz.

Alisen and McKenzie trailed in the rear. There was something about the fact that they were trying to be stealthy that seemed to steal their speed. Alisen felt as if her legs were lead, and her breathing came short and raspy. She could hear McKenzie panting. Though they were not running quickly she could hear the soft, padded footfalls of Kale's shoes and the heavy tread of Yavuz's boots. The constant thump-thump became wearying. She saw that the others pulled ahead, that she was being left behind. She tried to keep up, but the effort was too great. It was like she was a player in a dream, a terrifying nightmare with no end in sight . . .

"Alisen!" cried Kale.

His voice broke her thoughts and brought her back to the real world. With a blink she steadied her wandering eyes and brought them to focus on him.

"Hurry up!" he continued. "Yavuz thinks we might have been missed!"

Alisen shot a quick glance at McKenzie, tapped on her shoulder to wake her from a similar trance, and then started running.

"Come on!" shouted Yavuz. "I can hear a stir in the camp! I believe they have missed us!"

There were only a few hundred yards left, and Alisen knew she could make them. She knew that once they got there they would be in danger, perhaps in even more danger than they had been when they left, but at least they would have a chance. A chance for freedom, a chance for a change, a chance for the final dream to come true.

Yavuz kept darting anxious glances back at the camp. Alisen could hear a vague rustling noise behind them, something which boded ill to Yavuz upon his return to camp. She tried to run faster, almost as if she was trying to run so that she could get far enough away from the camp to leave the sound behind. It kept coming closer, closer . . .

Yavuz stopped suddenly. "Run on," he whispered, panting heavily. "I'll say you outran me, or something. At least you'll get away."

"We can't ask you to do this," said McKenzie.

"Well, I'm telling you. Just go," he said. "It will be worse for all of us if they find me with you."

"Thank you," said Kale stiffly. "Really, thank you."

Yavuz nodded. "Now go!"

He waved to them and they disappeared into the trees ahead.

*****   *****   *****

Alisen could barely keep up with McKenzie and Kale. They ran on endlessly, regardless of the fact that the sounds behind them had stopped and they did not know where they were. Her feet began to drag, and several times she nearly tripped over them. Finally, she stopped, not caring if her companions left her. To her surprise they paused, breathing heavily from the run and staring all around as if they expected someone to jump out at them.

"Where are we?" McKenzie asked as soon as she had gotten her breath.

Kale looked around dismally. "I don't know," he said. "How it hurts!" He fell to a kneeling position, holding his sides. McKenzie gave a cry and hurried to help him. He waved her away as best he could but made no move to get up.

Alisen saw and heard all this as if through a shadowy veil. Nothing seemed to be real, nothing seemed to be happening. She would wake up, and find herself in bed at home . . .

"Alisen!" said McKenzie. "Are you alright?"

She shook herself, startled. "Yes, I'm fine. Honestly, McKenzie." She paused. "I'm starving. You know, we haven't had anything to eat in . . . it must have been days."

"You're right," said McKenzie. "At least there was water. We'll have to find food soon, or we can't keep moving like this."

Kale got up, pale-faced and obviously in pain. Alisen glanced quickly at his arm and cried, "Kale, you're bleeding again!"

He looked at it for a moment, then dismissed it with a sigh. "Not much we can do. The bandage will hold for a little while longer. Right now, we just need a place to rest."

"Right here's good enough for me," suggested McKenzie.

Kale shook his head. "Anybody could sneak up on us," he said. "Look, you can see where the trees thin up ahead. There's probably a clearing of some sort up there."

"I'll walk there with you," said Alisen, "but if there isn't anything there, I have to stop for a rest. Call me chicken, or whatever it is you say, but I have to. I'm exhausted."

Kale nodded. "I agree," he said. "That's what we'll do."

Wearily they plodded towards the clearing. Though it was not far away, it took them a while to get there. Each had to stop every now and then to catch their breath.

Kale gave a sudden gasp of surprise. "It's the C.A.P. hangar!" he cried.

Alisen and McKenzie strained to see ahead. They had returned to their starting point, after an absence of many days and the intervention of many horrific experiences. It seemed to Alisen eerily prescient. Through her mind flitted memories of the last dream, and she shivered.

"Look," Kale cried, "there are people going in. It's the cadets! They're having a meeting!"

"But the door is guarded by an I.P. patrol," said McKenzie doubtfully. "Kale—"

"I expect they've given permission," said Kale. "We should certainly go. That way we can communicate that we're alive and—"

"Kale," said Alisen desperately, "you can't go in! The dream!"

Kale paused uncertainly. Then he laughed, a pinched laugh which held no conviction.

"I'm hardly worried about us all disappearing," he said. "What I want is food, and a doctor. Maybe we can find some of those things if we go."

"Kale," said McKenzie, "don't do this. It's all true, I promise you."

"Nobody's going to disappear," said Kale, "and we have to go. This might be the only help we get for a long time, or ever. We have to take advantage of it while we can."

Alisen seized his unwounded arm. "All the other dreams came true, though the probability was ridiculously against it," she said. "The only thing standing between you and safety—"

"Is my unbelief," finished Kale. "I know. I've always known. But I still haven't seen any sign of God. He could fix all this, right? So why didn't He?"

"That's the whole point," said McKenzie. "He's about to. That's why these people are going to vanish."

"Are you going with them?" said Kale pointedly.

"Yes," they said together.

"Look," he said, seeming to lose his temper suddenly, "we're going in. We'll get help from the cadets, and nobody's going to disappear. Follow me."

Before Alisen could do anything to stop him, he bolted out of the trees with surprising speed and ran toward the hangar. For a single moment of shock Alisen stared after him, before resigning herself to following him to the fate she and McKenzie both knew.

When they reached the hangar, Kale had already gone inside. They were quickly and carelessly screened by an I.P. guard before they were allowed to enter. When they got inside, they saw the cadets milling around, the chairs in their accustomed places, everything how it was before, except for a large burned patch on the wall near the closets. Alisen wondered if this mark had been left by Amar when he had nearly burned them to death only a few days before. It had felt like months, but really it had been less than two weeks since the saga of pain and death started.

She looked around, wondering if Sadie had made it to the meeting. And then, over in the corner, she saw her huddled in a chair, looking dreadfully confused but comfortable and happier than she had been when Alisen had seen her last. Alisen ran over to hug her and congratulate her on getting free.

"I don't know why they let me go," explained Sadie, "but I was happy to get out any way I could, you know?"

Alisen smiled. "I'm so glad you made it," she said. "I really missed you. I missed our math and chemistry lessons."

"Believe me," said Sadie with a short laugh, "I would have given anything to get out of school while I was in it, but now that I'm out, I'd do anything to get back in."

Alisen heard Kale calling to her from across the room. The meeting was about to start. She hugged Sadie again and hurried to her place.

And now here they were, rushing with dizzying speed toward the end. Alisen watched as everything fell into place, but she was powerless to resist it, and she did not think she even wanted to try.

Things were different. Everyone looked pale and haggard, and some were missing altogether, and yet there was an odd lurking sense of familiarity. Alisen sensed the fear that pervaded the room, but somehow, she herself was not at all afraid.

The lieutenant colonel walked through the desks to the whiteboard. "As you all know," he began, his voice oddly shaky, "these last few days have been a horror none of us could have predicted or imagined. The I.P. has taken over our country. However, they are trying to revert from their sudden attack to facilitate the return of law and order as quickly as possible. That is why we're allowed to meet here tonight."

He paused and looked anxiously around the room. "Some of the members of this squadron are never coming back . . . "

Alisen remembered Jay's tragic death, and Naorin's heroic effort to free them from the I.P. prison.

" . . . and we will never forget them."

The entire room was deathly silent.

"There is a young member who wishes to address you tonight. I'm going to let him come up to the stage here and tell us what he thinks of this devastation. Anyone who can make any sense of all this is welcome."

***** ***** *****

A young cadet came through the aisle and stood before the whiteboard. "I'm sure you're wondering what I could possibly have to say," he said. "Did I know this was coming? Could I have warned you? No, but I should have been able to."

He paused. Nobody moved.

"All these events are predicted in the Bible."

Somebody in the back stood up. "You're going to preach now?" cried a voice shrilly. "When the I.P. is out there killing people?"

"'You will hear of wars and rumors of wars, but see to it that you are not alarmed. Such things must happen, but the end is still to come.' Quoted from Matthew 24:6," said the cadet quietly.

"What has that got to do with anything?" said another voice from the back.

"This verse from the Bible seems to summarize what's happening, doesn't it?" he said. "'Wars and rumors of wars.' And if we ever needed God, it's now."

"Get promoted to chaplain, did you?" sneered the first. "Preaching to us about the end times?"

Kale hadn't caught the drift of what the cadet had been saying. Rather timidly, wishing he had asked Alisen and McKenzie first, he raised his hand.

The cadet called on him. "Yes?"

"I was wondering," said Kale, "what did you mean about that rumors of wars thing? I mean, I've heard that before, but . . . "

"Well," said the cadet, "it's considered to be a sign of the end times. Another thing that many people believe will foretell the end is the disappearance of all people who believe in the one true God. That could happen any time."

"So, you're saying—" Kale stopped in astonishment.

A white light, painful to look at, suddenly enveloped the cadet. Heat burned on Kale's right shoulder. McKenzie shone brilliantly next to him. Over her shoulder, he could see Sadie, who was also illuminated in the brilliant white light. He turned to look the other way and saw Alisen glowing warmly, her face transfigured and infinitely surpassing in beauty anything he had ever seen before.

He tried to touch her, but she did not seem to notice him. She seemed to be enraptured with something that he could not see. He cried out and fell back out of his seat into the desk behind him, which tipped over and crashed on the floor. The light burned. He tried to cover his face with his hands, but still the light seeped through and wrapped him in its beauty.

Just as suddenly as the glow had begun, it vanished.

With it vanished the people who had shone so brightly.

The cadets around the room cried out with terror. There began a mass scramble for the door. Everyone ran over top of each other, heedless of protocol, rules, or regulations. It was a horrible moment.

Kale, crying for Alisen, was run down in the middle of the aisle and trampled on. He could not rise, much less make for the hangar door or try to search for his missing friend. Nobody cared about him enough to stop. They were far too terrified.

He lay on the floor, paralyzed, until everyone else had escaped outside. Then he screamed, a desperate, haunted scream. "Why?" he cried, over and over. "Why would You leave me here? What did I ever do to You?"

And in the midst of his pain and grief he knew that the fault lay with him, not God. He had not believed, and he had been hard on McKenzie and Alisen when they shared their faith. He had not listened, and now he would have to pay the price.

He raised his tear-stained face to the ceiling. "Seven years," he said, his voice raspy and hoarse. "Seven years of horror and pain and death."

He tried to stand up, tripped over something, and fell to his knees. Sobs, painful and choking, escaped him rapidly and he could not suppress them. Finally, he knelt with his forehead to the ground and whispered, "God, forgive me for being so stupid. Help me get through this. I know I can't do it alone. Oh God, please, please help me." Then he burst into a rain of pitiful and wailing tears.

He had missed his chance. His friends were gone, and he was left alone, to face the seven most horrific years humanity would ever endure.

CHAPTER XXII

GRACE SAT STRAIGHT UP IN bed and screamed. Her mother, frightened, ran into her room. Grace sat on the edge of the bed, tears running down her face.

"What's wrong, Grace?" her mother asked, sitting down beside her.

Grace huddled against her mother's side and closed her eyes. "I had a dream," she said. "It was about God, and the end of the world, and something called the Civil Air Patrol. It was the most horribly clear dream I've ever had. I'll never forget it, ever. And it was so terrifying."

"Maybe," suggested her mother, caressing her gently, "maybe you had too much pizza for dinner."

"No, no, I know it wasn't that. It was all so, well, *clear*, like a movie or something."

Her mother smiled. "Or maybe there's a message in the dream. Shall we pray about it?"

Grace nodded.

"Dear God," her mother began, "we give up to You this dream Grace has had. If there's a message You want her to hear, then please reveal it and make it clear. If there was any evil in it, we pray in Jesus' name for it to be removed from Grace and from this house. Please give her peace about anything that frightened her. In Jesus' name, amen."

Grace opened her eyes and sat up straight. "Can I tell you about it?" she asked.

Her mother leaned back against the mound of pillows and smiled. "I'd love to hear it," she said.

"Alright." Grace began, "It started off with this girl named Alisen, who was preparing to leave her house to go to this thing called Civil Air Patrol. She had just finished braiding her hair and wound it into a bun. She admired herself in the mirror for a moment. She really was very pretty, and I think she knew it. She gave her bun a last twitch and started down the stairs . . . "

––––––––––––––––––––––––––

For more information about
Lauren Smyth
&

Stories of the Night
please visit:

www.laurensmythbooks.com
@lsmythbooks

For more information about
AMBASSADOR INTERNATIONAL
please visit:

www.ambassador-international.com
@AmbassadorIntl
www.facebook.com/AmbassadorIntl

If you enjoyed this book, please consider leaving us a review on
Amazon, Goodreads, or our website.